The Hidden Queen

E.M. Jaye

Contents

Summary

She was Claimed to be his Queen...

Eleanor never thought that her life would be anything more than the poverty she grew up in. But fate had other ideas. On her twentieth birthday, Eleanor reported to the claiming ceremony. All women are required to enter, she never knew that she would be claimed.

Now she is more than just a mate to an alien warrior, she is a mate to *the* alien warrior. Danion Belator of Old, king of the alien race that saved humans from extinction, is now her mate. She fears she has traded one master for another until Danion transforms her.

She never knew she had the strength within her, but Danion knows she does and will not rest until he awakens it. He brings out the fire hidden within. Where once she was meek, she is assertive. Where once she was afraid, she is brave. Where once she was alone, she now is mated.

He has found his Queen...

Danion waited for an eternity to claim his mate, and when she was finally within his grasp his enemies attempted to kill her. He swore bloody revenge against them.

But their assassination attempt uncovers hidden secrets about his young mate. Things that defy all reason, and that could very well mean the death of the galaxy.

With war upon them, Danion and Eleanor must fight for not just their lives, but all life in the galaxy. Danion needs Eleanor's help to win this war, but his mate is unaware of her own strength. No worries, he will help her discover the queen hidden inside her.

Dedication

To my wonderful parents, who shaped me into the person I am today.
Without you I would never have started this wonderful journey of sharing my love of
books with the world.
I love you both.

Geldon Language Pronunciation and Definition Guide

Abiciant—(Ab-iss-e-ant) Rare sublineage that allows the weaver to channel their mental energy upon another and control them.

Animare—(An-a-mare) Term of endearment given to a mated male from his female. This term is the highest form of respect one mate can give to another.

Aninare—(An-a-nare) Term of endearment given to a mated female from her male. This term is the highest form of respect one mate can give to another.

Aniun—(An-ee-um) One of the six great, or main, lineages, this is the control of the power of water. Warriors gifted in this often exhibit calm personalities.

Atelean—(Ate-lee-on) The family name of the founding Gelder ancients, once the most powerful family in all the galaxy.

Beb—Term of endearment used in the Star language, usually reserved for a couple that are in a romantic or sexual relationship.

Belator—(Bell-a-tore) The power name of the high warrior king, belator appeared upon the king when he came into maturity.

Bellum—(Bell-um) Term that refers to securing something, commonly used as a multilayer weave that allows a room to be locked securely.

Caeli—(Say-lee) One of the six great, or main, lineages, this is the control of the power of air. Warriors gifted in this often exhibit joyous and carefree personalities.

Cerum—(Sear-um) Word that designates a ceremony of great importance.

Chakkas—(Cha-kas) Invisible points that run throughout the body that channel the energy of the cosmos.

Cognata—(Cog-na-ta) Familial relations that means cousin.

Deim—(Dem) Curse word, profanity.

Erain—(Air-ens) Race of aliens that thrive on the pain, suffering, and death of all races other than their own. They attempt to commit genocide on any planet they come across. Normally impulsive and historically prone to fighting among each other.

Fiefling—(Fef-ling) Curse word, profanity.

Hael—(Hail) Sublineage that gifts the weaver with healing abilities. Gelders who are strong in this line commonly become medical doctors. Those gifted in *caeli*, *vim*, and *simul* often possess strong gifts in *hael* as well.

Ignis—(Ig-nis) One of the six great, or main, lineages, this is the control of the power of fire. Warriors gifted in this often exhibit passionate personalities, and are commonly quick to anger.

Itumnis—(It-um-nus) The fountain from ancient Gelder, known for its eternal life.

Lacieu—(Lass-ce-o) The one original lineage, known as the lost line. No one alive is thought to possess a gift in it.

Massa—(Mass-sa) Title of honor to a warrior who possesses mastery in a lineage.

Medate—(Meh-date) Form of meditation that only the most disciplined warrior can perform. It allows the weaver to access every fragment of information they have ever come across, even something that they did not consciously know they observed. Performed incorrectly it can destroy the mind of the warrior who attempts it.

Memien—(Mem-ee-in) A physical manifestation of power, it can function as a power source and can protect, attack, or provide energy to the weaver.

Merate—(Meh-rate) Lighter form of meditation that warriors who are adept with mental skills can achieve.

Myo—(My-oh) Meaning my or mine.

Praesidium—(Pray-seed-ee-um) A group of six warriors who are masters in their lineage that are pledged to protecting their pledge holder.

Ratshult—(Rat-shult) Derogatory name.

Scimaar—(Sim-mar) A blade used by the Gelders in battle.

Starskies—(Star-skees) An alcoholic beverage that is so potent even a Gelder can become inebriated.

Tatio—(Tat-tee-oh) Unique mineral that is necessary for Gelders to be able to weave their power.

Terra—(Tare-ah) One of the six great, or main, lineages, this is the control of the power of rocks and minerals. Warriors gifted in this often exhibit stoic personalities, and are commonly levelheaded and serious in nature.

Prologue

Danion

"Dane?" a voice to my right asks. I can't tear my eyes from the still body lying in the healing pod before me. I sit at the bedside of my beloved *aninare.* My mate. She seems so frail inside the massive pod. Jarlin, her doctor who happens to be the highest-ranking *hael* officer, assures me she will recover from this assassination attempt. As if I can just turn off my concern. I cannot help but worry. This is my *mate,* and she nearly died. Because I failed to protect her.

The stark white qualities of the infirmary that surround her cause her delicate features to appear pale. So very pale. As if she is on the very brink of death. Her slender frame seems even smaller in the pod designed to hold the much larger bodies of Gelders. Our bodies are designed for battle, muscular and tall.

Her light appearance is a sharp contrast to the dark looks that we all favor. Her long, light blonde hair nearly matches the white sheets she lies on. So at odds with the dark black hair that I, and all Gelder warriors, have.

"Dane, my king, you are needed." I finally acknowledge the male to my right. It is Golon, not only my second in command but also my cousin. He is one of the two warriors I trust implicitly. Trust does not come easy when you have spent millennia waging war.

Golon is a formidable warrior, second only to me, and is adorned in the standard warrior attire for his class: tight brown leather pants lined with concealed steel blades, and a thin shirt that has *memien* threads woven into the cloth. The shirt hugs the upper body like a second skin. The *memien* threads are a physical manifestation of our power that only masters can weave into cloth. The color of your house, therefore, is dependent on your lineage control. Golon, like myself, is a master in all the lineages and can wear any color of his choosing in social circumstances.

But this is no social circumstance. This is a time of war. And during war, we wear our warrior colors with pride. Mine being white, as all kings before me have, and Golon in a purple so dark it appears almost black. The attire that a Gelder wears is for more than just appearance; not only can the wearer draw power from the cloth but it also tells of the wearer's rank in our society. The more skin exposed, the more powerful the being. A statement to all that this warrior is strong enough to defeat any foe, weapons or no weapons. Golon's sleeves go just past the shoulder, while my shirt has none. In battle, I rely on nothing but my sheer power alone. I need nothing else to protect me.

As king, it is my duty to announce to all that I need no assistance in protecting what is mine. Very different from the casual wear we sport when not in battle status.

"Golon. I cannot leave her." Even to my own ear, I know how desolate I sound. I recall how badly I handled my mate. How I let the bond madness drive me to harm the other half of my soul. She has become so precious to me in so little time.

I berate myself for allowing the argument we had to stretch on for so long. Maybe if I had made more of an effort to control the raging emotions our unfulfilled bond caused in me I could have prevented that fight. A thousand possibilities of what I could have done better race through my head.

"Dane." I sense Golon's movement across the room and moments later I feel his hand on my shoulder. "I know how difficult this must be for you. I can't pretend to know the struggle you are facing as I have no mate of my own, but you are king. You do not have the luxury to sit here and wait. The Erains have dealt us a hard blow, they decimated our defense network." Golon squeezes my shoulder. "You need to react. Strike back against this new threat and protect life. That is our mission, to guard any and all life in the galaxy against threats they are not prepared to face themselves. That is the way of the Gelders."

His words sink deep within me. As king, I am the supreme defender. I defend all beings no matter their race, sworn to protect and cherish the beauty of life throughout the cosmos. At this moment I would throw it all away if it would allow me to stay here with my mate. But I know Golon is right. If I fail to defend our bases that the Erains are attacking more than just my mate will perish. Trillions of souls will die.

"I will not leave her unprotected. The traitor who dares attack her has not been captured yet," I say to Golon.

"Amell and her entire *praesidium* are standing alert outside. No one is allowed to enter this room except for you and Jarlin." I let out a defeated sigh.

"Alright, I will be there shortly. Give me one moment of privacy." I turn from him before I even finish speaking. Absently, I notice that he leaves the room, but the entirety of my focus is on my mate.

"I will find this *infer* who tried to harm you, Eleanor. I will keep your planet and all the mortal planets safe. This I promise you." I lean down through the healing weave, surrounding her like a veil, and press a kiss to her forehead.

I turn and exit the room quickly. Once outside I see all six of Eleanor's *praesidium* standing guard. These males represent the strongest mastery of each of the main lineages. They are the elite guard to their queen, my mate.

I turn my attention to Kowan, the master of *simul*. He can weave all six of the lineages, making him the leader of her guard.

"Protect her well, Kowan," I say to him. I then turn my attention to the only other warrior I trust above all else.

"Amell, my friend." I place my hand on his shoulder, keeping my arm locked as straight as an arrow. A warrior's greeting. "I know you wish to aid me in the battle plans, but I cannot leave my mate at this time without knowing that you will be guarding her. Keep her safe for me." Amell, the master of *terra*, or earth power, nods.

The rest of her *praesidium* line the hallway and I make eye contact with each one. My eyes settle on Arsenio, the master of *ignis*. The fire lineage. The male who lusts for my mate and was the reason my mate and I fought so fiercely before.

Adjacent to him is the *anium* master, Malin. No warrior in existence is stronger than Malin in the water lineage. He has the unique ability to actually merge with his element. He can live underwater with no assistance or need for oxygen.

My eyes continue down the line and find Etan, the master of *caeli*, the air lineage. The gravity of the situation weighs heavily on this warrior's soul. Etan's eyes are normally full of laughter, his face exuberant. Today his entire being exudes worry and he stands stiff and alert. Posed to block any attempt on the queen's life.

Finally, I meet the gaze of Griffith, the master of *vim*. The life force lineage. The one being here who can hold my mate to life even if she tries to fade away. I feel comforted that he will be here to monitor Eleanor.

"*Praesidium*, the one who you protect lies defenseless in that room." I see all the warriors stand on alert. "I know you will do everything in your power to keep her safe. Do not let her pass from this life. I need updates as Jarlin gives them."

"Yes, my king," Amell answers me.

With a brief nod, I turn and head down the hall toward the battle room to make plans for the war.

Chapter One

Danion

"What is our next move, my king?" Shemir, the chief guard captain of my fleet, asks me. I ignore him. I am busy studying the display of our crashed defense network, trying to determine how we missed this massive hole in our system. A few well-placed attacks on only six communication outposts and the entire system crumbled. Useless. The entire system is useless now. I try to keep my mind on this network, my mind keeps wandering to my mate and how she is still being kept in a deep, healing sleep.

It is not safe for her to be awoken yet. Her body is still struggling to fight off the effects of the poison. Jarlin, her doctor, is assisting her body in every way he can. But still, she fights. It has been over one Earth week since she fell prey to this traitor's attack. I never even suspected an attack on her life. Not here on my ship. I never thought a Gelder would attack their queen.

I am told that as long as she is in the healing sleep her life is not in danger. I should be by her side, holding her hand, lending her my strength. Not here, listening to the incessant pestering of a lower warrior.

But I am a king. I have to uphold my duties to the galaxy. To protect the galaxy from this Erain vermin. For the first time, I resent this responsibility. I want to be with her. Hold her.

"My king? How do you want to proceed?" Shemir's high-pitched and nasally voice prattles on again. I have to work hard to hide my impatience. How I wish Amell or Golon were the ones with me now, but I have them on much more important tasks.

Amell is overseeing the constant guard of Eleanor, and I assigned Golon to ferret out our little stowaway. It's been over a week since my mate was poisoned and nothing has come of our search for the rat.

"My—"

"Enough! Shemir, who are you?" I cut him off.

"I am Shemir—"

"I know *that*. Your title. What is it?" I ask him with curt, abrupt words.

"I am chief guard captain. I am responsible for the guardianship of all the Gelder outposts," his nasal voice says.

"Yes. So tell me, Chief Guard Captain. Who am I?" I ask with deadly calm.

"You are king." I raise my head and meet his eyes for the first time. Holding them until he breaks contact. He knows what I am waiting for. "You are the high warrior king, Danion Belator of Old, elite rank master of *simul*, the protector of all kinds. The supreme defender."

"Yes. Yes, I am. If you know my title, and you know yours, why are you questioning me on my strategy? I will make my decision when I am ready. Once I have compiled all the facts and determined what the best course of action will be. Not a second before. And unless you wish to grow a considerable backbone and issue me a challenge, you will learn to show the respect that our respective titles require." At this, he flushes and looks down at the floor. I can smell the mortification on him like a heavy cologne. A sign of weakness. I would not expect this level of weakness in a warrior of his rank. He should be much stronger.

"Leave me. Your weakness is a stench in the air and a distraction I cannot afford. Be prepared to be under review; you dishonor your position with your words and your actions. Proving yourself unworthy." I say this last part with a challenge.

Shemir surprises me by actually meeting my gaze this time. I can see he is weighing his options. I am anxious to release some tension, and a sparring session with this warrior would do well to relax me. Any warrior worthy of the name would not let such an insult pass. He is obligated by duty to challenge me. He will defend his title and let me work off some tension.

"Very well, my king." He says this with a look at the floor and exits the room.

What?

His actions shock me. How did he walk away from his post, how did he let himself be called unworthy and not issue a challenge in response? Even being his king does not make me exempt from challenges upon honor. Something is not right.

"Jedde, find Golon and have him report to the war room immediately," I send out to the ship's communication liaison. Jedde is the eyes and ears of my ship. He can communicate with everyone from his command station on the bridge. Of course, our little Erain rat was concealed from him as well. Whoever this *infer* is he is well-informed about our behaviors and protocols.

"At once, my king," Jedde answers.

I don't bother responding. I force my mind onto the task at hand: trying to determine how I move forward protecting not only my world but also all of the worlds within the system. Our old, outdated communication system is being reconfigured after decades of neglect and will hopefully be functional within three more Earth days. My young, sweet *aninare* saw the dangers of relying solely on the new grid system.

Eleanor, a young human woman was more astute than all of my warriors combined. Myself included.

My mate, who has become so precious in so short a time.

Now that we must rely on the old archaic system, we will be hours behind the action, but that is better than the days we are right now. It takes *days* to hear about any updates from the war. I cannot understand how this happened. Erains are impulsive, it goes against their nature to band together, but that is exactly what they have done.

I shift my gaze to the new display, the one I have created to showcase what battles our people are waging. Right now, we know that every mortal world we protect was attacked. Several moons, outposts, and even emmortal races are also under siege.

They launched a full-scale attack on all sides. We simply don't have the resources to handle this, not without the grid to help us hinder their movements, take out minor threats, and predict their targets. If we knew what we were dealing with we might still manage to put up an effective defense against such staggering numbers.

Currently, the only battle we are successfully fighting and able to monitor is back on Earth. I traveled so close to this planet that we can receive updates from the defense grid every few hours. Since Eleanor was there, I had a very large force protecting that planet, from a distance. I did not want to alarm the humans, so the fleet was stationed nearby and monitored for ships entering the solar system. It seems the Erains were not prepared for such a large defense. However, our other mortal planets are not faring so well.

The shields that surround each planet are all holding up, as of two days ago when the last update came to us. We have lost ships and warriors to these battles. Warriors we cannot replace. My mind turns once again to my mate, trapped in the healing sleep. If she never awakens, I am not sure what I will do. How I will go on and fight this war without her?

By willpower alone, I push my worry away and instead focus on how to defend our territory without losing even more precious lives. I study the grids for several hours, making decisions and battle plans to be sent out on scout ships and delivered to our worlds.

I have mapped which outposts we know have been attacked and make a list of which ones can be forfeited. Those that we have no hope of saving should be evacuated so I can relocate their resources.

With this, I can reposition three Solar Class War Vessels, two full legions of Gravity Drone ships, and twelve Lunar Class War Carriers. The two mortal worlds that have lost all defenses, except the shields, only had three Gelder ships in orbit each when they were attacked.

Of these three ships, one was a civilian spacecraft that housed families of the warriors stationed there that had only minimal defenses. The other two were minor war machines. Since we did not expect a new attack on these worlds, major defenses were not present.

I decide to send one of my available solar class ships to each planet along with a quarter of the drones. This should be enough to fight off the Erains that are battling for those planets. If we are successful, we can take those planets back and save the lives of those on the surface.

I send my thoughts to the Powers that the shields have held strong and the mortals still live by the time we can get those ships there. Even though we would have lost several thousands of Gelder souls we cannot replace, I hope the billions of souls we were protecting have at least been spared.

I am debating where my third solar class would be the most useful when the doors are flung open.

"What is the meaning of summoning me, and through Jedde no less, when you know I am trying to track down that slime that poisoned my queen?" Golon demands.

"Are you implying that you are more concerned for the welfare of my mate than I am? That you feel more deeply for the wounds done to her?" I ask with deadly calm.

"Of course not!" Golon seems to shake himself, then breathes deeply. "Apologies, *cognata*. I am only frustrated at how well he has hidden. A whole *pallie* has passed since the queen was poisoned and I have not found a single sign of him." Frustration is evident in his voice.

"Yes, that is why I called you." I look at him pointedly. "I understand your frustration and therefore will overlook your outburst. But never forget, I am Eleanor's mate first and king second. I would not have summoned you for anything less than her needs."

"Again, apologies. What have you uncovered?"

"Shemir, the chief guard captain. He was acting most strange this evening. Acted in ways no true warrior ever would. Allowed me to question his honor and say he is unworthy of his position without challenge. Just accepted my words and left. No warrior with so blatant a weakness would have climbed to such a title as chief guard captain. Follow him and see what you can uncover. He may very well lead us to more clues," I instruct Golon.

"You challenged his worthiness and he merely left?" Golon questions with a peculiar look on his face.

"Yes, I let him know to expect a review as he is not worthy of his title. He left the room with no challenge issued."

"The Shemir I know has always been so focused on proving his worth. He would not have allowed such a slight to pass without defense. I will investigate and let you know what I can bring to light." With a hasty bow, Golon disappears from the room.

I turn back to my plans. Once I finalize the defense of our territory I can return to my mate's bedside and aid her in any way I can. With that, I focus again on the boards spread before me in the air.

Where to put that last Solar Class?

Ellie

I open my eyes slowly. I feel so worn out. My limbs feel like lead. My head feels like someone used it to set off a gong. My mouth is full of cotton. I feel awful.

When I finally manage to open my eyes and register my surroundings, I see I am under some sort of glass box. There is writing in a blue light-up display that I cannot read on the box. Outside of the glass, I see white everywhere.

"Eleanor? Can you hear me?" I turn my head to the voice. I see Danion, my warrior, looking at me from the side of the glass. His hand is holding mine through some kind of glove that connects from the outside. It is not rubber or thick like the ones I have seen back on Earth Nueva, but it seems to be part of his hand, a living part of him. Just a haze around his hands. It appears almost as if the glass is wrapping itself around his hand.

"Eleanor?"

"Yes, I can hear you," I croak out. I can barely form words with how dry my throat and mouth are.

"I have summoned the doctor; you have nothing to worry about now. I will keep you safe." His words barely register. My eyelids are falling again, and before I know it the world is black again as I am swept into the peaceful nothingness that consumes me.

Danion

"Why did she fall back into the healing sleep? I thought you said she would wake up?" I demand to know why my mate has succumbed to sleep once more. Out of the corner of my eye, I see Amell, that mate-lusting bastard Arsenio, and the rest of her *praesidium* back away. Well, let them. I am in no mood to fight my rage. My mate has slipped away again.

"We cannot control her body's needs, Danion. It is a miracle she is still alive at all. We have her remarkable heritage to thank for that," her doctor states.

"Have you discovered where she comes from?" I ask of him. The only reason the poison did not take my mate's life was because of her mixed heritage. We thought her human, but upon inspection of her DNA, we found that she is in fact only half-human.

"Yes, and it is the most surprising thing I have ever seen. Such a seamless fusion of two radically different genetic makeups is truly fascinating. In truth, I have no idea how it was possible. How it even came to be—"

"How what came to be?" I interrupt his musings. I need answers, not to listen to him fawn over her genetic history and wonder how she came to be. "She is my mate, and your queen, not some science experiment to marvel at. Your job is to heal her. Now, what have you uncovered?" Jarlin acknowledges his error with a stiff nod of his head.

"She is half-Gelder, and not just any Gelder but *ancient* Gelder. A very old, very powerful Gelder line. Prior to the transition that made us immortal, if I had to hazard a guess with so little data. There are some odd markers in there, bits that are not accounted for in either genetic makeup, so I am still looking for those origins and—"

"How is that possible? Half-Gelder means that one of her parents was one of us. The ancients died off several millennia ago, so how can my human mate, who has only lived for twenty Earth years, have one parent who is ancient Gelder?"

"Your guess is as good as mine at this point. No warrior would have a child outside of the protection of our ships. All warriors bring their mates to a Gelder stronghold for safekeeping once they are with child. They also would have been careful with who they left in charge of her care." Jarlin frowns before he continues.

"Obviously she was mistreated in her youth. In addition to the evidence of breaks in her bones that never healed properly, I can see she has not had proper nutrition for a substantial part of her young life." His lip curls in disgust and my stomach burns with similar revulsion.

I can practically feel the anger radiating off her *praesidium*. To mistreat a child is one of the very few crimes punishable by death to the Gelders. Children are revered, due in part to their rarity.

His words are like lightning through me, and my mind whirls with a mixture of rage and confusion. Who will I kill for her mistreatment? Why did she not tell me of her abuse? I tamp down my rage and force myself to focus on the problem at hand: how to treat her now that we know her lineage.

To truly ensure her health fully recovers we need to know her parentage. How is she half-Gelder? The ancients were not immortal. They aged and they died. They would not be alive still, even if they were stranded out on one of these remote planets. It was several thousands of years ago that we transitioned. At least five thousand. The transition occurred two generations before my own birth. None of the first explorers who set out to map the galaxy would still be alive to give life to a child. They would have died off thousands of Earth years ago.

"Keep trying to find the origins of those genetic markers you are not sure about. Maybe they can shed some light on her heritage. I will be back soon; I have to find Golon and inform him of this. Keep this quiet for now." He gives me a disgruntled look at this last command. I suppose it is unnecessary, but I am taking no chances. Not when my mate is stuck in that blasted healing sleep pod.

I caress her hand one more time and then lower my head through the weave and allow the threads to wrap around me to keep her safe. I place a small kiss on her forehead.

"Sleep well and heal fast little one. I will try to be back before you wake," I whisper into her ear.

As I rise from the pod's silvery weave, I check that the threads are knitting back together in an unbreakable seal. Only I will be able to penetrate the weave I have threaded. I can reach through it, allowing the threads to wrap around my hand like a glove. I trust no one else to weave this for her. Of course, I was right next to her at dinner and I was unable to stop her from being poisoned. I am hesitant to leave my mate unprotected.

"Griffith?" I summon the *vim* master in my mate's elite protective guard.

"Yes, my king." Griffith walks to join me. I study the warrior before me. He is tall by Earth standards, but still several inches beneath my height. He exhibits the standard Gelder characteristics: black hair, and brown eyes, with strong almost severe bone structure. Nothing like the delicate features of my mate.

His clothing matches that of the rest of her *praesidium*: battle leathers that encase his legs and conceal the blades he carries, and a *memien* woven shirt. His sleeves fall to the mid-bicep, the sign of a master-class warrior. No social class is higher than the warriors before me, except for myself and Golon.

I glance back to my mate in that healing sleep pod, just looking so small. She is still dressed in the casual wear of my rank and she even wears the color white, which is associated with my name, just like she wore at our *cerum fuse*. Her bodice is adorned with a white cloth woven into an X design. The way the material cuts across her shoulders leaves them exposed, the fabric making them appear stark. It only adds to her small presence in the pod.

I long to see her walking again. Feel her skin against mine with no weave between us.

"I need you to be stationed inside Eleanor's room beside her healing pod, not outside at the door," I instruct Griffith.

Since the poisoning, no one has entered the room without having to pass through the guards. But with this new information about her heritage, I am worried all over again. She may not react well to any treatment we can give her. She is of a unique physiology. I fear that even as powerful as Jarlin is he will not be able to heal her.

"Of course, I will not leave her side," Griffith readily agrees.

Eleanor has made such an impact on us in such a short time. It is no surprise that her *praesidium* is anxious over her health and safety.

"Griffith, there is another task I would ask of you."

"Yes, my king? What is it?"

"I would ask that you keep a constant monitor on Eleanor's life force. Being the master of *vim* I trust that you would be able to sense if she was beginning to fade away. Or if she begins to have a relapse."

I know I have no right to ask this of Griffith; *vim* is one of the most taxing lineages to weave because it takes a severe toll on the body. It is impossible to weave *vim* without draining your own life force. However, I must ask this of him. I cannot leave her without a guarantee that she will not slip away in my absence.

"I will guard her with my very life," Griffith says gravely. In this instance he is not merely saying this, he is literally using his own life to guard hers. To anchor hers to this world. With a nod of gratitude, I exit the room.

Chapter Two

Ellie

There is a piercing pain in my head. I try to open my eyes but that makes it even worse. I slam my lids closed to protect myself from the blinding pain.

"Are you alright, Eleanor?" I hear a voice to my left. I cannot open my eyes, but I do not need my vision to identify my guest. Griffith.

"Yes, Griffith. Just some pain in my head." I try to speak but I can tell my voice is barely a whisper in the large room.

"Here, let me take that from you," he tells me. I sense him approach me and I risk opening my eyes. Through the silvery, glittering screen I see Griffith hold out his hand above me.

I feel a strange, warm sensation surround my head. The pain gently recedes and I slowly open my eyes without pain.

"How did you do that?" I ask him as he lowers his hand, letting it fall at his side. There seems to be lines around his eyes that were not there before.

"As a master of *vim* one of the abilities I have is to take on the physical pain of others. I can relieve their pain by bringing it into my own body." He says this with significant less volume than when I first awoke.

"You took on my headache?" I ask him, baffled as to why he would do this for me.

"Yes. You need to heal, Eleanor. The body is less effective at mending itself when it's in pain. You are in a sleep pod, a healing sleep pod. That headache forced you awake. You need the healing sleep." His words are beginning to fade away.

I can feel my mind being pulled back into a deep fog. I try to fight it, to resist going with it. I attempt to reach for Griffith but my hand stays limp at my side. I disappear into the abyss.

Three Days Later

I am vaguely aware of my body being moved several times. How many times I am moved is anybody's guess. How long has it been since I have been asleep? I have no idea. I recall awakening several times and Danion was at my side for almost all of them.

As I look around this time, I notice he is absent. I try to fight my sense of loss. He is a king. I am sure he has more important things to do than be sitting by my bedside.

Perhaps I dreamed of his presence. Perhaps he was never here. I notice that I am no longer under the strange, glass-like box. I am now in a white bed that gently levitates on its own; it vaguely resembles a hospital bed. I quickly realize that I am not alone.

"You must be Eleanor!" a happy, chipper voice bellows so loudly it makes me cringe. "I am so excited to finally meet you! I do wish it was in happier circumstances. I am Joy Goldsire, Liam's mate. If it wasn't for Liam and his protectiveness, I would have been there to meet you at your arrival."

"Liam?" I ask. I turn toward the voice and see a woman in the bed to my right.

I know from my stay with the Gelders that clothing is very symbolic in their culture, and immediately notice how similar her brown and gold shirt is to my own clothing's design.

Since she is of a lower rank, she has an added layer of material around her midsection and sleeves that start just below her shoulders, leaving them bare. The sleeves are connected to her bodice by only by a small strip of cloth and cover her entire arms down to her wrists.

Even with her sitting in bed, I can tell she is several inches taller than me, not that it is hard to be given my small stature.

I am instantly enthralled with the raven hair cascading down her back, pooling on the bed next to her hips. It is so gorgeous, like a long, silky waterfall. Her warm, honey eyes sparkle with her smile. Incredible. I have never seen such gorgeous eyes. Aside from Danion's, of course. His piercing gray eyes are truly remarkable.

"Yes! My mate, Liam, I know you met him. He told me how lucky the king was to be gifted a mate. After all these years of waiting, his patience was finally rewarded." She says this last part with a smirk. "I now see he did not exaggerate. Female, you are gorgeous!"

"Female?" I am fighting the fog in my mind. I vaguely recall Liam mentioning he had a mate who was unwell, which is why I couldn't meet her earlier. I also remember she was from Earth Nueva as well.

"Oh, I'm sorry! I got used to the way the Gelders talk since I so rarely get to communicate with my great-great-nieces. It is a phrase from my Earth days, but we said 'girl' instead of 'female.' I have been known to combine the lingo of humans and Gelders," Joy explains, but my mind fixates on only one thing.

I can barely contain myself when I realize the importance of what she said.

"Communicate with Earth? Do you mean to say you are allowed to talk to people on Earth? How is that possible? How do you talk to people on Earth?" I ask quickly, my voice cracking slightly.

The possibility that I can speak with my family again is almost too much to bear. I miss my sisters so badly it is like a gaping wound in my chest. And Marilee, my best friend who I was abruptly taken from at the claiming ceremony.

I need to know that they are alright and that they are happy. If there is any way that I can talk with them I am going to do it.

"Well, of course, I talk with family. I wouldn't just leave them all behind, would I? Of course, everyone I knew closely has passed away now since I have been here for...let me think...one hundred and two years." Her eyes roll upwards to look at some invisible thing above her. Her tongue sticks out ever so slightly and she appears to do the math in her head.

"But I do have some great-great-nieces and nephews living on Earth and I like to check in every once in a while." She pauses for a moment, looking at me with concern. "Are you alright, Eleanor? You seem a bit pale. Should I ring for Jarlin?" I can't comprehend her words though.

"No, I am fine," I answer absently.

She speaks with her family, how is that possible?

I am about to question her further on how she communicates with her family but something she said grabs my attention. "You are over one hundred years old? How is that possible?"

"Oh, have they not explained about that yet? When you perform the *cerum fuse* you bind yourself to your mate. During the bond of the flesh, our physical bodies are connected. We are linked to our mates, so we age at the same pace as they do," she explains.

"So, if one of us dies, the other one does too?" The implications of how my life affects Danion come crashing over me.

This painful realization explains why everyone is so worried about my health. They are not worried about *me*, but what my death would mean to them. If I were to perish, so would Danion.

Even though Joy's next words should set my mind at ease, they don't. I can't get the idea out of my head that these warriors had a secondary motive for saving my life.

"No, nothing like that. Though I am told that physical pain is common if one mate dies, the other does not die along with them. The aging process is completely different. It is an intentional thing. Your mate purposely keeps your body in this youthful state. It is very rare for a mate to die along with their partner."

"But not unheard of?" I ask her as I notice her specific wording.

"Well...no." She seems hesitant to answer me. I continue to stare at her until she answers me. "Occasionally a mate can *choose* to follow their mate from this existence."

"What do you mean choose? They take their own life?" I query.

"In a sense yes. They spend their whole lives with their mate, sometimes that life spans more than a millennium. After that long together, they cannot imagine living in a world that does not have their mate in it." Her words are sad.

"Wow. I can't imagine knowing a love so strong that death is the preference over not being with them." I marvel at her words. It sounds equal parts amazing and horrifying.

A love like that can be very dangerous. While on the other side of the coin, it could be beautiful. I am filled with longing, and reticence, at the thought of possessing a love like that.

"Oh, but you will. It is the way of the Gelders. They love as strongly as they do battle."

"I suppose for some it is," I answer her. I can't imagine Danion needing me so much that he would choose death if I were to fall.

"No, it is true for you. I have seen how Danion was when he thought you might not pull through."

I am about to argue my point again, but the determined look in her eyes tells me she will not let this go easily. Rather than fight over this, I cede my point so we can move on to more important topics.

"Oh, alright. I suppose he does care for me in his own way. But we haven't known each other long." I am anxious to move past this topic of conversation. I have questions that she needs to answer. "So...you talk with your family on Earth? I didn't think this was possible. No one has ever heard from a woman once she has been claimed." I explain to her one of the most basic and well-known facts on Earth Nueva.

"What are you talking about? I talk with them at least once an Earth month. Just to check in and see if they need anything." Now she looks as perplexed as I do. "Why would you think we don't get to talk to our families? The Gelders aren't stealing us away, just claiming their soul mates. They want us to be happy, not deprive us of family."

I answer slowly, choosing my words carefully. "I can't speak for the Gelder side, but on Earth, we are told no woman who has been claimed has ever been heard from again." I can't shake the feeling that something very wrong is going on.

I do not know how to reconcile this new information. The longer I am here the more I realize that what I have long accepted as fact is not correct.

Every time I learn new information about my position here with the Gelders it contradicts what I have been taught my whole life. My inner bullshit meter is saying it can't all be a mistake. One side of this agreement is obviously lying, and I am leaning toward Earth being in the wrong.

"Would you mind answering a few questions for me? About what it means to be a claimed woman and how it affects Earth?" I ask Joy.

"Sure I will, but I have a nasty feeling I am not going to like these questions. I also have a feeling I don't want to be anywhere near Danion when he finds out." She says this with a mixture of concern and mischief. I smile over at her and silently agree with her. If what I suspect is true, and I have been lied to by Earth Nueva officials, Danion is going to be furious.

"OK, so you have covered that you can talk with family. Are there any limits to who you can talk with on Earth?" I ask with a thought to my best friend, Marilee.

"No, Danion has no concern with who you talk to from your old life. It is usually prepared videos though since we are often too far away from Earth to be able to establish a back-and-forth connection. We have the technology, but Earth refused to take any of it. Our communications technology is capable of incorporating a projection-based video so it would be like I was there with them. The videos were the Earth ambassador's idea actually, a form of compromise. I think it has been about eighty Earth years since I had a physical visit."

"Really? Why so long?"

"Well, I am an ambassador's wife. I share many duties with my mate and we are very busy. Also the last living relative I knew personally passed away. Accidental car crash." Pain clouds her face when she tells me this. "So, it just has not been a huge priority to make the trip. Especially since my nieces and nephews are a little unsure of me. Being so old, but looking so young." She gives a little laugh. "Whenever I mention coming to meet them, they respond with some excuse as to why it is not a good time."

"How old are you? I don't want to be rude, but you must be over one hundred and twenty years?" I ask her.

"I celebrated my one hundred and thirty-first birthday this year. But I am told I don't look a day over one hundred." She laughs loudly at her own joke, causing me to laugh with her.

"Well, I would have pegged you at eighty so you're doing well for yourself," I joke back at her. Her laughter has put me at ease. "But seriously, I understand where your nieces and nephews are coming from. I am so surprised that you can look so young. I never knew that we would not age."

"I can still hardly believe that no one told you. What did your preparer tell you before you traveled here?" She looks at me with confusion.

"Nothing. Well, she hinted that I was being sold into slavery—" I am cut off by her shriek.

"WHAT! Slavery? To who?"

"To the Gelders." Joy loudly scoffs at my words.

"This is ridiculous. They would not enslave us, they are a guardian race. They protect life above all else." She shifts in her bed to face me. "You better start at the beginning. Tell me everything about your stay on Earth."

And so I do. I start with the breakdown of the areas, what it means for me to be in Area Three, the continued Erain attacks we see in the sky, and the little we know about the claiming process.

Throughout it all her face gets more and more closed off. Void of emotion and sometimes even strained, as if she is diverting her attention between me and another person. I don't know who, as we are the only ones in this room.

Danion

"My king, I respectfully request an audience to discuss a rather urgent matter." I hear Liam's voice at my back. I turn away from my study of Golon's investigation report. It appears our *Shemir* is nowhere to be found. It is as if he just disappeared.

"Yes, Liam? What is it?" I motion for him to join me at the station I have dedicated to defense.

"It concerns your mate." I jump from my chair but Liam's next words stop my progress to the door. "Oh, nothing with her health," he rushes to assure me and I resume my seat. "Though she did wake up a while ago."

"What? Why was I not told?" I start to rise once again, anxious to speak with her, but his next words stop me dead.

"She awoke briefly and spoke with my mate. I understand she is sleeping again now. Jarlin did not know she was awake and she never called out to her *praesidium* either. It appears only Joy spoke with her." Liam pauses briefly, apprehension clear on his face, before he continues. "But, sire, the information Joy discovered about Earth needs to be discussed. It may affect your mate's happiness in the near future."

I have an idea of what Liam is going to tell me. I am just now beginning to realize that the human race has some rather nasty characters holding the seats of power. Using tactics that are so underhanded, even I as a jaded warrior cringe at them.

But still, it is important to gather all information. I am curious to discover what new crimes the humans have committed.

"What did Joy find out?" I ask with resignation, knowing I will not like the answer.

"It appears that the Earth Joy left is radically different from the one your mate lived on. So different in fact it is almost as if they come from different planets entirely. Something very wrong is going on there."

"Explain." I try to house my impatience but I do not succeed. The word is short and abrupt.

"Well, to start it appears that on this newly named Earth Nueva people are born into designated roles. They are never allowed to aspire to be more than what they were born into."

"Eleanor did mention something like this. While it is upsetting, we do not make a habit of judging or interfering with the societal systems of the worlds we protect." The exception being in situations where the world is divided, then we do require the whole planet to agree to our terms. Thus requiring them to dissolve any disputes between themselves.

I recall Earth was one of the planets where we did have to enforce this law. It is not surprising that some restructuring of their government ensued. They were massively divided. Hundreds of governments had to be dissolved and reintegrated into one new unified system.

"Yes, except this is not how Joy grew up. In any way. In her youth, she was encouraged to be whoever she wanted to be. To dream. And it was not just her country, it was in many countries. Freedom was highly regarded all around the world." Liam speaks quickly, barely breathing between words. "This is a radical change to occur in only a century. Even with the government restructuring, I cannot conceive of a situation that would net this result. I do not believe it occurred organically; someone has brought about this change in social structure. Most likely as a power play."

I contemplate his words. It is not strange, or even rare, for a world to experience radical changes to its social structure once they discover they are not alone in the galaxy. But this is more than a social change. This is a complete reversal in beliefs if I believe Joy, which I do.

"What could have caused this change in beliefs? Or enforced it?"

"I warn you that I have no evidence to support this, but combined with the other things our queen told Joy, I believe that their human ambassador has used fear propaganda to subjugate the people of Earth. And he used us to do it."

His words cause a fire in my core and a responding flare in my powers. Ever since Eleanor fell ill I have struggled to control my powers. The smallest amount of distraction causes my power to leap at its bonds.

"How? How could they use us?"

"Eleanor has a very long list of ideas about the Claiming Pact and the actions of what the Gelders will do to enforce it, yet none of it is true. Most of it can only be described, at best, as deliberately misleading." He takes a deep breath and I brace myself for his next words. "For instance, she believes that no claimed women have ever been heard from again. It is all but stated that we do these women harm. The entire planet fears what we do to the women we claim. Most think we enslave them or worse, rape and kill them."

"Rape our mates? The single being we pledge to protect above all others is being told we will *rape* them when they come to us? Why do they come willingly then?" After my heated outburst, I recall the revelation I had soon after meeting my mate. Liam reiterates my own beliefs.

"King, this is only the beginning, there is much worse to come. Eleanor told Joy that every woman who is claimed knows that if they refuse us anything, anything at all, we will terminate the agreement and let the Erains kill them all." I suspected this from my discussion with Amell, but to hear its confirmation raises a thirst for blood inside me. "And that they see *daily* proof of Erain ships exploding above them. That they are ever present and constantly trying to get through the Gelder defense shield we have in place around the planet."

"But the Erains have not attacked Earth since we fought them off a century ago. They attack now, but nothing before this."

"Yes, I am aware. But Eleanor is not. She also says that several *thousand* people die from Erain abduction and mutilation every year." His words lie heavy in the room. Thick with horrifying implications. I pause in stunned silence before speaking.

"You are saying that the humans are killing their own people, mutilating their own people? The Erains have been absent from their section of space for decades and nowhere near their planet since the war." My words are dark. "They are not responsible for these atrocities."

"I have no proof, but I fear that is what is happening. I imagine anyone who questions the authority of the government is quickly disposed of. It would explain why the humans who communicate with our women have not shared the fact that they hear from our mates with the rest of Earth's population. Also, it explains why so many of our mates' remaining family members all died accidental deaths eighty years ago." Liam says these last words ominously.

"They have killed our family." My words are bleak. "There will be blood for these actions." I sit quietly for a moment. "Why would they risk our wrath with this betrayal of the agreement? Let alone *how* have they kept it a secret all this time. No leaks. In a world that is advanced enough to possess global communication, it would be impossible to cover every story. To prevent this being reported on."

"There is no communication now on Earth. Of any kind."

"What? I recall global communication networks the last time I visited that planet. It is how we ratified the agreement."

"There were. In fact, there were extensive forms of communication one hundred years ago. Joy remembers freedom of speech and a system called the 'Internet' where you could talk to anyone in the world. But Eleanor had no idea what these were. They disabled the networks. There aren't even news broadcasts. Everything is routed through the government now. No way to talk to the masses without approval from the ruling powers."

"They have stripped the very rights of their people. Using us to do it. We have to put a stop to this."

"I agree, but there is more." Liam's words are bleak.

"More? What else could there be?"

"Joy said Eleanor told her of the rules all women must follow or they risk terminating the treaty with us. Rules like studying certain subjects only, letting men enter a building first, never contradicting a man in public, and an endless amount of tripe all geared toward making women feel inferior to men."

At his words I feel a rage that rivals what I felt when Arsenio dared try to seduce my mate. It is an all-consuming rage. Although this time I embrace the fire, gladly funneling the raw power that comes with the anger.

"Liam?" I speak with a deathly calm.

"Yes, my king."

"I am not going to kill the human scum responsible for this. I am going to torture him. When I find out who instigated this I am going to make him wish he had never heard the name Danion Belator of Old."

Chapter Three

Ellie

When I awake again I slowly open my eyes and blink repeatedly to clear them of the bright lights of the hospital wing. I look to my left and see Danion sitting by my bedside, grasping my hand. His face is stoic, making direct eye contact with me.

"Hi." Upon seeing his face I realize how much I have missed him. It also makes me realize that Joy's presence when I awoke last distracted me from understanding the implications of where I am. I think back to my last memory before being in this room. All I can remember is intense heat.

"What happened?" I ask the proud warrior who is my mate.

"I assume you mean why you are here? You were poisoned, Eleanor." Danion's words are hot, filled with unsaid anger. But behind it, I can sense his fear.

"Poison?" I feel my chest get tight. "How?" It is all I can manage to ask. It is not Danion who answers my question.

"We were able to identify that the spiced juice you enjoy was contaminated with a poison lethal to humans." The other male's words are heavy, laced with a meaning I cannot decipher. My mind is sluggish; all I can focus on is the fact that I was poisoned.

"I am happy that your medicines were able to keep me alive." I split my gaze between the two males in the room with me.

"We were able to manage your symptoms, but the circumstances behind this poison are beyond our medicines. We were not able to administer an antidote until three days ago, right before you awoke last time. You have once again been in a healing sleep since then."

"Jarlin, don't." Danion's words are full of warning.

"Jarlin? Who is Jarlin?" I ask. I am slowly gaining control of my thoughts. My brain feels like honey.

"That would be me, my queen. I am Jarlin. I am master of *hael* and a healer of the elite class." He says this with a small bow. He shifts his attention to Danion. "She deserves to know, Danion."

"Not now she doesn't. She has just returned to me. I desire some time with her. She needs to heal."

"What do I deserve to know?" I glance between these two bolstering males. "Danion, I am fine. If there is something you are concealing from me, I insist you come out with it." By sheer willpower, I am forcing my mind to clear. Danion meets my gaze with no emotion. I can tell he wants to fight me.

"Danion. I want to know. Jarlin, tell me." I turn my eyes to the healer. Jarlin's eyes flick to Danion. "Don't look at him, I am right here. It is my life. I have the right to know." Jarlin remains motionless. I turn my hot gaze to Danion. "Don't do this, Danion. I deserve to know whatever you know. I thought that is what you wanted, for us to be partners. Equals. We can't be equals if you decide what I am and am not ready to know."

"As you wish, Eleanor," he says after a pregnant pause. "Jarlin, I will be the one to tell her."

"I think it best if I stay so that I am here to answer any technical questions the queen may have."

"Very well." With that, Jarlin steps back to give us an illusion of privacy. My sense of dread magnifies. Whatever they have to tell me must be awful. Perhaps I am dying. Danion turns his attention to our clasped hands. "Eleanor, the poison you were given is one hundred percent lethal to humans. It is a death sentence. No one survives it." His words hang heavy in the room.

"But...I did. Obviously I am still alive. Did you bring me back from the dead?" I ask hesitantly. In one way, this is much worse than I thought. But in another way, I was fearing that I would soon perish with or without their advanced knowledge. So this is not the worst news he could have told me.

"No, you never died, Eleanor." His gaze is heavy on mine. Penetrating into my soul. As if he is willing me to grasp his meaning.

"Then how did I survive? How am I here?" I struggle to come to terms with what he is telling me.

"You survived, simply, because it is lethal to humans only. There are other races, such as mine, that are able to fight it off." His meaning hits me like a falling Erain ship from the sky. Right before it crashes into the shield and explodes.

"But...but I *am* human," I insist.

"No. You are *half*-human," he corrects me. "Apparently."

"How is that possible?" My question hangs empty in the room. I asked the question to no one in particular, but it is Jarlin who answers.

"My queen, if you permit me?" He produces a three-dimensional display that hovers above the floor. It is the only spot of color in this stark white room. The hovering model resembles me and Jarlin motions toward it with his hand, silently asking for my permission to explain the diagram. I nod. "Gratitude to you, my queen. Once you were brought in I examined you fully. Your core body temperature had skyrocketed to well over three times the survivable level for a human. After I forced your body temperature down to a more manageable climate, I pored over the data. Your DNA, while human in some ways, had genetic markers that are not in the human genome."

"How is that possible? I was born on Earth. My mother hates me; she wouldn't have taken me in out of kindness. I have never even met a Gelder before I was claimed. Or any alien for that matter. I have only seen them in government advertisements. Even that has been very infrequent." I question him with no small amount of force. My entire being is rejecting what he is trying to say.

"Your mother was indeed human. However, your father was Gelder. Full-blooded Gelder if I had to guess. And I never guess," Jarlin says confidently.

"No. Just no. You are wrong. You have to be wrong." I can't bring myself to accept what they are saying. "You have made some kind of mistake."

"Look down at yourself, your chest, how do you explain that?" Jarlin asks. At his words I look down at myself and don't see anything different. I look to Jarlin, then Danion, with a question in my eyes.

"Look at your bare skin, *aninare.*" Danion lifts the sheet and holds it up to block Jarlin's gaze. With one last look to both males I pull my top away from my body and freeze.

I can't believe my eyes. I blink rapidly, as if that will change what I am seeing. Starting under my left breast is an intricate tattoo, sweeping up and around my chest in a gentle arc. It is beautiful and graceful. It vaguely resembles an old, dead language I once came across in my studies.

I see the resemblance to the markings every Gelder carries upon their chests. Those markings tell the story of battles won. Of bloodshed. The stories of the lives they have taken. I feel sick as I look at the beautiful, yet macabre story that now is permanently a part of me. Tears gather in my eyes.

"How? Why? I have never killed anyone. Why did these appear on me?" I whisper to the room. Whoever I come across will think me a killer. That I took the life of someone else. "What happened while I was in that healing sleep you speak of? How did I kill someone and have no memory?"

"Kill someone? Why would you think you killed someone, for Powers' sake?" Danion's quick, scorching anger is like a balm to my wounded soul. A small piece of familiarity in an ocean of uncertainty. I cling to his anger like a life preserver.

"My markings. They are The Warriors' Blood Tale. A recollection of every life taken by a warrior, whether in battle or not," I explain to him.

"Where did you hear that? Who would tell you this? It is ridiculous. That is NOT what a Gelder mark is." Danion's hand cups my chin, forcing me to raise my head and meet his gaze.

"It's not?" I ask him, barely concealing the hope in my gaze.

"No." His answer is heavy with finality. "It is best if you forget every single thing you have ever been told of us. It is all a blatant falsehood. Our markings tell our history, our ancestry. It is a way that we can always know family. Our family trees are born with us, a part of us. Our flesh proudly displaying where and who we come from. Linking us to the lives lost and sacrifices that were made to gift us with life."

His words are beautiful. I struggle to accept them.

"Then why am I just now getting the markings?" Again, it is Jarlin who steps up.

"I believe that the poison is the reason for that."

"How so?"

"Since you were brought in here I have been monitoring everything your body has been doing, even on a cellular level. Your DNA is changing. Proteins that have long been dormant are being expressed. Proteins that resemble ancient Gelder proteins, not human ones.

"It is my belief that something caused your latent Gelder heritage to activate. Either it was the poison itself, an emergency response to your cells dying, or the heat that ravaged your body that sparked this change. Or some other unknown cause, I am still looking into what could have been the start of all of this. Nevertheless, the fact remains that you are of Gelder descent. Strong Gelder descent, at that. You are becoming more Gelder by the day, there is no question of that."

"So...my almost dying sparked my DNA to transform itself to save me? And my markings emerged because now my DNA is more Gelder than human?" I question.

"Not quite. A cell is a simple system; it responds to signals from the body to tell it what to do. When your body began to shut down, it signaled that the cells needed something. So your cells found a way to give you what you needed to survive. That something being your more resilient Gelder DNA."

"Why would I need the markings to survive? Is there some sort of function to the markings?" I ask Jarlin.

"No, they are as Danion said. They tell our ancestry, our history. But you cannot pick and choose what genes you want. Once the latent DNA activated, it triggered all of them to change. This is just one of many physical changes I expect to see in the coming days."

"I am going to look different?" I ask him with a hint of desperation in my voice. "I won't be me anymore?" I can feel myself beginning to hyperventilate.

I may not be anything special. My hair lacks any luster and my eyes will never sparkle like some, but I have always been me. If that changes, what am I left with? Not only am I different on the inside and losing the most basic part of me, my DNA, but I am also losing my body to this unforgiving change.

"*Aninare*, you will still be you. There are not many traits we have that you don't on the outside. The marking is one of the few. They began appearing almost immediately, yet everything else about you is the same. Your gorgeous, unique hair is still the same as the day I first saw you. Your eyes still have the same piercing beauty that makes me want to be a better male for you. Your mouth is still provocative enough to make me curse my stupidity for causing the divide between us." His hand cups my head. "You are you, and nothing can change that."

His words touch something deep inside of me. They bring me out of my panic. He is right, I am still me. Even if a few cells inside act differently. I am still the same girl I always was. No markings will change that. Nothing can change who I am except me.

I tighten my hand around his and thank him with my eyes. I now need to force myself to focus on the questions that are at the forefront of my mind.

"So these markings, they tell of where you come from?" I ask them, they both nod. "I have never known my father. My mother never speaks of him. I have imagined a thousand different scenarios in my head about what he may have been like, what kind of man he was. I would like to know. I deserve to know. What do they say? Where am I from?" I ask of both of them.

"Well, that is a little difficult to answer," Danion begins, but Jarlin picks up.

"Not necessarily," Jarlin says with an insincere look of apology for the interruption. "Your markings are in the ancient language but the characters are not quite the same. In fact, there are some rather significant differences to our ancient written word. I am not able to read them. Many of the markings appear similar to our symbols, yet they are distorted somehow.

"This may be because you are both Gelder and human. It could have resulted in a combination of both languages. There is only one word we are able to make out." I wait for him to continue, but he says nothing else.

"Well? What is it? What word?" I ask after it is clear he is done talking. Danion squeezes my hand to catch my attention.

"*Lacieu*. The lost lineage. It has been lost to us for over five thousand years. The first lineage. The original. The lineage that brought forth all of the others. The lineage that gave birth to the Gelder race. We believe you have it within you."

At Danion's words I would have had to sit down if I weren't already lying down. It has been a day for shocking revelations.

Chapter Four

Ellie

The next morning I mentally review everything I learned from Danion and Jarlin. After they dropped the bomb of my suspected roots, Jarlin left and Danion stayed with me until I fell asleep.

He even helped me walk around the room a little. I wanted to get up for a moment and stretch my legs, I just needed out of the bed. While he was concerned, he did help me up and stayed close to me the entire time. I was only up for a few minutes before he had me back in the bed to rest.

During that time we spoke of inconsequential things. Just meaningless little topics. For a king I am sure they were boring. But for me? For me it was everything. I recall the way Danion helped me fall asleep, with his hand in my hair. Singing me a soft, calm lullaby in a language I had never heard before.

I never knew he was so romantic. I am still smiling when the doors open and Joy is brought in. She is confined to her bed again. I wonder what it is that renders her bedridden.

"I tell you, Ellie, those guards of yours are no joke. They insist on doing a full search of me every time I have to come here for my checkups. It is getting real frustrating." Her words bring me out of my haze.

Before I fell asleep, I learned that I am connected to the lineage that they believed had died out several thousand years before Danion was even born. Now I'm stuck in a loop of anxiety wondering what this all means for me and the people I care about.

Strangely, the list of people I care about is significantly larger than it was before Danion claimed me. Before, only my sisters and Marilee were on it. Now it has Danion, Golon,

Liam, my *praesidium*, Joy... The list goes on and on. So many people have shown me kindness since coming here.

"I mean, do they think I am going to attack you? I come here every day to be examined. For the last week you have been unconscious while I am here and I have never harmed you. Overprotective for sure." She then smiles. "Not that I can say anything about protective males. Look at Liam, he insists I am checked out every day." Her words make me curious. "Though I do understand his concern." Her face speaks of deep sadness.

"Why are you being checked every day? Are you ill?" I ask her.

"Ill? Oh, Powers no! I'm pregnant." I notice now the glow they say some women have. She practically exudes happiness. At our first meeting I thought that was just her natural joy. As if she was merely embodying her name.

"In fact"—her voice lowers to a conspiratorial whisper—"I have made it into the second trimester. I am so excited; we have never made it this far before. I feel really good about this one."

"Made it? What do you mean?" Her face loses its glow and appears heartbroken again.

"Well, I am not sure if you know this, but the Gelders, well, their population is dying off. They are having fewer and fewer children. I have been mated to Liam for a century, and while we have conceived many times we have lost them all. Never made it past the tenth week. But this is my thirteenth week now." I can see the hope and longing on her face. She wants this baby so badly.

"I am so sorry for your loss. That must be unbearable. I will think of your unborn son or daughter and hope they are gifted a long and healthy life," I tell her with utmost sincerity.

"Thank you, Ellie. I just feel that this is the one. Jarlin, well he..." Her voice breaks as tears gather in her eyes. "He fears that after so many losses, this may be my last chance. It takes longer and longer to conceive now. We went almost a decade between conceptions this time. So I am not moving from this bed until I am holding my precious little baby. I am even transported here from my chambers in this bed. I am taking no risks this time."

"If there is ever anything you need, I am here for you." I look over at her. "Anything."

"Thank you, Ellie. Let us think of happier things." She fans her face, trying to stop her tears. "What do you think of my new *memien* band?" She lifts her arm and flaunts a bracelet that resembles the cloth on my bed. As I watch it starts to change colors.

"Joy, what is that? I have been seeing it everywhere." I recall my joining dress also changed color. Two minuscule straps of cloth connected only by a thin cord that resembles her bracelet. "Why do the colors change?"

"Oh, you haven't been told about this yet?" I shake my head. "Typical men right there. Doesn't matter what planet they were born on, they still think that nothing needs explaining. This material is woven, not just with cloth, but with power. It is why it is so rare. It is extremely difficult to create and stabilize. But once made it bonds to the owner and can read your emotions, diagnose your needs, and even provide you help if you are in danger or unwell."

"Really? That is remarkable. But why? Why would immortal warriors want that?" It seems that in a culture where gold is a useless metal and diamonds are only as good as cutlery, clothes and linens are more of a sign of power than anything else I have come across.

"Well, like I said it also reads your needs. So say you are in pain, any form of pain, it can draw on its own essence to heal you. Haven't you ever felt different when wearing some of this cloth? If you wear it, or own it, it was created just for you. Tailored specifically for you."

I think back to when I first tried on my joining dress. Before I put it on I felt terrified to wear something so revealing in public. Once it was on I felt empowered though, as if I could do anything. Be anything.

"Yes. I did feel different when I was wearing the dress," I tell her. She gives a somewhat smug smile in return. She is so forthcoming with information that it is refreshing after a month with the closemouthed warriors.

I have learned more in two days with Joy than all the time I spent with the warriors.

"Well, you see? I knew you would have some. Danion is one of only a handful who are strong enough to create the *memien* out of all the weaves. He gifted this to me as a way to protect this baby." Her hands float down to her belly. "Your mate. He is a good male." She smiles warmly at me.

Danion is a good man. Male. It would take someone of insanely strong character to have ruled for so long, to be all powerful and not turn cruel or greedy. To still hold the needs and desires of his people above his own. I certainly can't say the same for any human I have ever come across. Maybe there is some justification for the mistrust and disregard Danion has for humans. Maybe we are inferior to them.

Don't think that. Don't you dare think that. You are not inferior.

I don't mean me specifically. I just mean that... maybe there is some truth to his feelings for our race.

I don't want to hear it. There is never an excuse for thinking that you are better than anyone else.

I suppose, but I still think he is a good man.

I am pulled out of my discussion with my inner self by Joy's voice.

"Ellie? Are you alright? Should I call for Jarlin?" I can hear the concern in her voice.

"No, I am fine, just lost in thought is all. Yes, I believe he is a good male," I agree with Joy's earlier comment.

A noise at the door captures our attention. Jarlin comes in, his face disturbed. My blood runs cold with the sadness I am sensing in him. Despair is literally rolling off of him.

"Joy...I am afraid that we are getting some readings that are...worrying." His voice is filled with concern. Genuine concern. It is then that I realize that to him, this is a personal matter as well. All the Gelders know what is at stake. If they do not start producing children, and giving birth to the next generation, they will die off. Maybe not today or tomorrow, or even next century but one day in the not-so-distant future the Gelders will be nothing more than a memory.

"Worrying how?" Joy asks, her voice rough and scratchy. Filled with pain. Jarlin's eyes flick over to me.

"I have called for Liam. I will wait until he is here and then I will discuss this matter with you privately."

"I will wait for Liam, but I want Eleanor here." Her voice is breaking. "Where is Liam? I need him." Her gaze flits toward the hallway before she closes her eyes and gets a deep look of concentration on her face. Her brow furrows and then smooths out. "Liam is almost here."

I realize that she must have been speaking with him telepathically. Danion has mentioned that once I have fully accepted him as my other half I will be able to communicate with him this way. Instead of thinking of this with the obvious pleasure Joy gets from communicating with Liam, I am dreading it.

It seems like such an invasion of privacy. To have no secrets, no barrier to protect yourself behind. But I push away my own concerns. They are inconsequential when I fear we are about to get terrible news. My thoughts are interrupted by Liam barreling through the doors. Amell is right behind him, trying to keep him from entering the room.

"Release me! I must get to my mate!" Liam tries to shrug off Amell's grasping hands.

"Liam, please! I need you. Amell, please let him come to me." Joy is sobbing, grasping for his hand but Amell is steadfast in preventing Liam from getting to his mate.

"I am sorry but we must protect the queen. He needs to be checked first," Amell tries to convince them. "A few moments is all I will require."

"Amell. Amell. Amell!" I yell to get his attention. The entire room instantly quiets. Joy is no longer sobbing, Liam has stopped thrashing in Amell's arms, and Amell is staring at me. His arms are now circling the still Liam in an embrace that almost looks tender instead of bruising.

"Yes, Eleanor?" Amell asks me.

"You will release Liam and allow him to comfort Joy. Now, Amell!" I order him when he does not react.

"My queen, I must protect you—"

"I am fine, Amell, it is Joy who needs protecting now. She needs comfort. Only Liam can give her that. Now release him and let him do his duty." I stare Amell down. "I am fine, Amell, Jarlin is right here if I have a relapse, and you will be right outside. Now go."

Finally, slowly, Amell releases Liam. He takes a tentative step back as if he is letting loose a rabid wolf instead of a trusted friend. Once Liam is free he immediately closes the distance between him and Joy. He wraps her in his arms and places a gentle kiss on her head.

Amell bows low and exits the room. I can tell he is not happy with the arrangement but there is nothing to be done about it now. Liam and Joy need one another. Jarlin turns his attention to the couple embracing on the bed.

"Liam, Joy. I am afraid the baby is showing some signs of distress. I am concerned about what this might mean for the child. It is not a guarantee that the baby will be lost, but it does not look good. The life of the child is in danger and that is my biggest concern now." His eyes are steady on the two mates.

"What do we do, Jarlin?" Liam is the first to raise his head and ask the tough question.

"I want Joy to remain here, in the medical wing, around the clock." His eyes shift between the two embracing on the bed for a moment, and then settle on Joy's distraught eyes. "I know you are already on bed rest, but now I need you nearby for constant medical care. I want to be able to keep a close eye on you. I am also going to monitor you and the child so I can predict a miscarriage early. Hopefully, if we are fast in reaction, we will be able to prevent it from happening."

"Of course. She will stay here. However, I am worried about her being alone at a time like this. Do we have someone who can stay with her? At any other time, I would refuse my duty, but billions of souls will be lost if we do not turn the tides of this war." Liam sounds heartbroken over the fact that he is unable to stay with Joy.

"I will be here. Even if I am released I will make sure I stay and comfort her the best I can in your absence," I speak up. My heart is breaking from the despair on both of their faces.

"That is kind of you, my queen." Liam turns his gaze back to Joy. "I will return quickly. I need to inform Danion of this development. He needs to know. Perhaps he will have an idea of how we can save the baby. I will be back as soon as I can." At Joy's nod, Liam exits the room. Jarlin moves to the base of the bed and begins working on the interface.

"Jarlin? Could you move me over to Ellie?" Joy's voice quavers as she speaks.

"Yes, of course." Jarlin presses a button and Joy's bed glides over to meet mine. We are so close we can hold hands. This is just what Joy does, clasping my hand and squeezing so tight I will definitely be bruised. I can't muster the energy to be concerned with my hand though, not when Joy begins to cry such desolate tears.

I reach over and pull her head to my shoulder, coaxing her to rest against me. I run my hand down her hair the same way I used to soothe my sisters. It is all I can think to do. Soon Joy's cries turn to whimpers. Then they quiet altogether to be replaced by deep, even breaths.

I hear the door open and raise my head. Joy is still sleeping on my shoulder. Danion, Liam, Golon, Kowan, and Jarlin all enter the room wearing identical grim expressions.

Liam comes around and sits on the other side of Joy. He gently cradles her and moves her to lie against him. She does not even stir. Good, she needs the rest. She needs the reprieve from reality that only sleep can give her.

"Jarlin, what can be done? Anything in our power is at your disposal to save this baby. The war itself is second to that child's life." Danion's words carry none of the emotion I see on his face. He is grieving this child already. Probably in the same way he has grieved for countless others. My heart breaks anew at the horrifying image his words have painted.

"I know, Dane, but I am afraid I don't know what the next step is. I simply do not know what is causing the miscarriages. Everything I try is ineffective. Nothing is working, just a steady decline in the baby's health. Honestly, I thought the child would pass several weeks ago. It was doing very poorly, and then the baby all of a sudden made a change for the better. It suddenly had strong vital signs, virtually healing itself overnight."

"What caused this improvement?" Golon asks his eyes on Jarlin with a hawk-like focus. I can see the wheels turning in his head, trying to solve the problem.

"I do not know. I am still trying to determine this. Maybe if I knew I could save it now." His words are faint. As a healer, not being able to save a life is obviously devastating for him.

"When did this happen? Do you remember anything peculiar about when these changes occurred? Where were we at the time? Was our ship orbiting anything odd? Passing through any strange phenomena?" Golon asks.

"What does that matter?" Liam asks. His voice is raw and already grieving for the child.

"I am trying to find out if there are things we can replicate and see if that saves the baby. It could potentially prompt a similar reaction and help the baby's health improve. Maybe we passed close to a star in our travels, or maybe a certain food she rarely eats was served. Anything can be helpful," Golon explains. "Anything, even something small is clue enough for me to enter into *medate,* or even *merate,* and try to discover an answer we have missed before."

"There was nothing special about that day that I can think of," Jarlin answers, then he goes rigid. "Except that it was the day of the *cerum fuse.* Your joining, my king." Golon and Danion go still.

"You mean to say it occurred on the day that Eleanor and I joined together?" Danion's words are like ice, completely still in the room. Heavy with unspoken meaning.

"Yes. Yes, I am sure of it. I had to decline my invitation so that I could remain with Joy. I was sure the child would not survive the night. Joy was feeling quite unwell too. The next day though, she was doing so much better," Jarlin answers. Then his words become slow and thought out. "In fact, I believe the baby's health improved around the time the ceremony should have been taking place."

Danion and Golon turn to each other and stare in silent communication. There is a slight nod between them and then Danion speaks.

"Kowan, you will be responsible for Eleanor's safety while Golon and I enter into a *merate.* With this information, we may be able to save the child if we can find the connection. It is far too important for us not to discover the reasons why my bonding ceremony would help the child. We do not know how much time we have." He turns his attention to Amell. "You will be placed in charge of defending our territory against this attack. We will have a brief discussion before we submerge ourselves in our meditation."

"What is it you hope to find?" Liam asks. A small, tiny bit of hope is evident in his words.

"Before you is a child born of a union between a human and a Gelder: Eleanor." At the shock on some of the faces in the room, I can tell not everyone knew this already. "I believe that the fact that my bonding to her occurred at the same time the baby improved is no coincidence. Something we did must have helped the child. There must be a reason. We need to discover it. And we need to do so soon," Danion explains. Golon speaks up as well.

"Yes, normally I would enter into a *medate*, my special weave, therefore allowing Danion to remain available but since it was his joining I need access to his mind," I remember that Golon once told me that he is the only Gelder who can enter into a *medate*.

It is a deep meditation that allows him to access every bit of knowledge he possesses. After being alive for so many years it is hard to remember every specific detail that he has come across. The *medate* allows him to focus his mind and filter through everything he has ever read or seen. Even when it was something he did not actively observe. He can recall images from past encounters he only saw in passing. He has a perfect memory, nothing is lost to him.

"Of course. Kowan and I will fill in for you both. I will walk with you so you can brief me on the way. We cannot waste precious time," Amell says with a very solemn look. Danion nods. He comes to my side and leans down, placing a chaste kiss on the corner of my mouth.

"I will hurry. Please stay safe while I am in the *merate* with Golon. We both must enter one. The answer may be hidden away in either of our minds."

"Yes, of course. Just please, save the child." I look over at Liam and Joy, her sleeping face is streaked with dried tears. "Please, save the baby. Whatever it takes. Save the baby."

"If it is within my power, I will do it. Whatever it takes."

Chapter Five

Ellie

"Kowan, any word on Danion and Golon?" I have asked the same question every morning for the past three days. His expression tells me his answer will be the same.

"No, a *merate* can take weeks to complete depending on the difficulty of the question you are trying to answer. If it can even be answered. Golon has been calling on his *medate* weave to answer this question for centuries, and even then he has never solved this mystery. We have been working to save our children for over two thousand years. With the passing of our elders, we noticed the lack of our youth more starkly." His words spark a question deep within me, what happened to their elders? But now is not the time to think about those long gone, it is for trying to save the small life before us.

"I know, but I can still hope." I stand up and start slowly pacing. Just yesterday Jarlin told me I should try to take small unassisted steps when I can. Help build up my strength and increase blood flow to try to work out the last traces of the poison. It is a tricky little poison for sure, and it has stayed well past its welcome.

All of a sudden Joy's bed emits a loud, piercing sound, like an alarm of some kind. The whole room is masked in a deep blue color.

The door to my right explodes outward and Jarlin bursts through. It leads from the temporary connecting office he had set up three days ago. He is frantic at the interface to Joy's bed. He is adjusting settings in a panicked frenzy.

"No. No. No. Not now. We just need more time." He talks more to himself than anyone else. I am frozen in fear. Fear of what this means. I have never seen the cool and composed Jarlin so frantic.

Without warning Joy curls in on herself and grips her lower belly while howling in pain.

"No! Not my baby. I can't do this again." She begins to sob. My heart breaks. I know how badly she wants this baby. How much we all want this baby.

Tears come to my eyes and her pain compels my muscles to move. I cannot just stand by and watch her lose this baby. I move to her side and grip her hand tightly.

"Oh, Joy, it will be alright. Jarlin will find a way to stabilize the baby and then Danion...Danion will be back and he will know how to save it." I continue to whisper comforting lies to her while she cries. As much as I hope that Danion will be in time, I don't believe it. He will be too late. Too late to help this poor defenseless child.

A child who is so loved, who deserves to be born and know all these wonderful warriors who already would die for it. Maybe, just maybe, I am being a pessimist and we really can save the—

"Joy...I am sorry... Nothing I am doing is having any effect... The baby..." Jarlin's voice actually breaks and he has to take a deep breath. "The baby is not going to survive."

No. Denial shoots through me and settles within me as steely resolve. Something inside me seems to be urging me to take action. It is faint, so faint that I can barely discern what it is that I am being shown, but nevertheless, I follow my heart.

This baby will not die. I refuse to accept that. I was a baby no one wanted but I survived. I am a half-human, half-Gelder mix and I survived. So will this baby. I move one hand to rest on her belly and I then lean over Joy, placing my head right above the small, almost unnoticeable rounding of her stomach.

"Hi, baby. You don't know me but I know you. You need to pull through. There are so many people who want to meet you. We want to love you and spoil you. You need to be OK. Please be OK." I don't know when I started crying, but as I talk to Joy's stomach I feel tears gushing down my face.

Joy and I collapse into one another, we are nothing more than two women locked in our own grief. Leaning on one another in a vain attempt to find an escape from this relentless pain.

With both my and Joy's sobs echoing in the room it takes Jarlin quite a few attempts to get our attention.

"Joy! Eleanor!" Finally, the wonder in his voice grabs my attention. There is elation in his words.

"What?" we both say in unison.

"The baby, it's calming down. It's healing. Vitals are all stabilizing, readings are all coming in as close to normal as they ever were." He looks up with a grin on his face. "I can't say for how long, but the baby is going to be fine. For now." He says this last part with a smile so large it threatens to crack his face. The normally stoic doctor is so thrilled that the baby pulled through what we all feared would be a certain tragedy.

"I don't know what you did, Ellie, but Joy and I thank you." I look up at Liam's words. I didn't even notice when he arrived and came to stand on the other side of Joy.

"Oh, I didn't do anything," I try to explain to him.

"Yes, you did. I am not sure what, but you saved my baby," Joy says with a tearful smile. "I felt it. I felt you save my child."

I back away from them. I raise my hands up in front of me and shake my head. I bump into something behind me, losing my balance. Before I can fall arms catch me. I look up and notice Etan. I walked right into him in my retreat from the bed.

"No. Really, I didn't do anything," I try to insist.

"Look at your *memien*, Joy," Jarlin interrupts, shocked. Circling the entire band is a bright, glaring strip of pure white. It moves and interacts with all the other colors as if it was always there.

"What is that?" I ask cautiously, dreading the answer.

"That is a pure thread of *lacieu*, the dead lineage. You weaved it, and now it is linked into the *memien* that Danion gave Joy." Jarlin's words shake me. "This is the proof of your lineage. You are not only of the *lacieu* line, you are a master in it. An untrained master. And you used that to heal the child."

Danion

I am pacing outside Eleanor and Joy's room in the medical wing. After intense immersion into the *merate*, searching for answers to save the child, Golon and I emerged empty-handed and brokenhearted. With no solution, we knew that we would be saying goodbye to another child.

Only the child still lives. Healthier than ever. Eleanor wove *lacieu* over the child, wove a thread so strong that it actually manifested itself into the band of *memien* I created to protect the baby. Golon, who is leaning against the wall in front of me, seems likewise confused. Of course, his confusion manifests itself as deep concentration. He is dissecting everything we know that happened and working on developing a conclusion.

We have both been outside this wing since we emerged from the *merate*. We came straight here to console Joy. I also craved to see my mate. With the sadness that was heavy within me, I desired the comfort I can get only from her.

We have just been told of the events that transpired while we were locked in meditation. Both of us now have more questions than we had when we entered the *merate*, not answers.

"How could this be possible, Golon?" We are speaking in hushed tones so as to not wake the females within the room. Joy has been excessively tired since her baby's life has been saved, and Eleanor is still recovering from the poison. The physical toll of weaving such strong power has also exhausted her.

"I do not know, Dane. I do not know." Golon answers me with a look I can't decipher.

"Golon," I say his name warningly. "You always have an answer."

"Not this time. I truly do not know how your mate, a human no less, had the ability to weave such strong power and execute it with such precision. Let alone a dead power. Threading such power lines with no instruction or training should be impossible. It is a marvel, truly."

"You know something. I can tell. Share your thoughts," I insist of him.

"Danion." With a heavy sigh, Golon speaks. "Alright, here is what I can tell you. The facts are that she must have at least one parent who is full Gelder. Her DNA reads like a book. There is no hiding it, her parentage is clear as day."

"Yes, I agree." I am not sure where he is going with this.

"Yes, except how this is possible is beyond even me. No Gelder would have a child and then not bring them into the safety of our ships. Even if there was an ancient Gelder stranded on Earth for all of these millennia why would they not have reached out to us? We contacted Earth a century ago, the stranded Gelder would have known that. Long before her birth. Why did they not contact us and request to come home?" Golon asks me.

"Perhaps something was pulling him to stay on Earth. He may have fallen in love. Maybe they wanted to remain on the planet."

"Possible, but Eleanor was raised without her father. If he loved her mother why would he not stay to be with his daughter? Why leave her to be abused? Why abandon her to live a life with no protection? That is a question I cannot answer." With a dark gaze, he continues. "Also, how is it possible that an ancient Gelder, one that was born before our transition, was still alive to conceive a child twenty years ago? They should have been long dead. All these unanswered questions are connected somehow. Connected by a yet-to-be-discovered string."

"What would you have me do to answer these questions? If a *merate* cannot bring the answers to light, what can?" I ask of him. Golon is one of the few warriors I would trust my life with. Not only my life but the life of my mate and the life of the unborn child of the Gelder race.

My trust in him has little to do with our familial bond. His being my cousin is of little weight. It is his competence and his complete knowledge of both science and our history that inspires my trust. He has proven himself countless times over again. He is logical to a fault. I can always trust that Golon will do what is best for the many, instead of himself.

"We need to travel to Earth. We must investigate the circumstances of Eleanor's birth," Golon says after a long pause. "There is something we are missing. The coincidences are piling up and there is no such thing as a true coincidence."

"What do you hope to find there?" My question is pure curiosity. I know that Golon has a very good reason why he is investigating my mate's birth.

"Validation."

"Validation of what?"

"A hunch."

"Golon. These dramatics grow tiresome. Explain to me your hunch," I say with exasperation. Golon looks at me intently for several moments. His entire body is still as if frozen, not one muscle moving.

"Ponder this, *cognata*, our people have been experiencing lower fertility rates since our transition. In the last thousand years, we have only had three children born to us, and almost all of them have been pairs who are bonded with a mortal being. Most have had several failed conceptions first. It has taken the most advanced medicines that we have to help these babies go to term." His words are grave.

"Yes, Golon. I know of our people's struggle." I bite out while attempting to keep my impatience from my words. But I know it is a losing battle.

"Then how, on Earth, with no advanced medicines of any kind, did Eleanor come to be? A perfect blending of the two races. With strong powers, let alone the ability to weave the dead lineage. No half-child that has been born to us has exhibited even a fraction of the power she has. They all possess an exceptional resemblance to their mothers and little to no Gelder traits."

"Yes, that is true." My words soften as I begin to see where Golon is going with his hunch.

"According to Ellie, her mother did not struggle to conceive her. So probability leans toward her pregnancy being easy. How was it so easy when we can barely conceive children with mortals, especially humans, let alone have them go full term?" he asks me.

"You believe that it has something to do with the transition? That when we evolved and achieved our immortality we lost our ability to have children?" Fear grips me with the thought. If that is the price the Powers set for immortality there may be no way to save my people.

"Possibly." His tone is contemplative, I know he is hiding something. I just don't know what.

"What else could it be?" I ask anxious excitement courses through me. We are on the verge of something great. Potentially, this may lead to the cure of our infertility. Or, it may prove that it is untreatable.

"No more questions, Dane. I am not ready to share my theories. We will wait until I have more information." Golon turns and begins walking down the corridor.

I hope he is wrong about our infertility being linked to our transition. I need my people to survive. I have dedicated everything to them. I would rather take a *scimtar* and repeatedly gut myself than face a world where the Gelders fade into nothing more than a memory.

A dark, painful emotion rises within me. I turn to the door. I need my mate. I know she sleeps but I will just sit with her. Watch over her. Draw comfort from her presence.

I enter the chamber and stride silently to her bedside. I take a moment and just gaze at my mate, rejoicing in the fact that she is still here. Alive and well.

I take a seat in the chair adjacent to her bed and I sit by her side for hours.

"Wake up, *aninare*." I gently smooth my hand down Eleanor's head, softly waking her.

"Danion?" She starts to rise from her reclined position. "What happened? My entire body aches."

"That is common when you have expended too much of your lineages. You pulled from your own essence to save Joy's baby. You have both been asleep for well over a full day. Joy actually awoke before you." I cup my mate's chin, tilting her head toward me so I can see her beautiful eyes. Blue eyes so clear it is like looking into water. The peace she brings me is unrivaled.

"What?"

"You saved the baby, *aninare*. You wove life into her using a lineage older than even me," I tell her with a grin. My grin grows into a full smile when I see the surprised denial forming on her lips. "I swear to you, you did. You are an enigma, my mate."

"How..." She stops to clear her throat. "How do I have power? I know about my DNA thing but... How did I weave something I don't know about? How is that even possible?"

"Remember when I locked you within your body the day we met?" I ask her with a grimace. I cannot help but think back on that day with disgrace.

"I will probably never forget that experience," she says with a small shiver down her spine. Her reaction causes shame to flow through me. I dislike recalling the wrong I did to her. There is no defense I can use, no justification I can offer. Only regret and remorse.

"Yes, it is something we both remember poorly. I offer you my deepest apologies, once again, for the wrong I did you that day." I raise her hand to my mouth and press my lips to the cool skin briefly. "I did not know that I was capable of that gift either. Never before had I woven threads like those, nor did I know that I even possessed the ability. Yet I wove it all the same. Sometimes our bodies take over where our minds fail."

She seems to think that over, nodding slightly.

"I suppose. But I still think you may be wrong. There are other possibilities out there. Other things may be the real reason. Maybe someone else wove it, and it was them who just didn't know that they had that power. It makes more sense for one of you to have this power than me." I find myself once again smiling at her.

She seems to fight the idea that she is special at every turn. She outright refuses to believe that she is more than what she has always thought of herself. To me, there is no one more unique than my mate. She is truly remarkable. She just can't see the queen hidden inside. The queen I see every time I look at her.

"This power is known as the dead power for a reason, Eleanor. No bloodline, power line, or liege line has possessed it in over five thousand years. If someone here had that power, we would have seen it before this. Or at least seen a sign of this power's return. You are the new variable. Not only that, but your cells show signs of the physical strain they were under. Your body tells the story for you." I can tell by her expression that she is humoring me.

"I agree that you believe that. You will have to accept that I am not convinced yet," she says with iron in her voice. I simply smile at her and pull her hand toward my chest. I feel a wave of heat travel down my arm and through my body from where we are connected.

I move my gaze to her eyes and am trapped. Her eyes hold me more tightly than any bindings ever could. I see her gaze drop to my mouth, and my eyes follow a mirrored course on her face.

I know she does not feel well and that she is still recovering, but there is nothing that I can do to fight the attraction building between us. I need my mate. The matebond is a physical ache within me, driving me toward physical contact with this exquisite creature. It has been too long since our *cerum fuse* where we were joined. The bond madness pulls at me and needs to be calmed. Just one taste is all I will take. Just one taste.

All my good intentions are gone once I feel her mouth on mine. As soon as I taste her sweet, intoxicating flavor I am lost in sensation. I take one taste, then two, then countless more. Her hand fights to be released and reluctantly I give in, anticipating the feeling of her hands pushing me away. I feel a poignant sense of loss with her withdrawal. Her rejection of me.

Her hand snakes around to the back of my head and pulls me tighter to her, rather than away. A feeling of triumph rockets through me. She wants me, maybe just as much as I want her.

I correct myself, maybe nearly as much as I want her. It would be impossible for anyone to feel such intense desire as I am right now. The desire coursing through me is more demanding than anything I have ever experienced. I need to have more of her body on mine. I slide into the bed and wrap my arms around her, immediately losing myself to her.

"I see that you are feeling better, Ellie," a sardonic voice says from behind me. "And Dane, you are in good form as well." There is definite laughter in his voice now. One day I really am going to kill him.

Not only does he interrupt my physical joining with my mate, he dares call her by a nickname. Implying an intimacy they do not have. At least, an intimacy that they better not have.

"Golon," I bite out. "Do you *want* me to kill you?" Eleanor's once passionate hands are now frantically pushing against me, trying to put space between us. Reluctantly, I sit up and move back to my chair near her bed.

"Hi, Eleanor. I am sorry for interrupting such a tender, yet passionate moment, but I felt you would rather be made aware of my presence than let me continue to stand here and enjoy the show." Eleanor nods, face flushed with either passion or embarrassment. I would like to think it is the former, but chances are it is the latter.

"Golon, what are you doing here?" I bite back the curse I want to throw at him.

"I thought it best that I be here when we talk to your mate," he says with a happy smirk. He walks over to Eleanor and sits on the edge of her bed so close that his leg rests against her thigh. I have to strain to hold back my power. It fights to be set free and lash out against the male who dares touch my mate.

"Talk to me about what?" Eleanor is slowly coming out of the fog caused by our passion, which is a real shame.

"Our upcoming departure," Golon answers. Eleanor turns her attention to me.

"Departure? Where are we going?" she asks me. I send a brief smirk to Golon. It gives me pleasure that she turns to me for answers and not my brilliant cousin.

"We are going to Earth," I answer her.

"Earth? As in Earth Nueva? My home?" Pain pierces through me to hear her call another place her home. Home for me is with her.

The very moment we met I knew I never wanted to be parted from her. It is a difficult thing, to reconcile the difference in our emotions. While I have committed everything about myself to her, she seems to be holding quite a bit back of herself.

"Yes, we have business to take care of there." I share a meaningful glance at Golon. "In fact, there are many things that we need to handle there."

"What kind of things?" she asks hesitantly. Anger churns inside me. She fears me. Fears what I intend to do. I know that she is still unsure of me.

She does not trust that I am not going to punish her people. Frustration is building within me but I tamp it down. I do not know what else I can do or say to prove my worth to her.

"Well, we need to inspect the defenses and make sure that they are able to withstand the attacks the Erains are lobbing at the planet." I see her relax at this statement. I have a long way to go before I win her over. "Also, there are several questions that need answers. Answers that Golon believes can be found there. I agree with him."

My mind turns to the abuse that she has suffered. There will be many people who will pay for what was done to my mate. Her mother needs to be held accountable, the ambassador who stole her fortune will be made to pay back his debt ten-fold, and the woman who was supposed to prepare her to start her new life needs to be made an example of.

"What kind of questions?" my beautiful mate asks cautiously. I suspect she knows exactly what kind of questions I want answered.

"Well, Ellie," Golon speaks up to answer my mate before I can. "I have quite a few questions that I would like answered myself. To begin with, I would like to sort out who your father was and where he came from. How is he on Earth, when did he arrive, and how is he still living, to name a few."

"Yes, Eleanor. These are questions we need answers to. They impact the future of our entire race." I add my opinion as well.

I dislike her turning to Golon for answers. I can give her everything she needs. This isn't the first time since I met my mate that I resent my cousin for his cheery attitude and considerable knowledge. I wish he was gone from here and not sharing smiles with my mate.

"Will I be able to speak with my family? Since we are already going to be there?" she asks of me. I smile in triumph. Good, don't look at that blasted attention-hungry bastard. Look only at me.

"Of course, we can see your family. In fact, we can stop there first if you prefer. Before anything else, we can visit your childhood home. I would enjoy a visit to where you grew up."

I keep quiet about the fact I desperately want to meet her mother and her husband to question them. Let alone see for myself where she was raised. The stories I was told did not paint a pretty picture. I want to know why they mistreated the delicate, yet perfect creature before me. I need to know how they were able to do such a thing to a child so innocent.

A smile blossoms on her face. She reaches for my hand of her own accord. An all too familiar heat rises within me at her gesture.

"When do we leave?" she asks me.

"We are planning on leaving this afternoon. As long as Jarlin checks you out and everything comes back normal. We will travel in the shuttle you arrived in since it is the fastest ship in the fleet. Meant for speed but still has a wealth of weapons and shield generators as well. A larger vessel will follow behind us with more supplies and larger living quarters."

"How long will it take us to travel there?" She asks of me quickly. Her excitement at seeing her family again is reason enough to travel to the planet.

"Eager little thing, aren't you?" Golon interrupts, dragging her attention away from me. I turn my gaze and glare at him. The sultry, seductive tone of his words causes me to lose the grip I have on my power. It slams against Golon, but an outside observer wouldn't know it. Golon withstands the blast admirably. Just a small, almost unnoticeable flinch around the eyes.

He throws me a cocky, satisfied smile. That bastard knows exactly what he did to me and is happy he was unharmed in the attack.

"What are you doing to Golon?" Eleanor's voice beckons me out of my jealous rage. I turn my gaze to my mate.

"What do you mean?" I ask with confusion. How would she know that I did something? Golon handled the blast well. The rotten bastard.

"You just did something. I saw a huge wave of color flow from you and blast into Golon. It looked like an inferno. What was it?" Her words shock me. By the look on Golon's face, she's shocked him too.

"You mean to say you saw my aura?" I ask her, disbelief heavy in my tone.

"If by aura you mean the cloud that is always around you then yes. I have seen them since I arrived. It is hard to miss." She says this like it is an everyday occurrence instead of yet another outstanding revelation of her ability. "Doesn't everyone? I mean it is really noticeable. Yours in particular. It fills up this entire room practically."

"No, not everyone can see them," I respond. "In fact, very few can."

"Come on," she says. I look at her with no emotion. "You're not kidding? Some people can't see it?" Her voice is shocked.

"No, Eleanor. Only a very select few can physically see auras. Very few. It is an extremely rare gift," I explain to her. "Rarer than even *abiciant*, the mind control power that I accidentally used on you."

Golon, ever the scientist, has more detailed questions for her. At least he has dropped his flirtations. Finally. Nothing like a mystery to pull his attention away from my mate.

"What do these clouds of color look like?" he asks. "Be as descriptive as you can. When do you see them? Where do you see them?"

"Well, let's see." Her face scrunches up, forming a little V in between her brows. "All of my *praesidium* has one. But not all the time. Sometimes it is almost like a trick of the light. I think I see it out of the corner of my eye, then I look again and it is gone. Danion, you always have a color cloud around you. Some objects even seem to have a faint one. Like the bracelet that Joy has, the *memien* one that is designed to protect the baby. It is kind of like a haze that surrounds you. But it is fluid. Constantly moving around..." She trails off.

"Can you describe the haze more? What do you mean by it being fluid? Is it always there, is it ever solid? Faint or bold?" Golon asks. I can tell he is trying to guide her into telling him what he already knows. Trying to have her confirm his suspicions.

"In my *praesidium,* it is like a hint here and there, with occasional waves coming from them. Danion's is like a swirling storm around him all the time, and just now it looked like a powerful burst of the cloud flung free of its chains and went barreling into you. Except it disappeared when it reached you." Eleanor glances at Golon, studying him pensively. "You don't have one. I have never seen you shrouded in color. I once thought I saw it around you, but then I looked again a second later and it was gone."

"A very apt description. You are able to see auras as clearly as others see ordinary objects." He smiles to himself. "Once again you prove yourself to be a worthy mate to our king."

"Another powerful sign that there are some very important mysteries to solve regarding your parentage. No human bonding could result in such a powerful offspring," I say. "Golon is one of only two beings I have ever known who can see them as clearly as you describe. The other has been dead for over two thousand years." Disbelief is apparent on her face, I see it clearly.

"But I have heard several people referring to auras. I am sure a lot of people can see them," she protests. "Liam even described them to me before our *cerum fuse.* If he can't see them, how did he know how to describe them?"

"While it is true that we are all aware of auras, not all of us can physically see them. Many of us can sense an aura, and even weigh the strength of the owner based on the aura alone. But few can actually see it as a physical thing," I answer her. "Few of us can see the metaphysical manifestation of our power."

"Is this true, Golon?" Her lack of faith in me almost causes me to lose control once again. Somehow I manage to contain my rage, though Golon's words do little to calm me.

"Yes, sweet Ellie. Before you, I have never met anyone else who can see the auras with as much detail as I can. No one has ever described the auras in the way you do, the way that I myself would describe them." He says it with a grin. "I believe that is because no one else sees the auras the same way that you and I do. No one else is capable. It is a very powerful defense to possess." I wonder at his wording. How does Golon use his aura sight as a defense?

"How so?" She asks him the very question I was just pondering.

"It allows you to track attacks as well as see them coming. With in-depth knowledge of aura sight you can see an attack forming long before it is ever lodged against you," he says with a smirk to me. "No matter how controlled a warrior is, he can never hide his true emotions from an aura seer. A warrior can spend years perfecting a mask of indifference, but when we can see the storm raging within, we know to be prepared."

I am frozen in my seat. For centuries I have asked Golon how he can always sense an attack before it happens and he has steadfastly refused to share his technique. Even though it would have been a tool that could save thousands of warriors on the battlefield he refused to share it.

Now I understand that no one else could use his technique. I know now his defense is born of his aura sight. It also sheds light on his uncanny ability to know just how far to needle me without pushing me over the edge.

"Really, Golon?" Eleanor is looking at him in wonder. My Eleanor is looking at another male with wonder in her eyes. I do not like it. I dislike it so much that I cannot prevent what I say next.

"Yes, Golon. Keep telling Eleanor all the wonderful things you share. All the wonderful similarities between you and my mate. You might want to look at my aura though before you continue," I snap at Golon with ill-concealed resentment and jealous rage.

I know that I am being petty and selfish, acting much younger than my three thousand years, but I cannot help it. I have so few moments with my mate that I resent Golon for intruding into this one. I also cannot stomach the things they are sharing in my presence. If this is how they interact when I am here, what goes on when I am not in their company?

"Danion, relax. It is just some harmless fun," Golon scolds me. Acting as if I am the one in the wrong. My anger continues to burn beneath the surface. But of course, Golon pays no mind to this fact. He continues as if nothing is amiss. "Now, how about I take my leave and summon Jarlin? I think we need to start the exams if we have any hope of leaving on schedule." With a bow to Eleanor and a cocky wave to me, Golon leaves the room.

I turn my attention to Eleanor as soon as I am sure he has left the room. Even before I spoke I knew what I would say would cause another wedge and add even more distance between us, but I could do nothing to prevent it.

"You are not to flirt with males, Eleanor. You are mine, and you would be wise not to forget that," I all but snarl at her. On some deep level, I know I am being unfair, but fairness has no place in a male undergoing the pain of matebond madness.

Ellie

"Excuse me?" I can barely stifle my indignation.

"You heard me, mate. Don't. Flirt. With. Males." With every bitten-off word he gets closer to me until he is so close I can feel his body heat and his breath against my face. "If you want to flirt so *fiefling* much, you can flirt with me. Your mate."

He is unbelievable. Without fail whenever I think we are making progress toward something better between us he goes and messes it up by being himself. By showing me his true colors. Mocking me for ever thinking he might change. The kiss we shared was hot enough to almost make me forgive his high-handedness, his arrogance, and even his derision of humans. But luckily I came out from under his spell in time.

"You don't own me, Danion. I can do whatever I want." He tries to interrupt me but I don't let him. "Talking to someone is not flirting."

"The way you were talking is flirting. You know how you look. Every male on this ship covets what is mine. They cannot have you, and you need to be less cruel and not lead them on." His words are so insulting that it takes a few moments to interpret them.

"What? Lead them on! That is what you think of me? That I am some shallow, attention-hungry floozy who needs to be fawned over constantly?" I can barely get the words out I am so angry. "I will talk to whoever I damn well please and there is nothing you can do about it."

"You will not!" His hands grab my upper arms.

"Let go of me, you brute! You are insufferable! I refuse to bear more bruises because you get off on manhandling women!" I try to shrug him off, but at my words, his hands fall away so quickly my arms fly up with the sudden lack of resistance. I look like I am imitating a chicken my arms fly so high so quickly.

"Manhandle you?" He looks at his hands in shock. "Bruise you? I take no pleasure in harming you. Not in any way." His words are so soft I feel myself weakening. I force myself to fight off the compassion rising within me and to hold on to the anger. I can't lower my guard again. I have to remember what happened last time.

"Then why do you hurt me? Words are cheap. Actions are what really matter." I put all the anger I can muster into the glare I level at him. The look of desolation on his face makes it hard to hold on to the anger though. I feel vaguely like I am kicking a puppy. A ridiculous thought considering the male before me is the most powerful warrior ever known.

"It is not that I want to harm you. I would never knowingly seek to cause you harm. You must know that. It is just that…" His hands make a small wave as if he is searching for the words. "Well, that the matebond madness is stronger than I ever thought it would be. Sometimes the rage is more in control than I am," he says with a sigh.

I feel my anger melt away this time and I let it. Being angry does not come naturally to me and it takes considerable effort to hold on to it.

Joy described to me what this madness was. It affects the males in an incomplete bond. They go crazy at any hint of danger to a mate and they also become extremely territorial. While it does not make his behavior right or acceptable, I can at least understand where he is coming from.

"Look. I understand that the madness is not something you can just ignore, I also know it is not something that is easily controlled. But you can't use that as an excuse to insult me or to harm me. You need to learn how to reign yourself in and fight your instincts," I say, working hard to make sure there is iron in my voice.

"I know." He scrubs his hands down his face in frustration. "I know. It is just a lot harder than I thought it was going to be."

"Well, how about we just try to talk things out more," I offer in compromise. "Try to put a voice to our concerns before they erupt in an explosion of anger. Like you so often do."

"Talking? How is that supposed to help the madness?" His words, while gruff, are said in a tone filled with so much confusion I take no offense.

He does not mean to mock my idea, he has true confusion over how talking will help. I guess regardless of the species or age, a man is a man. I smile internally while thinking this.

"Yes, talking. You know? Communicating with one another. With our words. You tell me how you're feeling and I tell you how I am feeling. Less grabbing, more speaking." I smile at him, waiting anxiously to see how he responds to this idea.

When he smiles back I let out a relieved sigh. His face, normally so stoic, is a beautiful sight when he smiles. It softens the hard lines and warms up the coldness in his features.

The door opening alerts us to Jarlin entering the room.

"I hear I need to clear you for space travel," he says with a small smile. I realize now that he has been exceedingly worried about Joy and the baby. His overall demeanor is much more relaxed compared to when we first met as if he has shrugged off an enormous boulder of burden from his shoulders.

"Yes, that is right. How are Joy and her baby?" I ask while he once again starts interacting with the machine at the base of the bed.

"They are both doing much better," he answers with a large smile. "In fact, when the baby began showing even the smallest signs of distress, the machine traced the *memien* activating and sending aid to the child. Moments later the baby calmed right down." He looks up from the display. "It seems that whatever threads you wove into it are monitoring the baby and healing it as it develops. It is remarkable really. I honestly think the child will make it, thanks to you." He gives a bow to me. "Our queen and savior. You bring honor and hope to our race."

His words make me extremely uncomfortable. I don't know how to respond. Luckily Danion saves me with his own comment.

"Yes, she does at that. Hope for a brighter future. A better future." His hand finds mine and gives it a squeeze. "How do her reports look for a journey to Earth? I only want her going if we are sure she is well enough." I stiffen at his words. If he thinks that he is going to go to Earth Nueva and leave me behind he has another thing coming.

"I want to go. I want to see my family," I insist and try to pull my hand away. "I am fine. I feel fine. Wonderful even."

"Peace, Eleanor. I only meant that we will postpone the trip if you are not healed. We will not leave you behind, only wait until you are well enough to travel."

"Oh." His words calm me a little bit. But I am still anxious to go to Earth and see Marilee and my sisters.

"It looks like it is not going to be a problem. I see no reason our queen cannot travel. All traces of the poison are gone, and with the exception of some pain from the massive weave she threaded yestermorn, she should be fine," Jarlin says with a smile.

"You are sure? I do not want to risk her," Danion questions.

"Yes, I am sure. There are symptoms that could prove worrisome for her, so I will provide you with an itemized list of those. They are things that you can monitor her for. If they do arise while you are away from me, I know Malin and Griffith are both competent enough in *hael* to assist her if it was needed. Assuming that the remaining members of her *praesidium* are traveling with you?"

"Yes, they are. All but two of them. Kowan and Amell will remain here to handle my and Golon's duties. Golon and I will likewise cover the openings in her *praesidium*," Danion answers.

"What are Kowan and Amell going to be doing here?" I will miss them when we go. I have grown quite close to the warriors in these past weeks.

"Kowan will be managing the protection of Joy and her child, as well as assisting Amell, who will be handling the tactics of the war. He will be maintaining our defense and devising where we can strike back. Also, they both will continue the search for our traitor. Golon has made good progress in determining who poisoned you; it is just a matter of finding him now."

"Oh, I see." At the mention of my poisoning, I feel uncomfortable. It is hard to come to terms with the fact that I was so close to death and all the revelations that led to. "Who do you think it was that poisoned me?" I ask.

Danion casts a look over to Jarlin who, with a bow of his head, departs from the room.

"We believe that the traitor is one of our own. I am not sure how he was turned against us; I never would have thought any Gelder would work against his own kind." Danion speaks as soon as Jarlin is gone.

"Maybe he didn't turn against you," I suggest.

"How is poisoning our queen, my mate, not an act of betrayal?" he asks me incredulously.

"Maybe he was forced. Or blackmailed. We don't know really." As I say this I realize that I am attempting to defend my own would-be murderer. I grow quiet at this revelation. Danion seems to understand my hesitance and clasps my hand even tighter.

"It will be alright, *aninare*. We will keep you safe. We will also find all the answers." He says this with a small smile. "Now, if you are feeling up to it, would you like to go visit Joy and say goodbye before we make preparations to leave today?" Danion rises and holds out a hand to me.

With a small and tentative smile, I take his hand and rise. Maybe Danion and I can make this work. He may not have had a choice in picking me as his mate, but he seems willing to accept it. Maybe I can too.

It is hard to be constantly reminded how much I am lacking by spending time with the females on board the ship. Joy is such a strikingly gorgeous woman. I know that he would rather be with some tall, gorgeous warrior woman, like Joy. But if he is willing to accept my failings, I can live with that.

Liar.

Shut up, you. No one asked you for your opinion.

You keep telling yourself that.

With an inward eye roll, I refuse to respond to my own thought. Danion would surely be frustrated if he knew about the inner arguments I have with myself. What kind of queen talks to herself, anyways?

Chapter Six

Ellie

As the shuttle flies through space I reflect back to my first trip on this ship. That first time I was in here I was surrounded by large, silent warriors. I was intimidated. Scared. Isolated. But today? Today I have Danion, my mate, in the chair next to me with his hand firmly clasping mine.

I look up and make eye contact with the members of my *praesidium* traveling with me.

First I see Malin Mulus, the master weaver of *anium*, the water master. He meets my gaze and gives me a smile. Over the last several weeks I have grown quite close to Malin. We both share a love of the water and he has spent hours with me submerged in the pool onboard the main ship.

I enjoy his relaxed and easygoing attitude. Malin is calmer than the other warriors I have grown close with. I give him a small smile in return, then turn my gaze to the next warrior.

Sitting to Malin's right is Arsenio Tempestas, the master weaver of *ignis*. As I share a glance with this warrior I feel Danion tense up. I am reminded of the horrible fight that my bond with Arsenio caused between us. Well, that is not entirely fair.

The bond between myself and Arsenio was not the cause of the argument, merely the catalyst. While Danion can argue as much as he wants, I value Arsenio for the very reason he dislikes him. Arsenio's loyalty lies with me, not Danion. For that alone, I am grateful to him. With one last glance at Arsenio, I move on to the next warrior.

Griffith Vitae, the master weaver of *vim*. Griffith is reserved but very intuitive about people. Probably has something to do with the fact that he can control the life forces of the beings around him. Griffith is a warrior that I have struggled to read these past weeks.

He is always accommodating and chivalrous, but he has an aloofness to him that discourages me from getting too close. I offer a small smile to Griffith, but all I receive in return is a small nod of the head. I briefly think I see a warming of his dark eyes, but it is gone the next second. Must have been a trick of the light.

My eyes move to the last warrior of my *praesidium* with me, Etan Honoris, the master weaver of *caeli*. Etan has a lightheartedness that no one I have ever encountered possesses. He has a unique outlook on the world, able to turn any tale, no matter how dark, into a positive light.

I have enjoyed many days spent in his company debating philosophy. He also helped me let go of some of the anger I have against my mother. Not all of it, he is not a miracle worker, but he has helped me move past much of what was done in my childhood and come to grips with the past.

"Eleanor? May I ask how you are recovering?" I am brought out of my thoughts by a voice to my left.

"Thank you, Golon. Perhaps a little tired but overall I am feeling much better." I give him a small smile. Golon is one of my favorite beings. He is the only one who truly does not care about Danion's temper. We bonded quickly with one another.

"Wonderful. I was wondering if I could speak with you privately?" he asks me in a hushed tone. I look around at the spacious, albeit very public, shuttle we are on.

"Yes, but I am not sure how you would accomplish this," I answer him.

"If you permit me, I will thread a privacy weave around us." He says this with a small smile. He gives me an expectant look. I nod my head, indicating he is free to cast his weave. Right as he moves I see a deep magenta flow from his hands and form a cylindrical wall around us.

As the wall seals closed around itself, the last vision I see is Danion's face of outrage and his mouth opening in protest. Soon I am ensconced in this tunnel with just Golon.

"That's better," Golon says with a smirk on his face. "No need to have my dear cousin know all of my secrets, is there?"

"I suppose not." Now I am very curious. "What is it that you wanted to talk with me about?" And why would he not want Danion to know?

"You, my dear, you. Your powers are nothing short of extraordinary. The gift of aura sight is one of the rarest gifts we have. It is a gift that must be nurtured. Once it is truly mastered, there is no greater power. And none more deadly." His voice deepens ominously on his last words.

"How is it deadly? I just see auras. How are some colors dangerous?" I ask him. I really don't see how my seeing some colors every once in a while is dangerous.

"No, that is only what your untrained abilities allow you to see. You have not developed any control of your power. I have never before come across someone who shares my level of aura sight. No one can see what I can see. You may be the first. I would like to test you if you will allow it. To determine the strength of your gift. To see if you do indeed possess this gift as strongly as I do."

"Why? Why do you want to know the strength of this gift in particular?" I ask of him. "You didn't ask to do this when you found out about my alleged ability of *lacieu*."

"Because there is a reason I am second in command of the Gelder warriors, and it is tightly hinged on my gift of aura sight. Aura sight can open you up to a whole collection of additional abilities. I need to know if you too possess the full array of powers that come with this gift." The force of his eyes beat into mine. I have never seen him so ill-composed. He is usually so calm, projecting a laissez-faire attitude. He is very determined to test me.

"What will the test entail?" I force myself to ask. I am not going to just blindly agree, no matter how important Golon thinks this is.

"All I need is to touch your hand. You will feel a slight warmth on the skin, nothing uncomfortable, and then I will let you know what I find."

"Is that all? Really?" I fail to hide my surprise. My experience thus far with Gelder powers has been considerably more intrusive.

"Yes, I give you my warrior vow that I will do nothing else but what I have described." His words are warm, his face earnest. I believe him.

"Alright then, I guess." I need to know as much as I can about my powers. If I really have these abilities ignorance will only hurt me. Anything that might lead to more insight into my heritage is desired. I hold out my hand to him.

He grabs my hand and has it rest palm to palm on one of his hands while the other hovers just above it. I feel a slight heat, and the sensation is vaguely pleasant.

The heat travels down my arm and up into my chest. I can feel it spreading throughout my entire body. It is almost like it is penetrating deep into each and every cell I possess. It is steadily rising up my neck, traveling along my face. It is coming together around my eyes. The heat seems to climb up a notch.

My eyes succumb to the heat and my vision is shrouded with a deep honey color. Unlike before, it is not a color that comes from any one thing, it is more like a filter. As if the color is coming from within my eyes themselves. The heat continues to grow, and then just before the heat crosses into pain it stops.

Golon's face falls into deep concentration. The heat is holding steady on the precipice of pain. I realize I am holding my breath. My whole body is tense as I wait for his conclusion. Then a smile breaks out across his face.

"It is as I thought, Ellie. You are remarkably strong in aura sight. You rival, if not surpass, even my own gift." His smile makes me uncomfortable as if there is a secret he knows that I don't.

"Why do I feel like you are about to tell me something I am not going to like?"

"Because you won't," he says bluntly and with a smile. The same attitude I admire when he gives it to Danion is aggravating as all get out when he gives it to me. "You are resistant in believing that you have the power of any kind. You fight us when we state the facts. You refuse to accept that you are as unique and special as you clearly are. And while having this power is not quite as impressive as bringing an ancient lineage back from the dead, it is still remarkable in its own way."

I resent his words and his quick dismissal of my feelings. They are valid, regardless of how he sees them. Am I just supposed to accept all the claims that I possess some great power after a lifetime of being powerless? Fat chance.

"I can see on your face that I am right. You want to deny what is undeniable. You have power, Eleanor. Great power."

"What is so great about seeing auras?" Seems like a pretty pointless gift if you ask me. Not that any of these warriors ever do.

"Seeing auras is just how the gift manifests itself. More of a side effect of the true power. You can do so much more than just see an aura," he insists.

"Like what?"

"Remember in the *hael* wing, the medical wing, when Dane threw his power into me?"

"Yes, I do," I answer slowly. His words spike my curiosity.

"Remember how forcefully it was blasted into me? If that had hit any other being it would have thrown them through a wall. But I was able to withstand it. Able to take the full force of our *king's* aura and barely flinch." With his words, I realize the importance of that action.

"How?" I recall the blast of power that exploded from Danion; it is true it barreled toward Golon like a bullet. Then it simply dissipated when it touched him. As if it never existed.

"By seeing auras we have a remarkable advantage both defensively and offensively. With aura sight comes the ability to absorb auras that are thrown at us, internalize the power, and then use it for our own purpose." His words rock through me. "We can channel this energy into ourselves or outside of our bodies."

"Then no weave is a threat to us?" My mind is whirling with the possibilities of having this power. I do not even notice that I am no longer denying the fact that I have this power.

"Not quite. There are limits to what our bodies can withstand, and the amount of Danion's power that I had to funnel through me did quite a bit of damage. If he had thrown more at me I would not have been able to take it all." He laughs sheepishly. "Truly, I should not have attempted to take as much as I did. You have given him so much power that it is hard for me to keep up with him." He shoots me a rueful glance. "The most difficult limit to this gift is that you must be expecting the attack. You have to open your *chakkas* and be prepared to accept the aura into yourself. To channel the power into what you want it to be."

"What is a *chakkas*?" I ask him.

"Think of it as a network of focal points that run throughout the body. Almost like nerves. This system is where the power of our lineages travel within. This also makes it dangerous to open them up for long periods of time. That is why you have to predict the attack or the defense is useless. It is also why it can severely damage you if you try to take too much into yourself."

"What do you mean?"

"Each point through the *chakkas* system is equipped to handle only so much strain. They have very precise limits." Golon gestures to his upper arm. "Think of your muscles. A muscle can only lift so much weight, if you try to overexert that muscle, it would damage it. *Chakkas* are no different. If you were to take too much power inside of yourself, you could blow the *chakkas* points. Without these points, assisted healing is almost impossible. Your body rejects all power, having no way to let it flow through your body. Your own powers will become like an infection within your body. If too many are damaged severely, it is a death sentence." His voice is grave.

"Then why do you constantly challenge Danion? Aren't you worried about blowing your *chakkas*?" I ask.

"That is precisely *why* I challenge him. His power has climbed so high that I could not withstand an attack from him. That also means that I cannot absorb an attack meant *for* him. But by continually pushing the limits of my *chakkas* I am slowly increasing their strength."

I can't believe what he is saying.

"So you are doing this on purpose? Goading him into attacking you in order to increase your power?"

"Not mine. The power of my people. We need Danion. He has ruled for so long for a reason. Not only because he is the strongest among us, but because he is the best among us. While it is true that he is extremely powerful, this alone is not enough to prevent a challenge to the throne. If he was not the best king for us, he would not be able to rule. He places himself last, always. His people have always been more important." He gives me an intent stare. "His mate is more important to him than his own welfare. It is the way of a true king."

"I see." I murmur when in truth I don't see anything.

"I know you are still angry with him, and perhaps you have reason to be. But try to understand where he is coming from. Arsenio, while kind to you, earned the moniker of the 'Flaming Traitor' long before your time. And for good reason. He performed crimes against *vim*. A crime of the highest offense. He is lucky that he was forgiven when it became necessary for your *praesidium*." My face must have revealed my shock.

"Didn't mention that, did he? I thought he might leave that out. He serves his duty well now to protect you. But remember that in the past he has done real damage to not only Dane but our people as well. Danion has good reason to dislike him."

"What reason?" I cannot help but ask. This is not the first time that I have been told that Arsenio committed a heinous crime long ago. I have asked before but never received an answer. I have not found it within myself to ask Arsenio himself. I am afraid to risk the easy camaraderie that we have developed.

"It is not—"

"Your place. Yeah, yeah, that's what you all say," I interrupt him rudely. I am so frustrated with these arrogant males telling me only little snippets of information.

"It is true, Ellie." Ugh, how strange that after insisting they call me Ellie the nickname is starting to irritate me. Perhaps because the way Danion says "Eleanor" sends shivers down my spine.

"Is there anything else? We have to be getting close to Earth by now. I feel like I have been stuck in this tomb with you for ages." I know I sound petty and childish but I can't bring myself to care.

"Yes." At my glare, he is quick to amend. "Just one more thing. We will need to begin training you in aura sight. No one else can know of this. Only beings gifted in aura sight are allowed to know its secrets. It is forbidden to even write any of it down. No trace. We lost almost all of the great masters in the Great War. If I had not survived, this gift would have died those three thousand years ago." A look of sadness flashes across his face. I get the feeling that he lost someone he was close to.

"Alright. You will have to find a time and place though if we are to be training in private. I am not going to be responsible for this secret leaking out."

"Very well," he says with a smile. "Then once I have arranged for your first lesson I will come to find you. Now it is time to join the others. You were right, we are approaching Earth and will be there shortly."

Those are his parting words before he drops the barrier between us and the rest of the shuttle comes back into focus. The way he says them makes me smile. He is so disgruntled. As if he is offended I noticed the passing of time in his presence.

If I have thought it once, I have thought it a million times. Damn, arrogant warrior males.

Chapter Seven

Danion

"I insist you tell me what he spoke with you about." I am sitting beside Eleanor in a machine that is called a car. It is most strange, but it fulfills the purpose of transporting us to Eleanor's family home. On wheels. In a box on wheels. Humans are strange indeed.

She still thinks of this place as her current home. As opposed to my ship. Or by my side. Her true home. I vow that one day she will accept this, that she will take pleasure in my presence as I do in hers.

"If I told you, it would defeat the purpose of speaking behind a privacy weave, would it not?" Eleanor says to me with a little smirk in my direction.

I can hear a rumbling of humor come from the other occupants in the car. Golon is wearing an arrogant smirk I long to slap off his face. But a king never strikes his subjects. I used to be so good at following that rule, but since I have met my mate it is growing increasingly difficult to follow. Pummeling them with blasts of my power is not the same thing, but the line between them is so very fine.

I cannot stand to not know what was said. First Arsenio, now Golon. The matebond madness is difficult enough to contain without unmated males conferencing with her in secret. Logic tells me Golon would not have sought her out in front of me for romantic purposes, but the *infer* dares too much as it is. I am never sure what he is capable of. Family bond or not, I do not want him near my Eleanor.

"Eleanor. I need to know what was said between you." It is the closest I have ever come to begging in my life. Something in my tone must draw her attention because she shifts her entire body to look at me.

"It is not something I can discuss with you. But I promise it has nothing to do with whatever this is between us. It had to do with my powers and is between Golon and myself." Her words are intended to be soothing, I am sure, but it has the opposite effect. All I hear is her once again choosing another male over me. It is Arsenio all over again.

A dark, empty, pain-filled chasm opens up inside me. For my entire life, I have longed for a mate more than anything else. For the peace and companionship that comes with meeting your soul mate. No one ever told me that while a mate can bring you untold happiness, they also wield the ability to bring you untold pain.

"Oh, look, we are getting close to my family home now." Her words draw me out of myself. My glance out the window rockets me quickly and surely out of my wallowing and into the present.

All around me are decrepit buildings; they look like they are about to fall at any given moment. Garbage is littering the streets. Fires are burning in metal barrels lining the bumpy and hole-ridden road we are traveling on.

"This is where you spent your childhood?" I ask with barely concealed horror. She is so busy scanning the streets that she does not pick up on my tone.

"Yes. Oh, I am so excited to see my sisters. And Marilee. If you have time I would like you to meet her," she asks of me. "I think you will really like her."

"Yes, of course. If she is important to you I would like to make her acquaintance," I mumble distractedly.

My attention is still riveted to the horrific poverty that surrounds me. I have failed my mate in the most basic of ways. I see humans dead on the street. Not literally dead, but they will be soon. Death hangs in a heavy cloud over their heads, ready to claim them at any moment.

The thought of her living her life in this dangerous, run-down pit is a sign of how much I have wronged my mate. I can tell that many of the people here are starving. It causes me to look at my mate's own slight frame in a new light. I recall Jarlin's words about how her body showed signs of starvation.

"We are here," my mate says and opens the door to get out. My hand flies forward to catch her wrist.

"Wait. I will exit first and come around." I do not want her unescorted for even a moment in an area like this.

I open my own door and walk around the car and reach in to help her out. I keep her close to my side as we walk up to a building much worse than any other building I have seen so far. It is no more than a small square. One wall has fallen down leaving a large hole in the side.

There is what looks, and smells, like human excrement outside in the small patch of muddy gravel we cross to reach the hanging cloth that is used as a door. The four odor adds further proof that it is not mud alone that is filling this yard.

"Seems that my sisters have not been cleaning up after our parents like I did when I was here. I am sorry you are seeing this. It is normally much nicer." My mate seems concerned with the state of the "house."

I doubt that cleaning would make much difference. But to spare her the embarrassment she is feeling I send her a reassuring smile. It is all I can do. Apparently without my mate to care for her, her mother is living within filth. The sight of this house, a term I use loosely, only fuels my anger at the humans as well as adds to my own guilt.

Eleanor and I reach the ratty cloth that is hanging from the doorframe. Eleanor raises her hand and brushes the cloth to the side.

"Mother? Are you here? It is me, Eleanor," my mate calls into the room. A tall, lanky woman who is covered in dirt is standing on the far side of the room we enter.

"Ele-fat? What are you doing here? I thought you were living it up as a sex slave to the Gelders? Abandoning us to fend for ourselves with your typical selfishness." We step further into the room.

The woman does not lift her eyes toward me, let alone Eleanor. If she was not speaking, you would have no indication that she even knows we are here. "Figures you would be sent back here. Can't do anything right. Are we to die then? Be abandoned to the Erains? I always knew you weren't good for anything. A pathetic creature I should have let die years ago."

Eleanor shoots me a look of apology. Embarassed for the words, shame filling her eyes as she stands and takes this abuse. I am overcome by the rage I have barely been containing. I burst into the tiny, filthy room that this disgusting human raised my mate in.

"You dare speak to my mate in such a way, human? You would do well to take care of your words and show some respect. Do you know who I am?" I snarl at her.

Her eyes are wide as saucers and her mouth opens and closes. She is unable to form words. Eventually she reverts to just shaking her head back and forth. Remembering the reaction Eleanor had to hearing my name, I smile a feral smile at her.

"I am Danion Belator of Old, high warrior king of the elite class, guardian to all life." I watch as my identity dawns on her. Her eyes roll back and she collapses at my feet.

Seeing her collapse in fear helps my mood. Barely, but it is a start.

Ellie

"Was that necessary?" I ask Danion as I move forward to make my mother a little more comfortable.

"Yes." He turns to look at me. "You were supposed to have more than this. You were always meant to be my queen and should have been treated as such. I am profoundly sorry for what you have suffered." His words cause my back to stiffen. "No mate of mine should have come from this." His words shatter something inside of me.

I am sure he is appalled to have a mate that came from such obvious poverty. He must be embarrassed to have a commoner like me on the throne with no way to remove me from it.

It is a blatant reminder that he would never have chosen me. I am simply the biological match for him. Not an equal in any true way. I am just a poor girl from area class three. Always have been and always will be.

"It wasn't so bad—" I try to tell him.

"You have four sisters, correct?" he interrupts me.

"Yes, two sets of twins." I am about to tell him their names but he interrupts me again.

"And you all lived in this one room?" This is said with a curl of his lip.

"Well, Mother and Darryl have a private room..." I trail off as I notice that the area that used to be their room is collapsed and there is a large hole in the wall. "Actually, it's gone. But growing up us girls did share this room but not the same one as our parents." I wonder what happened to their room.

"Five of you. In here." His words are laced with venom. His eyes are scanning the room we are in with ill-disguised disgust.

I can just imagine what he is thinking. Appalled that he is stuck with me as his queen. Worried about his peers learning of the humble roots of his mate.

"Gather your sisters, wherever they are. I am surprised there is anywhere we cannot see them from where we stand. We are taking them with us. I will not leave children in conditions such as this." His words cause powerful, mixed emotions inside of me.

Shame washes over me to realize that he must be thinking about my childhood here, but that is quickly dwarfed by elation. My sisters are going to live with me. I will have them back. I can't hold on to the shame when such happiness is coursing through me.

"Do you mean it?" I ask him, my face splitting into a grin. Danion turns his attention to me and I watch the hard, stern lines of his face soften under my gaze. He has a small smile on his face. Even in anger he appears so perfect. I feel like any artist who saw him would immediately be inspired to create the most precious artwork in his image.

But his looks are so perfect it makes him seem unapproachable. Beauty that is best admired from afar. His hard jawline, dark hair, and gray eyes become even more distinct. But when he smiles it is a different matter altogether.

The lines in his face soften, his hair beckons for my hands to run through it, and his eyes become welcoming rather than cold. This is the transformation I see take place. His hand comes up to cup my cheek.

"My queen, my mate, my *aninare*. I truly mean it. We can bring your sisters with us. They will have a better life with us than anything down here on this rock of a planet." He smiles at me as his thumb caresses my lower lip. "I would do anything to make you happy. You have had little enough happiness in your life. If it was within my power you would never have reason to frown again."

I open my mouth to respond, but I am interrupted by my mother moaning on the floor. I would have moved her to the old, ratty couch, but the room is barren now. The couch is missing along with most of the furniture. I just laid her out more comfortably on the floor, using the jacket I wore over my Gelder clothing to act as a pillow for her head.

"Mother, are you alright?" My voice is empty, no warmth in it. I cannot bring myself to feel any real emotion for her. She is the source of my childhood torment. I do not wish her harm, but I also have no desire to speak with her more than I have to.

I look at this angry woman curled up on the floor. Her coarse brown hair so different from my own. Her eyes that once held such vibrant hazel color have faded to a drab and murky green. The lines that are set deep upon her face are caked with dirt. I feel a small stab of guilt. My absence has been hard on Mother.

She answers my question with a glare and her face gives away her hatred for me. It is comforting that some things never change. She opens her mouth to say something, most likely insulting, but then her eyes cut to Danion and her lips snap closed.

"My queen asked you a question," Danion all but growls. "You will answer her. Now."

"Yes, I am fine. No thanks to my daughter." Her lip curls with her last word. "Leaving me on the floor like an animal or a piece of garbage."

As I open my mouth to defend myself I am stopped by a maelstrom of aura erupting from Danion. Thanks to Golon I know that this means he is close to losing his temper. If not for his aura you would have no idea of the emotional battle he was fighting.

"A rightful place for you then." Danion delivers these words with finality. The look he gives my mother is filled with contempt. It is uncomfortable to witness. To see his unwavering support and defense of me brings me comfort though. It is something I have lacked all my life.

"Uh..." My mother is rendered speechless.

"No, you do not speak unless I decree it. Or I swear I will end your pitiful life. It is what you deserve for the crimes you have done against your queen."

My mother's eyes widen in not only fear but something else as well. Confusion maybe? Denial? She obviously does not accept me as her queen. Danion picks up on her feelings, even though she tries to mask her thoughts.

"Yes, she is *your* queen. Earth is part of the Gelders' Pact Worlds. You are subjects to the Gelder throne. Harming the queen is a crime punishable by death. I am the final judgment on these matters, and my judgment is that you are guilty as sin. If I so decide I can hold you accountable for your crime. Do you understand me?" He stares at her pointedly.

She gives a brief nod.

"I want to hear you say it."

"Yes." She can barely choke the word out.

"All of it. What do you understand?"

"You are within your laws to kill me."

"And why am I within the laws?" At her look of confusion, I see his aura flow from him and pin my mother to the wall. To an observer it would look like she is just hovering in midair against the wall. "Admit your crime."

"Because...I harmed your..." She stumbles at his dark look and rushes to correct herself. "My queen. I harmed my queen."

"Good. I will ask questions and you will answer them with complete honesty." He pauses to allow her to nod. "Good. Now, Golon! Enter." I am shocked to see Golon enter behind us. I glance behind Golon and see the other four members of my *praesidium* are standing guard outside the old, ratty cloth that acts as a poor excuse for a door as well.

I feel ashamed now that I know it is not just Danion who will see what I grew up in. But all of them. It is so radically different from the life on the ship. I have never really had to feel too ashamed of my background before.

The simple hierarchy of the social class here on Earth Nueva prevents that, as I was never allowed to speak to members of a high area rank outside of professional circumstances. While we were on the low side of Area Three, we still were close in circumstance to everyone near us.

Golon sends a look I can't decipher my way.

"King Danion." He gives a curt nod to Danion. Danion nods back. A silent communication goes between them.

"Incubator of our queen, I have some questions for you." I am shocked at the amount of revulsion Golon is able to pack into those words. Because of this, it takes me a little while to even realize what he called my mother.

My mother looks like she is going to protest this moniker, but then she gets smart and closes her mouth. I realize that they really dislike her.

"Tell me about Eleanor's father."

"There is nothing to tell," she says sullenly. Just one look from Danion has her opening her mouth again. "He was a sperm donor. Got me pregnant and then left. I didn't even know him."

I can tell she is lying. I know her too well. A small twinkle in her eye betrays her glee. She loves to lie. Lives for it. She gets a strange thrill out of deceiving others. I am surprised she would try that with these warriors. But then again, maybe that is exactly why she is trying. The greater the lie, the greater the high she gets for pulling it off.

"She is lying." I hear myself say the words and can barely believe my own ears. I have never spoke out against her. Apparently the strength that I have discovered since joining with Danion is not exclusive to dealings with him.

I can tell my mother is also shocked at me betraying her. I have never told someone when she was deceiving them before. The little girl I once was is long gone though, and the woman I am now needs answers.

"We are going to go through this one more time," Danion says. "You will not get another chance. We have other means to get the answer we seek; we do *not* need you." The threat implied with those words are enough to cause her to shake with fear.

I know it is wrong of me, but I have a small sense of satisfaction at the sight. My whole childhood she has laughed when she let her husband abuse me. Or when I shook with hunger and she would deny me one of the nutritional squares until I was so malnourished my muscles shut down and I was unable to perform my chores.

"Now, tell me about Eleanor's father." Danion asks this time. No offense to Golon, but Danion is a lot more intimidating.

"Alright." My mother seems resigned now. "I will tell you." She takes a deep breath and then looks at me. "You look just like him, you know. A constant reminder of what you cost me." I suck in a breath at the look of resentment that she sends toward me.

My view of her is suddenly cut off by Danion's back. He has moved in front of me to stand between us both.

"You do not speak to my mate. You speak to either Golon or myself." Power is slipping into his voice. I can tell he is close to losing control. I place my hand in the middle of his back and lightly rub it back and forth.

I feel him stiffen and then physically relax. I see his aura instantly calm. He may be an arrogant jerk sometimes, but I can find no fault in his protection of me. I have never felt desired or wanted before. But with Danion? He has a way of making me feel like I am the only person in the room.

I can feel a small part of myself thaw toward him. He is not perfect, but then neither am I. He is mine all the same. Did I ask to be claimed by him? No. But I am finding it harder and harder to be upset by the change in my life that being claimed has caused. And I certainly cannot complain about the male who claimed me. There is no other warrior I have met that I prefer to him.

"You speak of cost. Explain." This from Golon. He is either unaware of the silent interaction between Danion and me or he is trying to pull us both out of it.

"Before she came along, my life was so perfect. I had everything. I had him, her father." Her voice breaks on the last word. Never before has she talked about my father. I find myself hanging on every stilted word.

"His name was Jaeson. He was tall, fair, and the most perfect man you could ever hope for. Everyone was jealous of me. Everyone envied *me*. He was the catch of a century, and it was my hook that caught him." She speaks nothing of his character, only his physical appearance.

I long to ask what he was like as a person. Did he like books like me? Did he enjoy walking in nature? I will probably never know what my father was like. My heart breaks to realize that my mother only cared about him for his looks and the position he brought her in society.

"Continue," Golon prompts when she says nothing more. Her voice, when she continues, sounds surprised. As if she can't comprehend what else there would be to tell.

"Jaeson and I had been together for a year when he gave me an ultimatum about having children. He had been pushing for children since the beginning but I resisted. I did not want to have them yet. Possibly at all. I never liked being around children. But he threatened to leave if I didn't try for one. So I did." I hear her snort, but I can only imagine the look on her face since Danion has not moved from his spot between us. "I have never wished to be infertile so much in my life, but alas, I was not so lucky."

"Then what?" This from Danion. His voice gruff and domineering. What could I have possibly done to make this woman hate me so much?

"Then everything was perfect." She sighs dreamily. "He was so attentive, more so than he ever was before. He was so interested in every step of the pregnancy. We would talk about what we thought the baby would be and who it would favor. For the months I was pregnant, I was so happy. Then the baby came, and everything changed."

"What changed?" Golon asks.

"Jaeson did. His entire attitude changed once the baby was born." She speaks as if she has forgotten I am still in the room. Out of sight must mean I really am out of mind. "He held her in his arms for the first time, and then he left. Just up and disappeared right after that. So disappointed in the baby that he couldn't even stomach being around her." I go cold at her words. So neither parent wanted me.

I didn't know it until this moment but I was hoping to learn that my father cherished me. That at least one of the people who were supposed to love me above all else cared for me. I hardly notice that I have stepped closer to Danion, instinctively seeking comfort from him. From the one person who I know wants me in his life.

"I pity you, human," Danion says. "You were gifted something precious, yet you treated her like dirt. I don't even know your name, and I do not wish to. As Golon said, you are nothing more than the incubator that carried my mate. You best be sure you have told us everything about her father. You would not like it if I were to discover you concealed something from us, and made me seek you out again. Because after today you will never see my mate again. Never benefit from her light. Never taint the air she breathes.

"I am also taking your other daughters with me. They deserve more than this excuse of a life." It is not surprising that she does not utter even a token of protest over her losing her children. She does have more to say though.

"There is...one more thing," she says after a pause. As if she is debating about telling us. "Jaeson did...leave something for his child." She still speaks as if I am not in the room. From around Danion I see her walk over to the far wall and pull out a brick. She tosses the brick to Golon. "I don't know what is so special about it but it can't be damaged or destroyed. Believe me I tried. Whenever I tried to throw it out or leave the house with it, something would stop the brick. It can't cross the threshold."

"We will sort it out. Now, call for your daughters. We will be leaving," Golon responds tersely.

"I can't do that. They are gone." She says this with no emotion.

My heart shatters into a million pieces. Gone! No! My absence has not been that long, how are they gone? I must have made a sound because she snorts.

"I don't mean dead." I swear I hear her mumble "idiot" beneath her breath. "They don't live here anymore. That *friend* of yours refused to give us the money you left for the girls so we kicked them out. I believe they are living with her. Probably much better than we are since you left them a nice little nest egg. I am sure they are quite comfortable." For the first time she is directing her words to me again. She speaks with gleeful malice as if she knows something I do not.

"Leave. Now. You may return when we are gone," Danion tells her.

"This is my..." She trails off at the look Danion must be giving her. I can feel the anger rolling off him in waves. Without another word or look in my direction she leaves.

The small house feels suffocating now. I never realized how much my mother despised me. I feel that something is off, as if something about what I just learned is not the truth. I can't pinpoint the exact source of my feeling, but I just know that something is not right with her story. Before I can voice my concerns Danion turns around and wraps me up in his arms, pushing the thought out of my mind.

"I am sorry, *aninare*. I wish I could take all the pain you suffered and carry it on my own shoulders." I lean on his strength for a few moments more, a luxury I have never had before. I have always been the strong one for my sisters. After just a few moments being comforted by his strength I step away from him.

"So my father left me a brick? What could he possibly want me to do with a brick?" I can't keep the disappointment off my face. Maybe it was some sort of symbolism. Like I am worth nothing more than one single brick.

"More likely he hid the gift inside. From what the human described I would say he wove a protection weave that only you can break through. That is why it could not be destroyed or taken from the home. A blood weave to keep it safe," Golon answers.

"How do I break it then? The weave I mean, not the brick. How do I break through it and see what he hid? If he actually hid anything."

"I don't know. There are many different blood weaves he could have used. We might have to spend extensive time researching the matter. I must warn you, blood weaves are tricky. It may takes weeks, possibly even months, before we can break through the weave." I extend my hand out for the brick. Reluctantly, Golon stops his observation of the brick and hands it to me. As soon as I touch it, the brick begins to dissolve.

"What is happening?" I almost drop it but manage to keep what is left of the quickly disappearing brick in my open hand.

"Fascinating." Golon's voice comes to me filled with excitement. "I have never seen this weave in person. Only read about its existence. I tried to replicate it several times but it was simply impossible." Golon looks at me with wide, fascinated eyes. "It is a weave only known to the *lacieu* lineages and only a master in the line can weave this thread. It is called the *blode leete*, or loosely translated it means 'blood seal.'

"It is designed to be locked until the intended recipient merely touches it. A simple contact with the object from the holder of the blood seal and it opens. Nothing else could destroy that brick. The entire planet could explode and it would still be floating in space, unharmed. Waiting for you to open it." As Golon is talking I see the beginnings of a small heart-shaped locket emerging from the dust.

I smooth the remaining brick remnants away and transfer the locket to my other hand, marveling at how warm it feels. The brilliant light blue color is so pure it almost appears clear. Engraved throughout the body are colored metal markings that resemble the tattoo on my torso. I try to open it but can't. There is no lock that I can see, but there is a seam running along the locket.

"May I see that?" Golon extends his hand. I am hesitant to release it but I know it is logical to let him look it over as well. He might know how to open it. Somewhat reluctantly, I hand over my locket.

"This cannot be," Golon says, surprised disbelief dripping from his words. "It is blessed." He continues to study my locket but does not say any more.

"Are you sure? It can't be. Truly?" Danion seems shocked.

"Why is that surprising? What does blessed mean?" I ask anxiously. I hate not knowing what they are so concerned about. Is it bad to have a blessed locket?

"To bless an item it requires a part of your soul to be shared with it. It is considered an extremely private gift. Extremely private and extremely sacred. It is almost never done, and always, always the gift is given in person." Both warriors stare at the locket with a mixture of awe and misgiving. I must still look confused because Danion expands on Golon's explanation.

"A blessed item connects the wearer to the creator. It can be used for various purposes. Protection, a power source, or even communication over great distances. The blesser actually links the item to his soul, the very energy that defines him as a being. Because of how significant this act is it is exceedingly rare to come across blessed items. It is quite dangerous to have a blessed item out in the galaxy. Once created it can never be undone. It will exist forever. Your father left a part of his soul for you." Danion's words shock me.

"Why would he do that?" I cannot reconcile the man who took one look at me and decided to abandon me with the man who placed a part of his soul into a locket for me. They cannot be the same man. It is impossible.

"Eleanor. Your father cared for you. He would not have left you this locket if he did not. What drove him away is yet to be seen, but I am sure it is not as your mother said it was. He would not willingly abandon you only to leave his soul behind for you. We will find out what truly happened to him, I promise," Danion assures me.

"OK." It is all I can bring myself to say. I stare at the locket, trying to decide what I should do with it. I decide to place it in the pocket of my pants for now. I am not ready to wear it, to let it rest against my heart. "Can we go pick up my sisters now?" I am desperate to change the topic. My emotions feel raw and hyper sensitive like an exposed nerve.

"My king? We have an approaching party." We are interrupted by Griffith. I look up with surprise at Danion. He does not seem to be surprised at all. Was he expecting for us to have uninvited visitors?

"Who is coming, Danion?" I ask.

"I imagine it is a delegation from High Ambassador Lexen," Danion says calmly.

"What?" I ask, both confused and scared. The high ambassador is not someone you want to be on the wrong side of.

"I did not notify him of our arrival or respond to the many queries he has sent my way. Nor about his desire to know the new defense strategies I have set up since this heinous attack began, or about my business here on the planet."

"Why would you do that? Can you do that? I thought that you were bound by the same treaty we are."

"If this human ambassador feels he can pick and choose which parts of the treaty he has to follow, I can do the same." I realize now that what I mistook for calmness is actually a carefully crafted facade to hide his bone deep rage.

We all step outside to meet the delegation. There are no fewer than a dozen army vehicles coming down the road. They all stop in a semi loose circle around our own vehicle and my house, effectively blocking us in.

Two men dressed in all black, right down to even wearing black sunglasses, step out of the closest car and approach us. I can't help thinking that they are trying too hard to be intimidating. It is nothing like the natural power that Danion and these warriors have in spades. A power so strong that you can't help but feel apprehensive.

Standing anywhere near these warriors you are compelled to feel uneasy. When in their presence it is as if you are in a cage with a tame wolf. It knows how to act around you and you trust it to behave as expected, but in the back of your mind you know it is capable of tearing you to shreds.

The agents stop a few feet from us, standing with their feet spread shoulder width apart and clasping their hands in front of themselves. The taller of the two speaks first. He is tall compared to me, but next to these six warriors he looks frail. The height difference is so drastic it's almost childlike.

"Gentlemen, I am Agent Dolph Henderson and this is Agent Michael Rodriguez. We are with EGAET, the Earth Guard Against Extraterrestrials. You are in violation of the treaty and accused of high crimes against Earth Nueva's best interests. We are going to need to take you all in for questioning." There is stark silence. I have to hold back a bark of laughter.

I honestly can't believe their nerve. The only explanation I can think of is that they do not know who it is that is standing before them. If they did they would never be foolish enough to speak to him that way.

This is the king of the strongest warriors the galaxy has ever known. Strictly speaking, he is *their* king. I can't imagine what their plan is, or how they expect to bring these warriors in if they don't want to go.

Apparently Golon shares my disbelief, because I am soon distracted by him throwing his head back and laughing. Not a good-natured chuckle, not a laugh you give when something is truly amusing. No, the laugh he gives is more like the laugh you give to a child when they do something naughty and you are indulging them.

"You are going to bring us in? For violating the treaty? There is not a single thing you humans can do to us, let alone a cell that can hold us. Apparently we can add 'stupid' to the fast-growing list of faults we are finding within the Earth government." All traces of laughter disappear from his face as if they were never there. "We are within our grounds to annihilate this entire planet for the violations done by *your* government. We go nowhere but where we want to go. We do nothing but what we wish to do. You cannot stop us, and I wouldn't even care to see you try. It would be that pitiful if you did."

I look at Golon in surprise. He is normally who I can rely on to be pragmatic and calm, but I can tell even he is barely containing his anger. I wonder why he is so angry? Danion is always angry, I expect it from him. Sure enough, when I glance at Danion I see his aura is at its flash point again. My glances at my four other warriors show they too are battling their auras.

"It is our job—" Agent Henderson breaks off quickly by a very angry warrior king.

"You will not speak with us again. You will not attempt to stop us. I will be going to see your ambassador but it is most definitely not so that I can beg his pardon. It will be to discuss dissolving the current treaty, since there seems to be some confusion about our race and the insults we will tolerate." He steps menacingly forward. "You humans seem to think that we will allow insult upon insult to be piled upon us with no consequence. Your actions prove you are unable to rule yourselves so we will have to do so for you." Danion's words are aura heavy and I can tell he is holding the agents and all of the unseen agents still with his power.

I see a flare of power in his aura and then the army vehicles that are blocking our own are flung away as if they are made of paper. I hope that the people inside are not harmed, but I don't have a lot of time to give to this thought as we are all moving again. Danion grabs me by my arms, lifts me up, and moves so quickly that the next thing I know we are inside our vehicle.

"Take us to the shuttle. We will travel to the ambassador via the shuttle, not this tiny little box on wheels." I try to put a little space between Danion and myself but he grips my hand and then pulls me even closer. After everything I learned from my mother and the confrontation with the agents, I admit I crave some physical comfort so I stop resisting his pull.

Chapter Eight

Danion

As we are docking in the ambassador building, my mind travels over all of the information that we learned from Eleanor's mother. It goes against everything I am to call that vile woman her mother. Her life force was tainted. One of the few souls that are so self-absorbed it has begun to degrade the energy that makes up her life force. She was so badly contaminated that it could actually be sensed.

I want answers in regards to the treatment of my mate and I will take no prisoners. I will never leave the entire planet to fend for themselves against these Erain attacks, but I will not let these humans continue to abuse our treaty without consequence. I cannot fathom why they have done this. They cannot be so delusional to think that we would never learn of their deceit or that we would not punish those responsible.

My mate seems very nervous and keeps running her hands over her clothing. She is dressed finely in a warrior's daywear: dark brown leather pants with a sleeveless shirt made of *memien* to match mine. Tight, finely woven *memien*. It is a very powerful fabric, the threads being a physical embodiment of our power. No Gelder would ever doubt her rank by looking at her, but I know she feels nervous to face this human council. Humans find pleasure in lording position and title over those they deem to be beneath them by showcasing wealth: wearing fine clothes and worthless baubles.

To make my mate feel more comfortable I weave her a wreath of diamonds to encircle her neck. For reasons I cannot conceive, humans seem to value these worthless stones. So be it. If my mate needs some crystalized carbon to feel more confident that is what she will get.

"You look gorgeous, mate. Exactly how a warrior queen should. As I look at you I can find no fault, nor would any Gelder. You bring honor to our race. But if you feel better with these stones, I will have a dress made out of them for you. With or without them, you bring honor to us all," I tell my mate. She looks at me with pleased shock on her face.

"Yes, my queen. Nothing but honor," the traitorous, lustful Arsenio seconds. I shoot an annoyed glance his way. He answers this with a smirk and a rude gesture once Eleanor is no longer looking at him.

If it was not for my feelings toward my mate I would return his gesture with one of my own. A very powerful gesture that would rocket him outside of this planet's gravitational field. Let him float away into space. I take a few moments to enjoy this thought.

All of the warriors on the shuttle express their pride in her. Finally, after each warrior has spoken, I see her relax. She takes a deep breath and smiles out into the shuttle in general, wrapping all of us in the warmth of her soul. A warmth she so readily shares with the rest of us.

"It is all of you that bring honor to me." She reaches out and caresses my arm. Fire shoots through me and I quickly throw down my barriers. It is all I can do to keep my reaction a secret. A knowing look from Griffith, that he quickly hides, shows me I did not manage to hide my reaction from the leading master of the *vim* lineage. Masters in what is known as life force are notorious for their intrusive insights.

I am able to distract myself from my lustful thoughts by the shuttle finally finishing the docking procedure. It should never have taken so long to gain clearance to unlock the docking bay doors. This ambassador is walking a fine line; he must be incredibly stupid to blatantly disrespect the Gelder race. I am surprised a man of his low intelligence level was able to climb high enough to claim his title.

I stand as the doors of the shuttle open. I extend my hand out to Eleanor and help her rise from her chair. As we move to exit the shuttle, the other five warriors fall into a circle around us. They make the move look seamless. These humans do not know it yet, but before them are six of the strongest warriors in the cosmos.

Guarding a female who, I am beginning to suspect, will prove to be more powerful than all of us combined. A female who was abused by these very humans.

A tiny, frail male tries to stop our entourage. We spare him no more than a glance. We move with determination toward the ambassador's office.

Once we reach the office, a petite female who reeks of silicone also tries to halt our progress. Again, we ignore all protests and open the doors to this so-called leader's office.

Inside we find a small, pasty male sitting behind a large desk. He seems remarkably calm about our arrival. No matter how stupid he may be, he must know that we come for vengeance. No human should be this calm when standing against just one warrior, but he stands before six of them with a composure that I can't help but admire. It won't help him, but I admire his courage.

"Gentlemen, I have been expecting you." High Ambassador Lexen has the voice of a weasel. He is a man of slight build. No taller than Eleanor and almost just as thin. His white, thinning hair flaunts patches of bald skin. He stands and comes around the corner of his desk. His arms are open in a way that I suppose is designed to seem welcoming but have a hint of danger as well. However, on his thin and bony body the gesture just looks foolish.

"You will address your queen or it will be your head," I say to him. With no small amount of pleasure I lace my words with my power and watch it snake up his spine. I let it encircle his neck, squeezing ever so lightly. Enough to let him know I could take his life right now. I see sweat bead on his brow. That is how you intimidate someone, I think to myself.

"My queen?" He looks genuinely confused. "Earth does not have a queen." His eyes actually search the room, taking in and discarding Eleanor with a glance. I see her stiffen with embarrassment.

"Yes. Your queen. My mate. You may have manipulated this planet into believing you are a king but trust me when I say you do not want me to treat you as such. Your planet is under *my* protection. The treaty clearly states that Earth is one of the Pact Worlds. That means that this planet is Gelder territory. Meaning you answer to Gelder law above all others. Especially false laws that you yourself create for your own nefarious purposes."

I fold my arms across my chest. "Ambassadors are set up to manage these planets. They have no other power. No other authority. Normally a member of their own race is appointed, unless they prove unable to handle the duty. You have proven yourself more than incompetent," I snarl at him.

"Have I? I think we disagree on that matter." He still is maintaining an admirable calm for a man so close to his death. "I think you are going to do nothing to me." He even has a smirk of confidence on his face.

For all he lacks in intelligence he more than compensates for it in courage. That will not save him, but still, he is not as weak as I first imagined. "In fact, I think you will be leaving this room without doing a thing to me."

"You must truly be delusional. No Gelder warrior would allow their mate to be disrespected, let alone harmed, without taking vengeance. You have allowed my mate to suffer untold abuse, experience starvation, and grow up in poverty when I provided a fortune to be bestowed upon her. I know she never saw this money," I accuse him.

"No, she did not see it. She had no need of it. I monitored her for you and saw that she was kept alive. A girl from Area Three would have no need for the fortune you sent. I saw no reason why your future whore would need such luxury. So I appropriated the funds to be put to better use." He says this while staring at my sweet Eleanor with blatant disgust.

This mortal human clearly thinks he is above my mate. I begin to weave a thread of power when a lasso of fire encircles the ambassador's neck.

It would be a simple matter to trace the weave back to determine who the caster was, but I have no need. Arsenio's signature weave is in the fire rope. He developed this weave centuries ago and no one else wields it. He has wrapped it so tightly around Lexen's throat that it is not only burning him but also cutting off his air supply. His attempts to scream are no more than gasps as he struggles for air.

"That is your queen you speak of. There is not a warrior in this room who would not die for her, so you best choose your words carefully. You have no power here. You have no leverage against us. For your transgressions against our queen alone we should take your life. Not to say anything of the laws you broke when you used the Gelder name to enslave your people." I see the rope cutting into Lexen and can smell his burning flesh. None of us try to stop Arsenio. For once, I am in complete agreement with him.

"Arsenio, stop this." I am shocked by Eleanor's voice intruding into the ambassador's punishment. "Now, Arsenio. You are not murderers," she says again when her first command had no effect. Slowly, Arsenio loosens the rope but leaves it circling Lexen's neck loosely.

"You cannot kill me. You cannot do anything to me." High Ambassador Lexen braces himself against the desk as he coughs air through his bruised trachea. "I have built Earth Nueva into what it is today. I have no desire to conquer other planets, but I have earned Earth Nueva and it is mine. You will let me have my empire."

"Why would we let you keep your position?" Golon speaks up. "We will strip you of your title, bring light to all your lies, and place a trustworthy Gelder in your place to begin building the people you tore down back up. A Gelder who will not abuse the power his position gives him." I marvel at this; Golon normally takes the role of observer in all matters that don't pertain to science. Yet several times on our visit here he has spoken out.

"You have done an unforgivable crime against my mate. There is no pardon for you," I say to the weasel in front of me, who is the reason my mate was so afraid of me, the reason she knew hunger, the reason she grew up in filth. I have to put considerable effort into containing the anger that these thoughts cause.

"You will not touch me once you hear what I have to tell you." He sounds confident. He tries to pull himself up and make himself appear bigger. It is a failed attempt. Nothing he can do would ever make his frail appearance seem large.

"What is it that you have to say?" I cannot help but feel curious about what has provided him with such confidence. He knows the assault he did against us, knew there would be punishment, but believes that he is immune. I want to know why.

"Because Eleanor is dying. Has been her whole life. Would have died years ago if not for my interference. I made a deal with her father to keep her alive. If you take Earth from me, I will stand by and do nothing. I will stand by and watch her die. And so will you." His words ricochet through me.

The entire room is frozen still at his words. Eleanor is the first one capable of speech.

"My father made a deal with you?" she asks. The ambassador barely glances at Eleanor and does not answer her. His body language is stiff and reserved. He believes himself to be too good to speak to my mate. The rage that courses through me obliterates my shock at learning of her dying.

"I will say this only once more, *infer*. You will treat my mate with the respect she deserves or it will be your head," I growl at him. I can tell Lexen tries to hide his fear but it is plain as day on his face.

"Then it will be her death as well," Ambassador Lexen counters. He is a brave human, I will give him that.

"Then so be it. If it is a choice between letting Earth be controlled by this tyrant and my life, I choose the freedom of my people." Eleanor's words drop like a lead weight. As a unit, all of the warriors in her *praesidium* turn and stare at her.

"Blast the Powers you do," I tell her.

Ellie

I can tell from the look on Danion's face that my feelings on this matter are not shared. Not one warrior in this room is my ally. They all would rather cave to this rat of a man's demands.

"It is my decision, Danion," I say forcefully.

"No, it is not. You are not allowed to sacrifice your life. On any account. For any reason," he tells me.

"I am not sacrificing it. Well, at least not without a fight. But we will *not* leave this world and these people to suffer under this horrible man." I will not budge on this. I recall vividly the stories Joy told me about her life on Earth before the Purge War.

People could dream to be whoever they wanted. They were not born into the life they would lead. They had choices. They could talk to anyone they wanted to, not just those in the same social level. Joy's world is a fairy tale compared to what I have lived. I want that world for my people. I want that world to exist.

"I will not let you die."

"Then what is your plan? Just to hand over these people on a silver platter to this disgusting excuse for a man?" I say with a curl of my lip sent in the ambassador's direction.

I can't help but marvel at the man before me. All my life he has been something to fear. But he is just a frail little man trying to hold on to power that was never his.

I can't help but compare him to Danion. Danion is a king that has held the throne by sheer power alone. He was not born into the crown but earned it by being the strongest warrior in the galaxy. By all rights he has no one to answer to, since no one would stand a chance against him. But he does not abuse his power. He chooses to rule with mercy and justice as a guide all on his own, adhering strictly to his moral compass.

But this High Ambassador Lexen is a miserable excuse for a leader. He leads so he can control while Danion leads so he can protect. He is a powerless man, clinging desperately to power he stole. To a power that should never have been his. Somehow he has turned a world that cherished freedom into a world that never questions the government.

And worse, in Joy's time he would have only controlled one country. People could have appealed to foreign powers to fight his tyranny. But in my world? The high ambassador is judge, jury, and executioner. There is no appeal process.

The ambassador has always said that he was appointed by the Gelders, implying that the treaty depended on him in his position. I now know that this is not true.

"They are not dying, they have lived this way for a century. We can think of other options later—" Danion begins to argue with me and I cut him off.

"No. These people have been oppressed for a century. A *century*, Danion. That is longer than our lifespan! And this existence is not a life. Not living by any true sense of the word." I can see he is about to argue again.

"I will not risk your life. You are our queen," Danion says forcefully. I decide to try a new approach.

"I was just in the medical wing for weeks. I had who knows how many tests done. For goodness' sakes, my DNA was screened. Did Jarlin find anything in all the tests he ran that indicated that I was dying? I was with you for over a month. Nothing special was done to me in all that time, and I was not dying. He is lying. I say we call his bluff," I explain to him.

"I will not take the chance. *Aninare*, you are too important to me. I pledged myself to your protection above all others and that is a vow I plan to honor," Danion responds.

"I understand that. I appreciate that, more than you know. It means the world to me that you are so committed. But Danion, this is bigger than you and me," I insist.

"No, it is not bigger than us. You are my queen. Not in title alone, but in actuality. You are queen of the Gelder race, and by extension, queen to all the Pact Worlds. If you die, I may not be able to defend the trillions of lives I protect. We protect. We are all that stands between the people of this galaxy and death by the hands of creatures like the Erains. There is nothing in this galaxy that is bigger than you and me." He enunciates the last three words.

"That, Danion, is arrogance. We are only two people. Plain and simple. Our lives are no more important than anyone else's. When you start believing that, you are no better than this so-called ambassador. He believes he deserves more than other people do. He thinks that his so-called superiority justifies his actions. We can't be like him. I refuse to be anything like him."

I can tell my argument is having no effect. I am trying to formulate another argument when help comes in the form of Golon. And the words he says makes the ambassador look downright panicked. Good.

"Danion, I believe Eleanor is correct. No, don't get defensive. Stop thinking like a male in bond madness and start thinking like a warrior with logic. Eleanor has been living with us on your ship for several weeks. If she had some life-threatening disease that this human was keeping at bay we should have seen a sign of it." While Golon speaks his eyes are trained on the ambassador.

"What if her symptoms take longer to develop? Maybe she only needs treatment infrequently," Danion argues.

"Even then, Jarlin studied her physiology in great detail for weeks and saw no sign of any disease. Maybe joining with you healed her."

I have another theory.

"Or he is just lying. He is obviously not above that. What is to say he did not just come up with this? I have never seen him in my life. Never had anything special done to me that would be saving me from some life-threatening illness. I do not think there is any such illness." I deliver the words forcefully. Infusing as much confidence as I can into the words in the hope I can convince Danion to save Earth.

"No, I am not lying. Your father came to me right after you were born and told me of your condition," the ambassador insists, for the first time addressing me directly. "He explained what I must do to ensure you survived because he would not be able to do it for you."

"Then what is it?" I ask. I am sure he will not tell me.

"I will not reveal my only bargaining chip so early in the game." The ambassador speaks with a hint of smugness. He feels confident that Danion will not risk my life. He is confident that he will get to keep ruling Earth.

"Why not?" I ask him. "If you are the only one who can save me why not prove it by saying what it is that you have done for me?"

"There can only be two reasons he would not want to divulge his secret," Arsenio speaks up. He slowly closes the distance between him and the ambassador as he talks. "Either he is lying, and therefore has no answer, or he knows that it is something we can do for you as well, essentially nullifying his usefulness." Arsenio stops with barely inches between them.

"Very astute, Arsenio. I would not expect it of you," Golon comments. "We do have very advanced medical practices. If she did have a human illness we would most likely be able to cure it."

"That is not a gamble I want to take!" Danion still resists. I walk over and take his hands in mine.

"Danion. Listen to me. I have lived here on this planet under his rule. It is not a fate that anyone should suffer. I have never been sick a day in my life and never had any medical visits outside of the normal checks. I truly do not feel like he is telling the truth. But even if he is, there is obviously a cure. He has been giving it to me my whole life. So why would the Gelders not have that cure?" I reason with him. His hand comes up and cups my cheek.

"It is a chance, *aninare*," he tells me, his eyes troubled. I raise my hand to place over his on my cheek.

"If it comes down between trusting that Gelder medicine will save me or putting my life in the hands of this man, I will take the chance on the Gelders every time," I tell him. I see Danion close his eyes. Danion is silent for several minutes. None of us speak, letting him make up his mind.

"Alright." With this single word I glance over and see Lexen trying to flee the room. He has lost all color and the air of confidence has vanished. He truly didn't expect to lose this battle. He really thought that he could go toe to toe with this warrior and win.

"Not so fast, Ambassador. We still have other matters of your deceit to discuss," Danion calls over to Lexen without raising his head or breaking eye contact with me. I can see from Danion's aura that he has tethered the ambassador in place.

"What matters?" I ask. I thought Danion was only concerned with the crimes done to me. Are there more misdeeds to lay at the ambassador's feet?

"First, answer me this, Eleanor. How long have the Gelders been fighting the Erains in your skies? How long have we been waging a battle to keep this planet safe?" Danion asks me. I study his face for any clues to where this is heading.

"One hundred years. But you know this. Your warriors are the ones fighting the war. Aren't they?" I answer Danion's question slowly.

"Ambassador? Do you want to answer this question? Want to admit to your heinous crimes?" Danion asks Lexen with a raised eyebrow.

"I have no crime to admit to," Lexen answers, trying to appear confident and rebellious. The trembling in his legs and the quaver in his voice give away his trepidation.

"No? Then I suppose I will have to answer for you," Danion answers him, a harsh bite entering into his tone. "Eleanor, your planet was attacked one hundred and two revolutions ago. Or years, as you know them. We came, negotiated the treaty, and defeated the Erains. Within. Seven. Days." His words drop like lead in the room. I can't comprehend what he is talking about. "The Erains have not been back to this quadrant of space since then. Barring this most recent attack."

"But...that can't be true. We see the burning wreckage. The flaming remains that fall and get destroyed on the shield that you put up. Every day of my life I have looked up and seen the still-fiery remains of spacecraft. What are these remains if not Erain ships?" I ask with a stone in the pit of my stomach. I can taste bile rising in my throat. I suspect that I will not like this answer.

"Ambassador? Any comment yet?" Lexen shakes his head slowly back and forth. His face has grown even whiter though. The face of a man who has committed horrible deeds but never thought he would have to face them.

"Danion? What has he done?" I ask my mate and king. I dread the answer but know I must hear it.

"Are you aware that every year the human population gets smaller rather than larger? Even though your birthrates are higher than they have ever been?" he asks me.

"No, I didn't know that," I answer, somewhat confused as to where he is leading with this. Then it hits me, but I wish it didn't.

"Thousands upon thousands of human souls are lost every year. By Erain abduction, allegedly." Oh, no. No, no, no. No one could be this evil. I shoot a look of horror over to this tiny cowering man. Danion cannot be saying what I think he is saying. "Except there are no Erains, are there, Lexen?"

Danion stares at Lexen for quite a while. When he still gets no response I see a thread of blue join with a thread of red aura and shoot around Lexen. He finally answers.

"No." A single brief response.

"Tell us, Lexen. Tell us what you have done." Danion speaks with hard words. The threads grow brighter briefly and then Lexen is talking. Telling a tale so dark it turns my stomach.

"There are revolts in the middle areas. Of people who refuse to abide by the laws that I set. Those who are not cooperative are herded together like the cattle they are and shipped up to space in cheap transport shuttles. They are then fired upon right above Earth's orbit and we let the pieces rain down onto the shields." His voice is grim but unrepentant.

"My... I... For... Why?" It takes several attempts to formulate a response to such evil, and in the end all I can manage is a one-word query.

"It helped the cause. I used the threat of extinction to subjugate all you dogs beneath me. It never hurts to keep the threat alive for all of you. So simpleminded you all are. It was laughably easy to rule you." His words are bitter, foul. Evil.

"But why send people up?" I exclaim. "There are easier ways, surely? Why not just send the ships up unmanned. We on the surface would never know," I ask him. Lexen's lips form into a terrifying imitation of a smile.

"But that would be decidedly less fun. Any who oppose me deserve to die." He even laughs.

No true human being would find such morbid joy in this situation. But he does. He may have started out resisting to talk about what he has done, but by the end he is so caught up in his crimes that he is actually *bragging* about murder.

"You disgust me," I tell him.

"And you disgust me," is his simple response.

This spurs my warriors back into action. I think even these ancient, hardened warriors who have been at war for thousands of years are shocked at his depravity. As the last of his insult falls from his lips the males around me crowd him. I am struck with curiosity as to what they are planning to do to him.

"What will you do with the ambassador?" I ask.

"For his crimes against the crown alone, it is a death sentence. Adding to that all the pain and suffering he has caused to the billions of human souls here there is no question that he has forfeited his right to life," Danion answers. While I know he deserves this I cannot shake the feeling that doing so makes us no better than him.

"We can't just kill him. Regardless of his crimes, life is never something to be taken on purpose," I tell him.

"Then what would you have me do? We do not keep our criminals locked up. We have no jails," Danion explains.

"Well, what do you do with them?" I ask. I have to fight to keep my eyes from traveling to Arsenio. I know he was a criminal at one point.

"They are exiled to one of the working outposts. Put to work, made useful. We have only had a few that have ever committed a crime. Gelders are ruled by honor. Very few ever break our laws. No true warrior would forfeit his honor." I notice a heated glance between Danion and Arsenio.

"Well, couldn't we exile him then?" I ask.

"He would not be of use on any of the exiled worlds. There are no skills he has that would allow him to perform a worthwhile task. No world would take him," Danion answers.

"There must be somewhere you could send him. An advanced race such as you should not be practicing something as barbaric as killing as the only course of action," I insist.

To decide to kill someone without a trial or any kind of checks and balances seems wrong to me. What if their faulty justice system kills someone who is innocent only to later find that they acted rashly and no crime was committed? I can't agree with the decision.

I see Danion contemplating my words, gauging how serious I am in my conviction. I am one hundred percent serious. Killing him would be infinitely easier. It would also make us no better than him. Finally, after what feels like an eternity, Danion nods his head.

"You are sure you are comfortable letting him live after the atrocities he has committed?" Danion asks me.

"If you are asking me if I want to see him dead, then the answer is yes. He is a monster. But that is not our call to make. If you can find a place that he can be made useful that is the call we need to make. That is justice. Killing him is just too easy."

"Alright, you are my queen. My equal partner. You are also the one who suffered from his hand. If that is the punishment you would like to see visited upon him that is what we will do. We will exile him to one of the outer moon outposts. We will call for a shuttle from the ship and then send him there to be held until the next prison guildship is available. This vessel class is the only one equipped to transport prisoners. With the attacks we are suffering it may be a while before we can have him shipped off."

"Thank you, Danion." I smile at him. I feel immensely pleased with myself. That is two major arguments I have won against him. I am also pleased with Danion. He valued my opinion in handling an enemy.

"Griffith, I will leave you here to look after the planet's affairs, organize the transport of our prisoner, and appoint a temporary warrior to represent the planet's best interest while we work on getting a new ambassador permanently appointed. Also, once you have secured Lexen and you have seen to his transport to our long-range shuttle in orbit, make sure that we have him well secured in the lower decks. We will be taking the small-range shuttle back to the shuttle in orbit now. I do not want him in the same shuttle as the queen," Danion instructs his warriors.

"Malin, I have another mission for you. My mate should have been handled respectfully by the handler assigned to her. It is my understanding that instead of that respect, she was insulted and lied to. Deliberately, for the sole purpose of scaring her into dreading what her future may hold. She will be punished, you know of whom I speak?" He asks of the water master. I am struggling to follow the conversation. Who is he talking about?

Malin does not share my confusion, he nods his head. "Yes, my king, you speak of Lady Annabeth. I believe petty jealousy motivated much of the cruel comments and lies she spewed towards our queen. What would you have me do?"

Danion's face turns into a feral smile, "I want you to apprehend her, and make sure it is public. I want the people of this planet to know that we do not mistreat those we claim, and we will not tolerate lies being spread. Turn her over into Griffith's care." Danion turns to Griffith, "I am sure you can find a suitable punishment here on Earth for her."

Griffith nods his head, an angry look on his face. "Yes, I will strip her of her high rank and confiscate the material goods she so cherishes. We begin rectifying this society today."

Danion nods his head, then turns back to Malin. "When we get to the main shuttle, you will report back to the ship and request a briefing with Kowan and Amell. Golon, Etan, and I will be escorting the queen to pick up her sisters. We will meet you back on the shuttle in no more than a half rotation." He turns toward the door and holds out a hand for me. I take it and we head back to our small-range shuttle.

Lexen

As these warriors are securing me for transport I reflect on how perfect that played out. That couldn't have gone better if I had planned it myself. Oh, wait. I *did* plan that myself. The laughably incompetent Gelders played right into my hand. If the whore girl hadn't been there it would have been another story.

Of course, I knew she would be there for this first, but in no way final, showdown. She will be their downfall. What do they expect when they appoint a low-class peasant stock girl to be their queen? The thought of her on a throne sickens me.

Power is for those who deserve it. Power is for those who are better than the rest. Like me. I was born to rule these imbeciles. Humans crave subjugation. I have been planning my rule for a century.

However, I am approaching the end of my life. My human life. I can have anything I want on this planet, but the one thing I need is not on this planet. There is one place and one place only in the galaxy I can get what I need.

If it wasn't beneath me I would thank that foolish girl the Gelder rats dare to call a queen for doing just as I wanted. For sending me exactly where I wanted to go.

Ellie

"Thank you, Danion. For what you did in there," I say to him shyly as we walk toward the shuttle. He meets my words with a curious frown.

"For what?" he asks me.

"For listening to me. For valuing my opinion."

"*Aninare*, you need never thank me for that. That is my job as your *animare*. It brings me pleasure to do so for you."

"Well, then thank you, *animare*." Danion's body seems to lock in surprise, and his face smooths into an expression of extreme pleasure.

"Could you...say that again?" Danion asks me. I look at him with confusion.

"Thank—" Danion interrupts me before I can finish repeating myself in expressing my gratitude.

"No, call me that again." Oh, now I see.

"*Animare*," I say to him quietly, shyly. Meanwhile I give the hand within mine a small squeeze.

"You have no idea how long I have waited to hear that word from your lips, *aninare*." Danion raises our joined hands to his mouth and places a small kiss on the back.

"I am glad you are happy," I tell him shyly.

"This is a great gift you have given me. You do not understand; my entire existence I have been a warrior. Admired for my strength. While this pleases me, I have longed to be more than a weapon. You give me that. For you, I am not a warrior. I am your *animare*, your mate."

Danion's entire body is radiating heat. His aura is so full of open, wide arcs of sweeping motion I almost don't recognize him. His aura has always been violent before, tempestuous and swirling.

I realize that this must be him at peace. For once, Danion is truly content. I realize how important this is, me calling him *animare*. He has always been fighting for control of himself, literally waging an internal battle inside himself, and with one word I have calmed him.

My warrior may be fierce, but he is also lonely. If me calling him *animare* can bring this much peace to him, I will be sure to call him it more frequently.

We continue walking hand in hand, both lost to our own thoughts. As we approach the shuttle my mind turns to what he said as we exited the office.

"How long is a half rotation?" I curiously ask Danion.

"You would call it twelve hours." I must have been showing my confusion because he explains further. "Here on Earth you have what we call a solar-based reference of time.

Meaning that you based your units of time off your planets relative position in space and to the star you orbit.

"One day is one rotation around this planet's axis. A year, however, is one full orbit around the star, which takes three hundred and sixty-five days. I am not sure how long it will take your sisters to pack, so I allotted a large amount of time, twelve hours. I try to use your expression for time, but sometimes I fall back into old habits," he explains.

"That is fascinating," I say.

"Didn't you know this about your time?" he asks me.

"No, I had no idea. In my schooling the basics of science I was taught did not include anything about our measurement of time. So why do you refer to time in hours and days if that is not how you measure time by?" I ask him.

"It is criminal the things that were not taught to you." These words bring some shame to me. I know he does not intend for them to be hurtful but I cannot help but feel inadequate. His knowledge of the universe is so vast and mine so minuscule.

"To answer your question, I use these terms to make you feel at ease. Time is relative, not a set thing. Every world we come into contact with measures time differently. It is an easy matter for us to convert our time into your terms, but not so easy to teach you an entirely new system," he explains.

I smile at him a small smile of gratitude. I am grateful for everything that these warriors have done for me to feel accepted and welcome. They just want me comfortable in their lives. But I want to be so much more. I want to be useful and helpful.

"Could you teach me?" I ask him. "Your method? Do you think you could teach me how to use it?"

"You want to learn our time system?" he asks me.

"I am smart enough to learn it, I promise," I insist. I know that Area Three citizens are not believed to be smart enough to handle the harder sciences and that is why we are not taught them, but they are wrong. I am capable of learning.

"I would never doubt your intelligence, *aninare*. I am simply surprised you want to learn it. I am fine using your time measurements." At this time we have reached the shuttle and he helps me into my seat. He presses the button on the arm that crosses the security harnesses across my chest and takes the seat next to me.

"I do. I want to know what you know," I insist.

"You are starved for knowledge. Understandably, as these *infers* have done a horrendous job on your education," he says derisively. "But yes, I will teach you. Maybe soon we can begin our lessons. The war and determining your origins is a pressing matter, but hopefully we can squeeze some time in for just us," he says with heat in his eyes.

I feel a flush come to my face. I know he means more than studying time mechanics. I know that we are in a better place than we were the morning after our *cerum fuse*, but I don't feel confident enough in our relationship to jump headlong back into a physical relationship with him.

"Danion, I am not ready for that part of our relationship again," I whisper to him, very aware of the other warriors entering the shuttle behind us. I can tell from his expression that he is battling his instinct to object to putting any distance between us and forcing his rational mind to listen. I try again to explain my reticence.

"Danion, try to understand. Before we joined, I felt like I was in a fog. Looking back it looks like I lived a half-life before our minds joined. I always did what was expected of me. Never refused any command. Never defended myself against slander. Or abuse." I whisper the last part to myself. I take a breath and search his face for understanding.

"When I woke up after our ceremony I felt like a different woman. A woman who would not blindly agree to whatever was asked of her out of a misguided sense of duty. In part, I went along with the ceremony so soon because you told me it was what you wanted and needed. And I wanted to do as I was told." I see Danion's face tighten, pulling in at the corners around his mouth and eyes.

"You are saying I forced you to share bodies with me. That I gave you no choice?" I can see a look of revulsion roll over his features. I rush to correct his misconception.

"No, not that. I promise, Danion. It was as much my fault as yours. More my fault. I believed what I was told growing up, that claimed women had to do what their warrior asked or the world would be destroyed. Instead of discussing with you my fears and concerns, I never put a voice to them. You can't fix a problem I refused to tell you."

"A good mate would have sensed a problem. A worthy mate would never have needed to be told that you were being rushed." His words are stark. Self-hatred is evident in his expression.

"Danion, you are a worthy mate. I don't look back on that night with any feelings of remorse. I only wish I had more time spent with you in a less physical sense. Maybe if we had cultivated a more meaningful bond between us the morning after that night would not have proven to be so disastrous." I try once again to make him understand.

I can't find the words to express that I feel like I am two different women. The old girl who followed blindly and the new girl I am now who refuses to back down on her beliefs.

My hesitance is that I am not the same girl he claimed. I feel better. I feel stronger. I feel like I could conquer the world. In a way I just did. I defeated a tyrant who has ruled over this planet for decades with surprisingly few obstacles. I built him up in my head as some superpowered villain; I expected him to be harder to best.

He barely protested losing his rule of this planet. I guess when you have six Gelder warriors at your back no one is that difficult to take down. Still, I feel a small sense of worry about how little he protested his loss of power. Almost like he was hoping it played out the way it did.

I shrug off my concerns. I am sure I am worried over nothing.

"I understand what you mean. That if we had a stronger bond outside of the physical pleasure we bring each other we would not have had the fight that caused our month of silence." He looks at me intently while he says this.

"In a way, but I am actually mostly at fault for the longevity of the silence. I just felt so free having a choice of my own. I was worried that if I went back to you so soon after our fight that I would revert back to my old self."

"I understand. You felt that fighting with me was the key to your independence," he says.

"Yes. Yes, that is it exactly. And now that we are at this point in our relationship I would like a chance to get to know one another. Have the chance to *decide* to be together, not because we have to be but because we want to be."

I am sure he will one day realize that I am not the woman he wants to be with. And when that day comes I don't want to be any more in love with him than I already am. Sleeping with him will only make that worse.

"I do choose to be with you, Eleanor. No one is forcing me." It is all I can do not to challenge his statement. Biology is forcing him, biology chose me as his mate, not him. But I hold my tongue, it is not a battle I want to have right now in a shuttle filled with other warriors.

I glance over at them and I see that they are all sitting as far from us as they can, trying to give us as much space as they can to afford us even a modicum of privacy. I also notice that the shuttle is moving. When did we leave the ambassador building?

"Danion? When did the shuttle take off?" I ask him.

"We left a few moments ago. We need to drop off the warriors in the long-range shuttle that is in orbit above the planet before we fetch your sisters," he answers.

"We traveled in this shuttle, didn't we? When did another one reach us to get into orbit?" I ask.

"I had this one come behind us. A long-range shuttle is orbiting us because they are larger. I had it come fully loaded with supplies for the warriors in the war vessels above us. This planet may have withstood the Erains' initial attack but this solar system is quite a bit difficult to defend. Many planets are useful for hiding behind, and with no network grid we are searching blind for their movements. We need to be ready for the next attack." Danion gestures to the ship we are traveling toward.

"In addition, these shuttles are also equipped with much better communication ranges. With the delay we are experiencing communicating with our fleet I did not want to add several days of being out of contact. Unfortunately, these shuttles are quite slow and I did not want to travel in that alone here. So while we were handling our business on the planet it was traveling here," Danion explains.

"Oh, I see. When are we going to get my sisters? I thought you, Golon, Etan, and I were going to get them now?" I ask. I am anxious to see them again.

"Yes, we will be retrieving them as soon as we drop Arsenio and Malin at the ship. They will be turning it into our base of operations while we are here on Earth, equipped with everything we need. They also will prepare chambers for your sisters to stay in," he says.

"How long are we going to be orbiting here on Earth? I thought we would be going back to the ship soon," I ask, a little eager to get back to Joy. I want to be near her if I can and support her during this pregnancy.

"No, we have something to find here first. We can't leave until we have found it," Danion says.

I rack my brain trying to think of what could possibly be here that Danion would need. I come up blank.

"What are we looking for?" I ask him finally.

"Your father's ship."

Chapter Nine

Ellie

We are walking up a narrow flight of stairs to reach Marilee's apartment on the eighth floor. The stairwell is so slim that I barely have space to walk straight. I don't know how the warriors behind me are managing to make it look so graceful. Their shoulders are so large that they twist their bodies to compensate for their size.

I am excited to see my sisters and Marilee, but I am concerned that they have been living in Marilee's very small apartment. Her place is even smaller than the house I shared with my family. I am surprised they did not relocate somewhere larger.

My four sisters are a lot to contain in one tiny space. I think about how wonderful it will be for them to have individual rooms aboard the ship to call their own. They have never had their own spaces or been able to adjust to their own comfort.

As we reach the door to Marilee's apartment, I can't help but feel that something is off. I cannot place the feeling I have, but I suddenly feel nervous. With a deep breath I knock on the door. I use the secret knock that Marilee and I used as children. We designed it so that the other person would know who was on the other side without having to look. A childish game, but one we enjoyed well into adulthood.

I can sense tension radiating from the room. I realize that Marilee must be worried about how someone knows about our knock. She would not assume that I am back on Earth. After several very tense pauses the door opens ever so slightly.

All I can see is the hazel green color of Marilee's eyes, and then the door is thrust open so forcefully that it bounces off the wall behind. Surely it must have caused damage to the wall on impact but Marilee pays it no mind. Her arms are thrown around my neck and she is sobbing into my shoulder.

"Ellie! Oh, Ellie!" Her body feels frail as she clings to me desperately. "I am so happy you are here! I don't even care about how it is that you are here with me. Damn the world if that is what it takes to have you back! It has been awful and I need you here." Marilee's words become lost as she breaks down into hysterical tears and collapses against me. I lock my legs so that I can support her entire weight. A weight that feels much to light.

"Marilee, what has happened?" I try to ask her. The only answer is stronger crying. Her sobs are those of someone whose spirit has been broken. Hearing such a sound of distress coming from my dear friend tears at my heart. Golon, who seems to be surprisingly stiff all of a sudden, moves to take her into his arms and she tightens her hold on me.

"No! You cannot take her from me. Ellie, tell them you are staying with me. Please! I cannot lose you again," she wails. I understand where her hysteria is coming from. While my family left something to be desired, Marilee's family is all gone. She was the sole survivor of a horrible accident in our early teenage years.

Back then I was the only constant person in her life. I was there when she needed a hug or to listen when she needed to scream at the injustice of it all. I am all the family she has left. And I was taken from her.

I wrap my arm around her back and start to slowly inch her backward into her apartment. It is a single room, so small that I immediately spot my sisters are not here right now. It can barely fit the four of us. Both Danion and Golon are twisting their bodies to stand and not knock into anything. I wonder where my sisters are.

I glance around the space and my eyes freeze on the kitchen counter. I use the word *kitchen* lightly as it's really a single counter in the far corner. It has a tiny sink and an Instawave oven. That is the only thing to fill the small wall. Besides a tiny couch on the adjacent wall the room is completely barren. How has my family been sleeping in here?

"Marilee. Tell me those are not weekly nutrient cubes I see." The stark fear in my voice brings both warriors' attention on me like a pair of hawks. I cannot help my worry, those are substance cubes. A horrid invention and the cause of nightmares that have plagued me my whole life. I still suffer them to this day.

"What are weekly nutrient cubes?" Danion is the first to ask. Marilee is still unable to speak and I do not truly need her confirmation. I know them when I see them. They were used as a means to torture me for my entire childhood. Not something that is easy to forget.

"They are a small block of vitamins, minerals, and energy-packed protein to prevent the body from starving. It was the cure to world hunger, you know?" I say with as much scorn as I can. "It has all the nutrients your body needs to consume in a week so you only have to take it once every seven days. But it does nothing to hold off the hunger pangs. Nothing to prevent your body from craving sustenance or to stop the body from *feeling* starved. Muscles still get consumed, but it gives you enough nutrients to prevent organ damage." I detest the weekly nutrient cubes.

In my childhood I was only given those to survive. My mother said they were special just for me and I wasn't able to eat any of the daily cubes they had for themselves. Daily cubes are three times the size of the weekly cubes. Weekly cubes are purely meant to keep your body functioning.

Daily cubes on the other hand have more substance to them. They give the sensation of feeling full to make the day more pleasant. I am interrupted by Golon's angry voice.

"So they sustain the body but make you feel hungry? Why?" He seems to be losing control of his temper for the first time that I can recall. His anger is filling the room, much like Danion's often does. I have no idea what happened to affect the cool warrior so much.

"The weekly cubes are only for the lowest social classes. Areas One and Two mostly. The top area, government officials and the like, designed them so that the people in these areas would be able to survive and serve the upper classes but not use any resources that the higher levels would want or need. The reason given was so the people would still feel the desire to improve their circumstances by working harder. It would prevent them from growing lazy," I try to explain the ugliness that permeates this entire planet.

"So to encourage them to improve their situation, they make them starve?" Danion asks when Golon seems incapable of speech. Before my eyes I see Golon's aura for the first time. It is as violent as Danion's. Without warning Golon turns and leaves the tiny space. I look at Danion questioningly but he does not answer my unspoken query.

"Marilee, how long have you been on these cubes?" I have moved us to the small couch and wrapped her in my arms to offer her the little comfort I have. She has slowly gotten control of her sobs.

"Since three days after your departure. Ellie, I have no idea how you are here but I am so glad you are. I don't know how much longer I can manage." She is making small hiccupping noises between words. "The girls, when I went to talk to your family about you being claimed, your parents wanted to know why I wanted to speak with the girls separately. They seemed to know somehow that you had left something for the girls. They wanted their cut."

"I am sure they did; they knew I always looked after my little sisters. But why are they living here with you? Why did you not relocate to a new place? What happened to make you so desperate for money you are taking the weekly nutrient cubes if you had the money I left for them?" Her situation surprises me.

I left enough money not only to provide them housing but also to cover purchasing the daily food cubes until the girls were able to work and contribute to the finances. I thought that my parents might kick them out or refuse to spend the money on the dailies just like they did to me. Just in case, I wanted to make sure my sisters were cared for.

"Your parents declared lack of support of the girls." Marilee lets the words hang dead in the room.

I am so beyond shocked I cannot speak. Never did I suspect them capable of that. To declare lack of support... How could they?

"Lack of support? What does this mean?" Danion asks. "Explain." He asks again when his first question is left unanswered. I am finally able to answer him.

"It means that they officially stated that they are not willing or able to care for the girls due to the girls being defective. Making them unworthy of their current area level and needing to be dropped down to one of the areas that are on more government assistance. All the levels are on some kind of assistance, but the further down you go the more dependence there is."

I still cannot comprehend why they would do such a thing. They could have just kicked them out. To declare lack of support is almost unheard of. Sending someone down a class level is unimaginable. It is worse than a death sentence. Those people are always shunned in their new lives. Outcasts. Pariahs.

"Marilee. Why would they do that?"

"To force me to use the money you left. They were so angry when they realized you left it for the girls and not them. They wanted to make you pay," Marilee answers.

"I did not leave nearly enough money to cover buying the support of four girls," I say, shocked. I can't believe that Marilee saved my sisters. The price of taking on four girls' support is astronomical to someone in our position. "How did you even afford the payment on them? I left you half of what would have been asked."

"I used my own savings as well as took several small loans from some disreputable people. Between all of it I was able to purchase the rights of their support. But after I make the payments to all the loan holders and deduct my normal monthly expenses I have almost nothing. Luckily the weekly cubes are so inexpensive we have at least managed those." I see the bags under Marilee's eyes. She is running herself to the point of collapse. I can see her body shaking.

I do the math in my head and realize that she is short money. There is no way that she is covering all the expenses and managing five cubes a week.

I study my friend. I take in her dull hair, once a lush and vibrant auburn. It is now a drab and lifeless brown. Her eyes once bright green are now pale and tired. Her skin no longer possesses the golden hue it once had.

"Marilee, have you been eating the cubes?" I ask her, fearing the answer. It is one thing to feel starved while consuming the energy you need to survive. It is another thing to actually starve.

"Well…" The way she averts her eyes is enough for me to know the answer.

"Marilee. How many cubes are you able to buy a week?" I ask her. I need to know how bad this has been for them.

"Two. Most weeks at least. I do sometimes manage to get three of them." Her words fill my stomach with lead.

"Two?! How are five of you surviving on two one-week cubes? One per person a week is the absolute minimum anyone should have." The pain she must be in. The hunger.

"I have the girls split the two so they each get half. On those weeks I don't have one. When we have three I normally take a two thirds of the third cube and then we rotate who gets the other third. We are trying to stretch out the nutrients and lessen the pain for all of us." Marilee's voice is so weak I can barely hear her.

"Marilee? When was the last time you were able to get a third cube?" I ask. By the looks of her I am afraid the answer is going to be quite a while. She averts her eyes.

"Three weeks." Like I feared, it has been much too long.

"How have you survived?" It is amazing to me that her body has not shut down completely from lack of nutrients.

"Last week I took a small bite of the cube from each set of girls. I was worried about who would be here for them if I passed on, so now we are trying to just make the two cubes stretch to all five of us." I cannot stomach how hungry she must be.

I turn to Danion to ask him to get something for her to eat when Golon bursts into the room with unnatural speed. He is holding something in a container with Gelder writing on it. The smell draws Marilee's attention.

"Here, I got food for you," Golon says stiffly.

I glance at Golon, curious to see his facial expression. His face is showing his inner turmoil. He seems uncomfortable. He normally is so well composed it seems strange that he looks and sounds so nervous.

Marilee looks up, shocked.

"You brought me food?" she asks in wonder. So few people in our area actually help anyone. No one has anything to spare this far down the social ladder. Even more, it is rare that people in Area Three eat actual food. Most of us live off of dailies. Marilee has only experienced real food a handful of times in her life, which is considerably more than the times I have had it. Before being claimed by Danion, I had only had real food once.

"Yes, I know you are hungry. I went to the supply storage in our shuttle and got you some of our rations." He hands the container to her, waving his hand to remove the lid. The lid folds back in on itself and reveals something that looks like a type of dried, shredded meat inside.

Marilee just stares at the meat. I can tell she is nervous or unsure what to do with it. Or how to eat it, perhaps. Or maybe she is simply frozen in shock.

"It is a highly nutrient-rich plant from a jungle planet we discovered in a dual star solar system. It is very pleasing to the senses and can help you gain back your strength," Golon says to Marilee. Danion watches Golon with a strange expression.

Marilee gives me a searching look and I nod encouragingly. This is the final nudge she needs because she falls onto the container with ravenous hunger. She takes a big handful of the plant and starts to put the whole handful in her mouth.

Golon's hand prevents her from placing it all inside.

"You will want to eat it slowly. This is a very filling food, which is why I brought it. You can easily overindulge on this plant. Try small bites and then bigger ones," he instructs.

Marilee seems reluctant to put some of the food back but she does. She then picks up a small amount, a mound of the plant that is about one inch across in diameter, and places it on her tongue. Her eyes widen and then her mouth works quickly.

"This is amazing! I have never had anything like this in my life. It is growing as I chew it."

"Yes, it is a delicacy of the galaxy. Very few people ever eat it. It is very difficult to extract safely, so few do. It has a rich, sweet flavor and triples in size while you chew, therefore needing only a small amount at a time. It is a very filling dish. One that is highly sought after across all worlds," Danion answers with another glance at Golon.

Marilee nods and reaches for another small pinch of food.

"What is this called?" Marilee asks.

"It is called *etnai lef* and it is my favorite dish. Something that I try to sample at least every lunar cycle," Golon answers.

There is a commotion at the door and then four young girls walk inside. My sisters' appearances are so radically different than when I left Earth that I am shocked.

The older twins are normally driven and self-confident, but Jessica seems exhausted and Jaime is near tears. And poor Samantha and Savannah. Normally the young girls are so exuberant and full of laughter with mischief frequently dancing behind their eyes. With one look at them it is hard to imagine that there was ever happiness in their lives.

When their eyes meet mine, four sets of eyes immediately begin to cry.

"Ellie, oh Ellie!" all four of them cry in sync and quickly run to jump on me.

"Hi, girls. Oh, how I have missed you." I open my arms wide trying to wrap them all up tightly.

"Ellie-Elle you can't leave again. We need you, it has been awful since you left," Savannah, the youngest of my sisters, says.

"I will never be apart from you again. I promise. I am going to take care of all of you from now on." I hug them even tighter.

"So you are staying?" Jessica asks me. "What happened to your enslavement? I thought you could never return to us?"

"She was not enslaved. She was mated to me. There is a difference, youngling," Danion says from his position near the door. "And she is not staying, you are all coming with me as well. I will take over caring for your well-being." Danion walks over to us and kneels down so he can try to limit how tall he is and attempt to appear less intimidating to my frightened sisters.

Even on his knees though Danion is at least a head taller than my sisters. They all lean a little closer to me, unsure of this giant in front of them. Not sure what to make of this stranger who promises to care for them. I understand their reticence. They have been lacking proper care for years.

"Girls, it is alright. This is my husband and we have come to take you with us. I know how difficult it is here and I want to provide you with a better life," I tell them with a reassuring smile.

"Why do we have to go? Why can't you stay here with us? I am sure your husband could visit," Jessica asks. Distrust is rife within the glare she throws his way. Leave it to my Jessica to stand up to the leading power in the galaxy and throw down a challenge to him.

"We would let him stay too," Jaime, Jessica's twin, adds with a small elbow thrown into her twin's side. Jaime, always the logical and pragmatic one.

"Because the life here is not the life you deserve. Danion can provide you with clothes, food, and shelter. He has given me a good life, one that I want to share with you. It's so much more than anything here." I can see the girls are still nervous to leave all that they know.

I do not blame them. Going with the Gelders has never been portrayed in a positive light on Earth Nueva. Danion's physical stature is not helping the girls feel any better either. He is so large, even on his knees, it is no surprise that it makes the girls uncomfortable.

I am just thinking of what I can say to try to make them feel more comfortable when Danion solves the problem. He does this by just being the man he always is—kind and caring with a determination to take care of those around him.

"I hear you girls are hungry. Golon happens to have some food brought here especially for you four girls." He holds out his hand to Marilee. After she grabs another serving she hands over the canister.

Danion does not realize the rare gift he is giving to my sisters. Food in itself is a treasure to them. Cubes are not pleasant; they're designed entirely as a form of sustenance. But actual food? It is the greatest gift that can be given.

"Go ahead, girls. Marilee is having some too." I nod encouragingly when they look back over to me for permission. "It will be very good, I promise." They slowly turn to Danion and take a shy step toward him.

"Now hold out your hands and I will give you each a little bit. All you have to do is chew it up. It is going to get bigger when you chew, but that is normal so don't be frightened of it," Danion explains to them.

Once all of their hands are facing upward he places a small amount into each palm. Slowly, tentatively, each girl puts it in her mouth and chews. The smiles and content sighs that explode out of them lighten the sadness that has been tightly wound around my heart since we got to Earth Nueva.

Soon the girls are laughing and asking Danion for more of the "magic food" that grows. Hearing the children's laughter is so refreshing. Even the terrible hardships they have suffered is not enough to crush my strong sisters' spirits. I smile over to Danion in gratitude. I let the girls have a few more moments to finish the second helping before I make the introductions.

"Danion and Golon, I would like to formally introduce you to my sisters and my closest friend. If you will permit me?" I ask, waiting for them to consent to being introduced. I have been picking up on certain social customs the Gelders follow. They both nod at me and I smile at them.

"First, Marilee Farcie is my closest and dearest friend, she also is the most loyal person you will ever meet. Marilee works as a social worker and specializes in Area Three domestic disputes. She is passionate in her work and competitive enough that no one is better at it than her," I say with a smile toward her. Her returning smile is warm, albeit weak from the strain she has been under.

"Passion in the work shows passion in the soul," Golon says with an intent stare at Marilee. I make a mental note to talk with Golon about his strange behavior. I don't want him making any of my family uncomfortable while they are with us. Marilee is just as much my family as my sisters are.

Marilee blushes and murmurs her thanks. She seems to be trying to avoid Golon's rather direct stares. I decide to try to steer the conversation away from my friend.

"Next, may I introduce you to two of my twin sisters? Jessica and Jaime. They will both be turning thirteen soon and are full of wonder and ambition. These two girls are going to change the world," I tell my mate and his cousin with a smile to my sisters. They are remarkable girls, and now that I am here I am not going to let anything bad happen to them ever again.

"It is pleasing to officially make your acquaintances," Danion says with a slight bow. This makes the girls both giggle shyly and try to imitate the bow.

"These next two beautiful girls are Samantha and Savannah. You would be hard pressed to find two happier children. Their smiles have the ability to light up a room." Danion repeats his action again and gets an even louder giggle from them. The sprinkling of laughter from my sisters makes me recall fondly the good times I had here, helping to erase the bad.

"It is very nice to meet all of you. I have heard so much about each of you from my time with Eleanor, but it is very pleasant to now know who inspires such stories of love." He makes eye contact with all the girls individually and I feel each girl become gradually calmer as they interact with Danion. "Now, we are on a slightly tight schedule so we should get packed and report back to the command center as soon as we can. Once we are there we can also get you all a more balanced meal and some comfortable sleeping arrangements," Danion says with a look of distaste around the room.

"Command center? I thought we were going to the shuttle?" I ask.

"The long-range shuttle is the command center I speak of. We will be setting up shop in orbit around the planet," Danion answers.

"We don't have anything to pack. We have just the clothes we wear. We sold everything else to help Marilee," Jaime says. This answers my earlier question about why the apartment was so barren.

"I am sorry, I didn't want to sell off their things but I didn't know what else to do. We had to eat." Marilee starts to explain further but is cut off by a very abrupt Golon.

"You do not apologize. For anything. This is not your fault. You are coming with us too. If there is nothing here that you desire to bring with you then we should leave now." Golon grabs Marilee's arm and tries to lead her from the room.

"Hey, let me go. I am not going anywhere with you," Marilee protests. I am happy to see that the hardship has not lessened her spirit.

"Do you need help packing?" Golon asks.

"I don't know if I want to give up everything and go with you. You're asking me to give up my life," Marilee says.

"I am not asking you anything, I am telling you. You are not staying here. I will not leave you here alone to suffer a moment longer," Golon insists. I can tell that this argument is quickly escalating so I move to intervene.

"Marilee, you should come with us. Please. I am not lying when I say it is a better life. An easier life. A life you deserve to have. You should come with us, with me. There is nothing holding you here. I would miss you terribly if you do not come," I remind her.

I can see Marilee thinking. She slowly looks around the room and then turns back to me.

"What about my work? The clients that I am working to help?" She asks me.

Before I can anser, Golon once again intercedes. "We are leaving a warrior on the planet, if you give me a list of who you need watched over I will personally make sure they are alright."

Marilee looks confused for a moment, "Why is a warrior being left here?"

I answer her this time before Golon can. "Ambassador Lexen has been removed from office. He has been lying to all of us, and Danion is going to make sure he can't hurt anyone ever again." I quickly explain all that we have learned about the Amabassador. His mass murders and his manipulation of the treaty.

Marilee's eyes seem dull for a moment. She holds her stomach as if she will be sick. I understand the feeling.

Then with one last look around she turns back to me.

"I don't like it here. I never have, really. I guess you are right. This is all I have in this life and it isn't much. I could go with you. You're sure they have a place for me? I won't be a burden?" she asks me. Once again, I am not the one who answers her.

"There will always be a place for you. You are coming with me." Golon speaks calmly, but with a will of iron.

"Alright then. I don't think I could say goodbye to you again, Ellie. I too have nothing here that I wish to take with me. Like the girls said we sold everything except for one set of clothes each."

"I am so sorry for what my absence has caused everyone. You are never going to go hungry again."

"OK, Ellie-Elle," all four girls and Marilee answer in sync. We move together silently and embrace each other. One big hug filled with sorrow, peace, and forgiveness.

"If there really is nothing you wish to bring, we should make our way back to the shuttle so that we can get going. There is work to be done and a war to be won," Danion mentions.

With that, I pull my sisters in close once again and we all begin to descend the narrow staircase out of this depressing box they have lived in and toward a brighter future for my family.

Chapter Ten

Ellie

"How are your sisters and your friend? Are they settling in? Do they find their accommodations satisfactory?" Danion asks me as I join him in our shared room on the long-range shuttle. This ship is about the size of an apartment building. While it seemed gigantic to my family, it is only a fraction of the size of the main ship I have been staying on. It is also much smaller than the warriors on board are used to living in.

I can see that they feel a little cramped. Only my family and *praesidium* have their own chambers. The rest of the support warriors that came here with this shuttle are sharing common rooms on the middle levels.

"They are doing well, thank you. They can't believe that they all get their own rooms. Of course, I am wondering if they are going to be able to sleep apart. None of them ever have. If it would open up space for your warriors, I am sure they would be fine sharing rooms while we are in orbit," I answer. Even if they had to share two rooms between all of them it is still more than four times the space they have ever had.

"They deserve to have their own space," Danion answers. "*Our* warriors will be fine sharing space. They have had the luxury of their own rooms for so long, they take it for granted. Your family, however, has never been so lucky. They will stay in their own rooms. If they wish to share that is their decision, but the rooms will remain theirs and theirs alone. They deserve some luxury after what they endured."

"Yes, they really do. Thank you for giving it to them. And Marilee." I walk over to him and I place my hand over his.

"The human showed great loyalty to you by the sacrifices she made for your sisters. She deserves this just as much as they do," Danion says. I find it odd that he does not say her name.

Perhaps there is some reason he doesn't speak her name. Maybe a custom that I am not aware of. I am about to question him when there is ping by the door, announcing that someone is requesting entry into our quarters.

"Enter," Danion says.

The door opens and Golon enters the room.

"Perfect, I am glad you are both here. I have something I need to discuss with you both. It is about your father, Eleanor." Golon's words shake me, reminding me abruptly about my father's parting gift and the mysteries still surrounding him. I temporarily forget that I wanted to ask him why he was acting so strange in Marilee's apartment.

"My father? What about him?" I ask.

"I believe there is a strong chance that his ship is somewhere on this planet." He looks solemn. "His ship may be able to answer some questions about the circumstances around your birth as well as shed some light on what the deal was that he made with Lexen. That is assuming that there was such a deal made. Before we leave this planet, we need those answers."

"But...is it safe here? Aren't the Erains attacking this planet? I don't want my sisters in any danger," I ask them both, my eyes moving between the two proud warriors.

"We are as safe as we can be. The warships here were able to defend themselves against the first wave and no new attack has come to this planet," Golon answers.

"In addition, this ship is designed by me. It has enough defensive and offensive power to go up against a fleet of Erain ships. Our power comes from our superior strength, theirs comes from their numbers. We can hold this planet easily," Danion answers with pride, but without conceit.

"If you are sure," I answer them both. I trust them to keep us all safe. "What are you hoping to find on my father's ship? If there is in fact a ship somewhere on the planet," I ask.

"There is definitely a ship here. Even if it is not intact there should be remnants of the ship. Your father traveled here somehow. He did not just appear," Golon answers me.

I am about to question him more about my father and what exactly he is hoping to uncover when a piercing noise begins blasting from the panel by the door. Both Danion and Golon look at each other with alarm.

"The *Cladem* bell?" Danion asks of Golon, shock in his voice.

"Yes. Yes, it is," Golon answers as he rises to his feet. Both warriors are wearing identical expressions of surprise and fear. My stomach churns with the look I intercept between them.

Danion quickly stands as well and offers his hand to me. Once I take it he pulls me to my feet and we hurry from the room.

"A *Cladem* bell? What is that?" I ask as I try to keep up with their much larger legs. We are racing through the halls, heading up several decks. We are moving so fast that I have no hope of tracking where we are. I have no idea what level we are on let alone what room we are heading toward.

"It is a warning bell, only used when we have lost a base that resulted in significant loss of life on our side. We haven't heard this bell in over two thousand years," Danion answers me with a hint of pain in his voice. He begins to move even faster.

"Danion, please stop. Slow down. I can't keep up with you," I tell him, out of breath from my attempt to match the speed he is maintaining effortlessly.

Instead of slowing down, he simply turns around and picks me up in his arms, and increases his speed even further. The walls are now nothing more than a gold blur as we speed past them.

"Danion, what do you think we have lost? One of the mortal worlds?" Golon asks Danion.

"Perhaps. We won't know until we reach the *bellum* chamber. Once ensconced inside its protected walls we can open the communication and find out," Danion answers.

"Danion?" My voice wobbles even though I fight it. I feel sick to my stomach with the question I am about to ask. I raise my voice and try again since I do not receive a reply. "Danion?"

"Yes?" Danion answers this time. His voice sounds distracted. No question about what is on his mind. Already I can tell that he is weighing the different avenues of response open to him and trying to formulate which is the best course of action for his people. Our people.

"What constitutes a 'significant' loss of life?" My voice is quiet, almost lost in the sound of air rushing by me as he races through the ship.

"Millions, Eleanor. The *Cladem* is only sounded when we have lost millions of souls." His words cause my body to break out in cold sweat.

Millions of people are gone. Never to see another day. All because of a group of extremists who worship chaos. A group who just want to watch people fall at their own hand. Drunk on the power taking someone else's life makes them feel.

The Erains believe that they have the right to take our lives because they think they are stronger than us. That they are better than all other life in the galaxy.

They are wrong.

And one way or another I am going to make them pay for the atrocities they have committed. Millions today are bad enough, but they killed over two billion humans in the first two days of the Purge War. They must be stopped. My only hope is that whatever base that has been taken is not too important for the Gelders and that we are able to strike back swiftly.

Danion

"Tell me I am hearing you wrong, Amell. We could not have lost the Paire Moon." I speak to Amell's three-dimensional figure.

Once we reached the *bellum* chamber I quickly contacted Amell and Kowan through our mirror table, a device that is connected through sub-space and capable of projecting a hologram of the receiver. Each paired seat is projected and gives the illusion of us all being at the same table. This is a necessary device that I require on all my personal ships.

"I am afraid your hearing has not suddenly failed you. We lost the Paire Moon. Along with every warrior and civilian we had stationed there," Amell's solemn voice answers. "Every single one. The defeat we suffered on the moon has accounted for well over ten million souls lost."

"What is significant about the Paire Moon?" Eleanor asks. I am unable to answer her. My mind is trying to process how we can win this base back.

Out of all our bases throughout the galaxy, it is the single most important one to us. It is unique. We searched the cosmos for a moon just like it for centuries and have never found another. This moon has been claimed as ours for over four thousand years.

While my mind works, I realize that Golon has answered Eleanor.

"Eleanor, the Paire Moon is a base that not only holds cultural and spiritual importance to our people, but it is also the one and only base that we are physically linked to," Golon begins to explain.

"What do you mean, 'physically linked to'?" she asks him.

"While we have explained that we can weave lineages or power, we never explained the strain that it has on our physical bodies. Weaving lineages takes an immense toll on the body. The strength required to absorb, manipulate, and channel the energy of the cosmos into and through our bodies causes significant damage on the cellular level. It is remarkable that we can survive the process," he says.

"OK." Eleanor waits patiently for Golon to continue. She is becoming used to the way Golon communicates. Taking long pauses between thoughts, therefore, giving himself time to sort through the massive stores of knowledge that he has in his mind.

"On our planet of origin, Geldon, we had a special mineral that was extremely abundant. Our ancestors mined this mineral since it had incredible properties. It could take in anything that it was exposed to and manipulate its traits, almost going through a metamorphosis.

"Our ancestors used this mineral so much that it contaminated the water, food, and air on our planet. It is believed by some to be the root of our abilities, binding to our very cells and allowing us to channel the powers of the elements. We call this mineral *tatio*." Golon takes another long pause.

This time, Eleanor does not comment or urge Golon to continue. Instead, I see her sharp mind processing everything she is hearing, compartmentalizing the information for later use. After some time Golon continues.

"*Tatio* was used so much, consumed so much, that soon it became essential to our physiology. Our ancestors needed it to survive. Without the mineral, our cells began to deteriorate and die. It was not long after we began to consume it that we were completely dependent on the mineral."

"If your cells die without this mineral, how are you truly immortal? I thought you said that nothing natural could kill you," Eleanor asks.

"My apologies, I mean our ancestors' cells would break down. Remember this is many, many thousands of years ago," Golon patiently explains to my mate.

"Oh, I see." Eleanor looks contemplative for a moment. "What role does this mineral play now?" she asks.

"It is essential for us to be able to thread our lineages. If we have not consumed this mineral then we lose the ability to use our powers," Golon answers. "Our cells cannot process the power without it. The pathways we use to weave our powers are simply closed to us."

"So you would be powerless without this *tatio*?" she asks.

"Yes. Completely powerless, outside of our ship weapons and hand-to-hand combat," Golon answers. Eleanor is quiet again for a moment.

I look around the table and see that the rest of her *praesidium* are also deep in thought. Even Griffith has been called up early from Earth. Instead of overseeing the correction of the government himself, I had him choose and assign a warrior to oversee Earth's corrupt government.

Only Golon seems to be inclined to answer my mate. It is times like this that I am grateful to my cousin. His mind is unrivaled by any creature in existence. He can answer all of Eleanor's questions while a part of him dissects the problem and forms answers in the background.

"What does this have to do with the Paire Moon base that the Erains have taken?" Eleanor asks. I smile to myself. My mate, always the clever one.

"This mineral, while abundant on Geldon, was a finite resource. It could not be replenished and it is impossible to replicate. Artificial copies of this mineral, while identical in structure, were always fatal to our ancestors. It was a problem we have been unable to solve either," Golon begins to explain.

"Thousands of years ago it became apparent to our ancestors that *tatio* was going to run out sooner than they thought. While many began trying to reverse our physiological dependence on *tatio*, another much larger group realized that we did not have the time to work around this need. They went down another avenue."

"What did they do?" Eleanor asks.

"They went to the stars and began searching for another supply of *tatio*. The search for this mineral is actually what started the Gelder Expansion. It is why we sample the resources on every Pact World. It is written into the treaties. We inspect every mined resource from every planet, searching for even trace amounts of this compound."

"That is why you process our supplies? You are not taking them for your own use? You are just searching for *tatio*?" she asks him.

"Yes, due to its ability to transform itself *tatio* is extremely hard to scan for remotely. It has to be inspected physically. The evaluation process does have a detrimental effect on the products themselves.

"For instance, we check the resource you call wood to determine if there are signs of *tatio* in the water or soil. If it is present in either the water or the soil there is a very definite trace in the trees. This process does damage a large amount of the wood sent to us. We can always supply replacement resources if we damage too much of course."

I now know why Earth Nueva always refused our offer of replacement resources. They always insisted that they had an abundance of supplies and that what we used did not harm them. Lies, I now know. The ambassador was simply using this as a reason to further demonize us. Stealing their goods and letting them starve.

"Have you found *tatio* on Earth Nueva at all?" my mate asks my cousin.

"No. That does not mean it is not there. As I said it is very hard to detect. Only one new source of *tatio* was ever found, but to avoid the same situation our ancestors found themselves in, we still search every day for an additional supply."

"So this moon, this Paire Moon, has this *tatio* on it? It is your one and only supply of this mineral?" my brilliant mate deduces quickly. It is now that I decide to weigh in on the conversation.

"Yes, it is the *only* source we have ever found and is an extremely plentiful supply. The composition of the Paire Moon is almost one hundred percent *tatio*. So while we are still looking for more sources, this moon alone can provide enough *tatio* for our people for millions of years," I explain to her.

It makes no sense why the Erains attacked this moon. I do not know how they would have even known to attack it. No one outside of the Gelder race has ever been told of *tatio* and the important role it plays in our biology. No warrior would ever speak of our need for it. While we will not die without it, we are rendered very weak without a constant supply. If we lose the supply of *tatio*, the tide of the war would most definitely change.

"I cannot discover the reason that they would attack the Paire Moon, Dane," Golon directs to me.

"Me either, *cognata*. How could they know of its significance?" I say.

"No, it is more than that, *cognata*. Imagine that they know of our need for *tatio*. What is the purpose? Every single ship, even this shuttle, is stockpiled with *tatio*. Since many ships travel for years without stopping for supplies each ship has enough to supply an entire army for one hundred years. It is a very long-term goal," Golon explains.

I realize he is right. Why would they attack the moon? It would take a century for us to feel the pinch of supplies. Many years ago, early into my rule, we had an algorithm in our navigation system malfunction. The entire fleet was affected.

No ship could travel; to do so was to risk ending up on the wrong side of the galaxy. Many warriors suffered since they ran out of *tatio* before we could fix the problem. Since then I have always made sure each ship carries a large surplus of the mineral.

"Maybe that is their goal. Maybe they are planning a long-term victory in the war?" Eleanor suggests. I turn to address her when that traitor Arsenio speaks up.

"Ellie, I admit the Erains have surprised us by finally coming together and coordinating a species-wide attack on us. But I think that is too much for their impulsive nature. At their core, they are impatient, rash even. It is also very risky to plan a move that has so much time for mistakes to occur. Too many things could go wrong. Even we would not attack a base that we would have to hold on to for a century before it became useful to us," he explains. "It would make more sense to simply destroy the moon from orbit, not capture the base and send agents to hold it."

I quickly bury the flare of jealousy I have when my mate gives him a grateful smile. I am again about to address *my* mate when Etan speaks to her. While I understand that they are her *praesidium* that does not mean they all need to be so familiar with her. She is *my* mate after all.

"Eleanor, the Erains must know that we will attempt to get the base back. It would be very foolish to plan an entire war around a single move that would withhold victory for a century. It is too long to hope that we will never get the base back from them," Etan explains with a warm smile. A smile that is returned and met with a sincere thank-you from Eleanor.

I don't know why her ease with her guardians makes me so angry, but it does. I should be happy; these warriors pledged their lives to her defense. Her being comfortable with them means they will be even more effective at protecting her. But I am not happy.

I am furious with these males for being so comfortable with my mate. More comfortable than I am with her. Whenever we speak there is still an underlying tension. With the warriors that are around me? No tension. They all converse with ease.

"Yes, *mate*. They must know that we would strike back to claim the base again. We must be missing something. Some hidden motive for their attack." I speak up for the sole purpose to draw Eleanor's gaze back to me.

"The fact remains, the moon has no other strategic advantages for them. Its location is not central and there are no weapons or other supplies stored there. Why did they capture the moon?" Golon asks.

"Does it matter why?" the lecherous Arsenio asks. "They have wasted resources along with leaving a large force on the moon to defend it. Let us wage an attack on these fools and take them out. We can take out a large portion of their army right there and get our base back."

"No, Arsenio, we underestimated our enemy before. The result was not only our entire network collapsing, but millions of lives. One of which was almost my mate's. We need to treat them with the cunning they have proved themselves worthy of receiving," I interrupt him.

"What is your plan, my king?" Amell asks of me. He knows that I would have only joined the conversation after I have devised a plan. While Golon spoke with Eleanor, I determined what I would do. Arsenio and the rest of these libidinous warriors who call themselves her *praesidium* can try to impress my mate with their battle knowledge some other time. The decision has already been made.

"We will use Sylva. I have already sent a request to her. She should be reaching a mirror table soon and will take one of the open seats and join us," I inform the group.

Sylva DeTalvasor is one of the fiercest warriors of the entire race. While female, she can take down any male. She is particularly skillful in covert operations. With an almost undefeated record, she is held in high regard by all. The only time she ever failed a mission was against a test of my own design. A test that is designed for the warrior to fail, so it hardly counts against her.

Every warrior has to enter into the Final Warrior's *Chorus* before they are granted the title of warrior and allowed entrance into the fleet. The *Chorus* is a challenge that is used to determine if a warrior is ready to graduate from training. It is the final stage for a trainee to pass in order to prove their strength.

I design the *Chorus* myself for every warrior, and it is always designed specifically for the individual who is taking it. It's meant to challenge them, force them to see their potential, and realize that there is always room for improvement.

It is designed for them to fail since the challenge is not to demonstrate who can conquer an enemy, but to show who can understand that winning a battle can sometimes lose you the war. Only Golon has ever overpowered this challenge and returned triumphant from his *Chorus*, much to my displeasure.

I will be using Sylva to travel undetected to the moon and discover the true purpose of the attack. Once she completes her mission she will return to us with a full report.

"Sylva, Dane? Do you think that wise?" Kowan speaks for the first time. "You know that the Erains are incredibly prejudiced toward females. If she were to be captured who knows what horrors they would inflict."

"Oh, Kowan, you are just too sweet. I am touched by your concern for my well-being," a sarcastic voice weighs in. We all turn to the newcomer and see the striking female appear as if she was here in the room with us the whole time.

Sylva, like most of our kind, is exceedingly tall and of a broad, muscular physique. Her strong facial features, as well as her dark hair and eyes, give her a more masculine appearance. My eyes trail to my mate and I take a moment to enjoy her small and unique looks. She is breathtaking.

"While I do appreciate your misplaced sentiment, I do not need protection from Erain soldiers. A true Gelder warrior fears no enemy." Sylva looks first at Kowan and then makes eye contact with the rest of the male warriors present.

"It is foolish, misplaced bravery like that which will be your downfall, Sylva," Kowan bites out.

For centuries these two warriors have been going head to head in competition. Each one always trying to triumph over the other. As young warriors, they were very close. They went through the academy together, then warrior training. They even served on the same squadron when they were new to the fleet. No one knows the reason for the falling out between these two.

"And it is hesitance like that which will never fail to hold you back, Kowan," Sylva retaliates.

"Warriors, need I remind you that we have a real enemy we need to fight with? Please, put aside this petty bickering," I intercede.

They both make apologies and fall quiet. I take this time to introduce Sylva to her queen.

"Sylva DeTalvasor, I am pleased to present to you your high queen, Eleanor Belator, my mate." She gives a deep nod and smiles in the direction of my mate.

"My queen, I am pleased to meet you at long last. Your elegance and poise are not exaggerated. I am honored to serve you," Sylva says with a second bow of her head so deep it almost touches the table before her.

"Sylva DeTalvasor, I am pleased to make your acquaintance. I also want to wish you good luck on your mission. I will be keeping you in my thoughts and hoping for your safe return," Eleanor says regally.

With the formalities out of the way, we begin to discuss the details of Sylva's mission, starting with outlining which warriors will accompany her and which path she should take to best avoid being detected. The planning goes on for several hours. When I ask

Eleanor if she is tired or if she wanted to leave she refused, insisting she stays just in case she can help with the plans.

My mate is a true queen in every sense of the title. Dedicated to her people, determined to prove herself worthy of being capable of leading them, and if or when she can't do that, resolved to learn what she does not know.

So I allow my mate to stay and to learn the battle strategies we use. By the end, she is more than able to keep up and even manages to provide useful suggestions. Never before have I met someone who has a sharper mind.

My mate is brilliant.

Chapter Eleven

Ellie

The next day, I am eating the morning meal alone in the chamber I share with Danion. While not ideal to share a room with Danion, there are limited rooms available on board and we have a large number of warriors present to ensure our protection.

I was nervous about sleeping in the bed with Danion again and being so close to him physically. I remember the response both of our bodies had to each other's last time. However, Danion controlled himself admirably. I too felt the struggle to remain distant from him. My body seems to crave him like a drug.

While I could see his inner turmoil by his aura, all he did was wrap his arm around my middle and hold me close throughout the night. I was surprised that I found it very pleasant, if not a little distracting. But I am so deprived of physical contact that it was well worth the distraction. I love the feeling of his arms around me.

My life has been sorely lacking casual affection that so many take for granted. While Danion and I have a long way to go in our relationship I can find no fault with his easy way of making physical contact between our bodies. He is constantly holding my hands, grasping my arms, or rubbing my back.

I am interrupted by my own thoughts by the door opening and Golon entering the room without waiting for a response. It is not polite to enter a private chamber without waiting for permission. That is very peculiar; Golon is usually very conscious of propriety. I wonder what is distracting him.

"Eating alone? Did your sisters not want to join you? Or perhaps your friend? Marilee, I believe her name was. Did Marilee not feel well enough to join you? Or did she have plans?" Golon asks. He is acting quite peculiar again. He seems to be intently studying the table design. Trying to appear as if he is not interested in the answer to his questions at all. If he doesn't care about the answers, I wonder why he asks them.

"Is there something the matter, Golon? I feel like you have been acting strange around Marilee. Is there something that worries you about her?" I can't imagine what could be causing him concern but I am obliged to ask.

"Around Marilee? A mortal? Don't be ridiculous. I just wondered why you are dining alone. I am allowed to be concerned for my queen's happiness, am I not? It is also logical that I am concerned with the well-being of your human friend since her health affects your mood. That is all." He says all of this defensively.

After a pause, he begins talking again while picking up a linen napkin and running it between his fingers. "I just thought that since she was so hungry she would not skip a meal and that she might be dining with you. Here."

"Well, no. I believe they are all dining together this morning. I was unable to go share the meal with them. Danion mentioned that we are to be meeting in the *bellum* chamber again this morning to discuss more plans about the war. I did not want to wake them early to eat with me only to have to leave them again so soon. They need some rest. I am hoping to have some time to spend with just them soon. As much as I miss my sisters and Marilee the war does come first," I explain to him.

"Yes, you are correct, of course." Golon seems to be fighting an internal battle. "We must focus on the war first. Everything else must wait for now." He speaks almost to himself. "In that regard, I wanted to update you on the search for your father's ship."

"Oh? Have you dispatched people to search for it?" I ask him. I don't know when he would have had time to do that; we were still up planning Sylva's mission in the early hours.

"Yes, I sent off the orders while we were in the *bellum* chamber last night. We have not had any leads. We scanned the planet for any of the metals that were used in our ancient ships but not even a trace amount was detected." He says this with a meaningful look at me.

"What does that mean?" I ask him.

"The metals that we used to build our ancient spacecraft are not foreign to your planet. There should be some traceable amounts in the soil. Even a small amount. Yet not even a fraction of a percent was detected anywhere on the planet," he tells me.

"Judging by your look I am guessing that you don't think this was a mistake." His look is grim, yet anticipatory at the same time. Golon does love a mystery.

Golon shakes his head at me in response to my comment. "Do you think that someone is hiding it?" I ask him.

"The only thing that makes sense to me is that they are hiding the metal from our scanners. We would be able to detect if there was some form of planetary net blocking us from sensing any of the metals. Since there is none someone must have a regional block set up."

"You mean someone has gathered all the metal in one place and is hiding it there?" I ask him. He nods his head. "Why would someone do that?"

"I have been pondering that question for quite some time now. Only one answer has come to me," he says. I mentally roll my eyes. Save me from dramatic warriors.

"What answer is that?" I am forced to ask when he does not continue.

"That the ship was damaged and your father managed to collect every ounce of the metal on your planet in an attempt to mend the ship. Which means that the ship itself must be shielded. If I am right, which I always am, it might be very difficult to find his ship. If not impossible. Our shields are practically impenetrable, even from our own scanners. I doubt we will be able to break through them and locate the ship," he says.

"Is it really so important to find the ship? I know we are worried about the deal the ambassador talked about, but I feel fine. I don't think there is a concern about me dying. Maybe we don't have to find the ship," I say nervously.

Be honest, you are nervous to learn about your father. You couldn't care less about the ship.

Of course, I am nervous about him. He abandoned me.

You don't know that. Look at the facts, he obviously cared for you.

Sure, he did. Cared so much that he left after taking one look at me.

Yes, but he also left you a locket that is embedded with part of his soul and made a deal with the devil to keep you alive. That is pretty good evidence that he cared more than you want to admit.

If you believe said devil about that deal to save my life. We have no idea if that is true.

You are just being stubborn. You know deep down that he cared more than you thought. Just not enough to stay...

I am pulled out of my thoughts when I realize that Golon has been talking for a while. "Eleanor? Don't you agree?" Golon is asking me.

"I am sorry, Golon. My mind was someplace else. What were you asking me?" I say to him.

He looks at me for a moment before speaking again, his face pensive. "I was saying that the ship could lead to answers about your parentage that could shed light on more than just your own life. It may lead to an explanation of what caused the *lacieu* lineage to die out and what happened to so many ancient warriors who never returned from their journeys," he says. "It is bigger than just you, and it could answer questions that will save millions of souls."

"Yes, I suppose that is true. We should look for his ship," I admit grudgingly. "What are your plans for finding it now?"

"We will be searching the planet for any weaves or disturbances. Anything that might indicate a shield is being used or any area we think the ship may be concealed naturally. It may be frozen or underneath the ground," he says.

"Alright. Is there anything you need me for?" I offer my assistance. While the thought of finding the ship fills me with a mixture of elation and dread, I know that both my inner self and Golon are correct. We need to find it.

"Not at the moment, but I will keep you updated on our progress and if I have need of your assistance later on, I will let you know," Golon says.

"Well, if you need me, I will be here," I say in return. "Should we go to the *bellum* chamber now? I am ready for today's planning," I say while pushing my plate away. While I did not finish my meal, I am no longer hungry. The turmoil caused by my father's ship has stripped me of my appetite.

"I can escort you, yes. I will alert Danion that we are heading that way. He has been responding to correspondence that came from the battle leaders. We have a line of communication open finally, but it does need to be noted that there is a significant delay. He just received sixteen urgent messages about current battles. Let us hope those bases have not already been lost." Golon offers me his arm and we exit the room, heading up several decks to the *bellum* chamber.

We travel in comfortable silence. Golon has a way about him that makes me very relaxed in his presence, despite my knowing him for only a short time. All these warriors do in their own way. They seem to have a knack for putting me at ease. I have never felt more secure in my life.

As we walk the halls, I reflect on what it is that holds me back from wanting to search for my father's ship. Internally I realize that my hesitance is because a part of me blames him for the pain I have suffered. If he cared so much why did he leave me like he did? How could he leave me to a cold and bitter woman who caused me so much suffering?

No matter the reason I cannot justify that. I would never leave my child defenseless and alone.

Before I know it, we are at the door to the chamber. Golon begins the lengthy process of unlocking the door. Danion explained to me yesterday that a *bellum* chamber is buried under thousands of privacy threads. Using the mirror tables that are housed within these chambers is the most secure form of communication imaginable.

However, using one comes with a price. It is extremely difficult to utilize; only Danion's ships has the ability, because he is the only one who can thread the weaves to use them without risking the lives of everyone on board. Etan explained to me that if they are used incorrectly it can rip a hole in the fabric of space. This is why the technology has never become commonly used.

Every *bellum* chamber has a mirror table inside and only the top-ranked warriors can enter. The privacy weaves keep out anyone who does not have clearance. This unfortunately makes for a very long process to gain access to the chamber. When we are finally through the weaves I see that we are the last to arrive.

The seats around the table are already filled with Danion and my entire *praesidium*. The only person missing from the group from last night is Sylva, but I know from our plans that she left this morning for her mission. It will take her seventeen hours to travel to the moon. With no way to send communication over such a distance we are not expecting an update for thirty-six hours. At that time she should be back from the moon and ready to debrief us.

I take my seat by Danion, who caresses my hand and places a blatant kiss to my wrist.

"Good morning, *aninare*. I am sorry I was absent when you woke. It was unavoidable." His words cause embarrassment to shoot through me. I send a quick, furtive glance around the table but see that no one is paying attention to us. It allows me to relax into my chair.

"It's fine, I know you had better things to do," I mumble quietly.

"I had things that required my attention, yes. But not better things," he says with a smile. "There is nothing better than starting the day with you."

I give him a small smile in response. While his devotion would be appreciated by any normal woman, I find it hard to accept such compliments. Throughout my life compliments have been few and far between. I can't find it within myself to believe his easy words. I am constantly on edge, waiting for the other shoe to drop. Apprehensive of when he is going to leave me or tell me I am inadequate.

"Today we need to devise a way of communicating with our fleet." Danion begins the meeting without waiting for me to respond to his seductive words. "We have been fighting blind since the communications grid has been crippled and it is limiting us. We are responding instead of instigating. Too many attacks are resulting in loss of life. By the time we know about it, the battle is already lost."

"Where are we in terms of communication?" Etan, who is sitting to my left, asks. I am also interested to find out where we are in terms of reestablishing communication.

"Right now we have the original system of communication set up, the one we used prior to our automated grid. As you know that system was fraught with inefficiencies and is severely outdated. Relying on this method of communication is resulting in a thirteen Earth hour delay at minimum between any messages sent to us. Meaning that we are twenty-six hours behind on a response."

"What is this old system? How are the messages making it to us?" I ask.

"We have some extremely fast, one-warrior-sized ships that can travel several times faster than the shuttle we took here. They are a bullet class, meant for speed and stealth," Danion explains.

"They are equipped with the longest-range transmitters we have. What we have done is stationed one ship within radio range of each battle we currently know of. When one receives a message, they travel out into space in direction of the intended recipient, more often than not that is me. So, most will be heading in whatever direction will get them closer to me. Once they are within range of another ship, they relay the message. That new ship will continue on the journey until they reach the next one and the cycle continues," he finishes.

"So essentially, they are moving the message between each different ship, like a chain," I clarify. My mind is a whirl with an idea that I am trying to pin down. "Could we bring up the old network on the display? The grids I mean? Can we repair the bases that we lost?" I ask. Malin leans forward and soon the table is displaying the collapsed network.

"It is a very inefficient system," Danion continues while Malin is busy displaying our destroyed grid. "By the time we know something has happened, we are more than a full Earth rotation behind the information. Our captains on the battlefields are handling their battles with no knowledge of what is occurring around them. They have no idea if the enemy is calling reinforcements or if we think they should abandon the battle. If we fail to recover some form of communication the war is over. We will lose, and with us, every mortal and emmortal life we know of will be snuffed out," Danion says gravely.

I lose track of the discussion after this. I am staring at the grid network that was destroyed the same night I was poisoned. The Erains targeted the six bases I noticed the first time I saw this network. They must have overheard what I was telling Danion about the design flaw in this grid.

The six bases were so integral to the design because they were the center of the web. While all the other bases had extreme overlap with their ranges, these six were necessary to connect all the threads together. Without them the arms of the network are working all by themselves with no command center to tell them what to do. The now collapsed grid was able to work on its own, responding to threats independently.

The idea of the chain of one-manned ships is smart; it allows for communication over great distances. Distances that are far too large to be able to receive any normal communication. But no matter how fast the ship the delay is too long. Essentially the network worked on the same principle, shuttling the message from one outpost to another until it reaches its destination.

The difference with the network was that it did so automatically, and since they were all connected it did it seamlessly. No delays of any kind. Each post also had scanners searching for activity in the area so that we knew if there were ships heading in any one direction.

"Malin? Do you think you could overlay this grid with a map of the planets, moons, and bases that we know are being attacked? Also all of the ships we have in the field and what mission they are on?" I ask him. The entire room goes silent.

I look up and see the table of warriors staring at me as if I grew another head. Slowly, Malin reaches forward again and there is a new map underneath the one already on the table.

"What are you thinking, *aninare*?" I barely even register Danion's words. I am so lost in my mind.

"Can you make it interactive? Where I can move the posts around?" My question is met with a look of confusion.

"Do it, Malin," Danion says. Then to me, "Whatever you're thinking, see it through. I trust you." I give him a distracted nod.

"There, all you need to do is reach out as if you were going to grab one of the projections. The sensors will do the rest," Malin tells me. After he demonstrates how to move one, I stand up.

I begin to circle the table. Almost without conscious thought I begin to move the bases around, pulling some from the outer edges and also pushing some outside of range of the neighboring bases.

I am lost in a daze, so focused on what I am doing I have no recognition of time. I am just a pawn to my mind's idea. I don't even know if what I am designing will work. I just move the bases around and keep moving, trying to minimize holes where I can and recover as much as possible.

Finally, I am done. I have no idea how long I have been at this. I step back and look around the room. Everyone is staring at me with shock on their faces. They seem baffled by my presence.

"What? Is there something the matter?" I ask them. No one responds. "What?" I ask again, wrapping my arms around my middle self-consciously. I am beginning to feel a little unnerved with all the staring.

"Eleanor. Do you have any idea how long you have been working on this?" Danion asks me.

"No? Maybe an hour?" I guess. I truly have no idea how long I was working. I felt a compulsion to finish my work, to bring the picture that I had in my mind to life on the table.

"Try twelve hours. You have not spoken a word to any of us or responded to anything that we have said. We even tried to physically shake you to gain your attention and nothing. What were you doing?" Danion asks me.

I have no idea how to respond. I had no feeling of time; I would never have guessed that I was working for so long. I definitely did not know that these warriors were trying to get my attention. At no point did I feel like they were shaking me. I was just lost to my mind's instincts. I was lost to the puzzle I was trying to solve.

"I felt this...this compulsion to solve this puzzle. The room faded away and I just needed to solve the puzzle." I try to put words to the feeling I had while I was working on the network. "I have always been drawn to puzzles and patterns. Something about this network drew me in. I could sense there was a way to fix it. I couldn't stop until I had finished it," I say lamely, with a small wave at the grid in the middle of the room.

It is a small excuse for the worry I obviously caused my mate and the warriors before me.

"What exactly did you fix?" Danion asks while studying the grid. Before I can answer him, Golon speaks up.

"She has found a way to repair the network," he says with a trace of admiration. "I did not think it was even possible for this to be done. Let alone so easily."

"Really? How so?" Danion points out specific areas throughout my new grid that are large open holes in space. "I see there are holes throughout the system. The way that these relays are designed...if there is a break in the data stream the entire message degrades. With these big gaps in the network the message would get interrupted and break down. How will the message stay intact to reach its destination?" he asks.

His words sound like criticism but his tone shows nothing but confusion and hope. He wants me to be right. It is with determination that I start walking him through what I did.

"The problem with the previous network is that there were six central hubs locked into place that connected each end to each other. Like you just said, if one goes down the whole network collapses. Anyone who studies the board enough will see that if they can disrupt enough of the bases they can collapse the system. Right?" I pause to make sure that Danion and everyone else understands what I am saying.

The room nods along with me.

"OK, so what I have done is I worked around the broken ones and shrunk the network. In addition to those six stations we lost we have had twenty-one more fall to the Erains. That really limited what I had to work with. Also, the overlap has to be extensive to ensure that they can't just target a few like they did last time." I pointedly look at Danion. "I would also recommend that no one, besides those absolutely necessary, have access to this map. So, no one can study it for holes." I pause here to take a breath. I'm nervous as to how they will respond to this next part.

"I was able to make these pockets of open space, so no edge of the field is connected by a permanent base. Doing that just makes that base a target for attack. So instead I propose we use the communication ships to fill these gaps. They are extremely fast, hard to find, and we can move them around. This will make them difficult to target." I indicate to the grid. "It will allow the currently collapsed system to reboot and all of the stations in the network will come back online. However, there is going to be significant loss of coverage." I survey the room and all eight warriors are trained on me. I keep going.

"I tried to centralize the coverage around battles we know about as well as big hubs that they might attack. I also tried to provide coverage around heavily trafficked areas, so we might even be able to monitor some of their army's movements. But I wasn't able to replace the whole system. We do lose about thirty percent of coverage, which is significant, but we can repair about seventy percent of the network. This would allow us to keep up-to-date on the battles as well as monitor for traffic near any of them," I conclude.

The room is filled with stunned silence.

"Eleanor, this is...remarkable," Danion says. "Truly remarkable."

There is a chorus of agreements from the other warriors.

"So, you want to do this?" I ask. "You think it is worth implementing? Wouldn't you rather one of you warriors look it over or something?" I say hesitantly.

I am sure that one of them have a better idea; I don't want them to use my idea just because I am queen. Even though I really think it is a good idea to use, I am open to hearing other opinions.

"Of course, we will move forward with your plan. No other solutions were discovered. We can't continue on like we have and hope to emerge victorious," Danion says.

"How long do you think it will take to get all of these bases moved and into their new positions?" I ask Danion. I know that time is an issue right now. With each passing moment more life is lost in this war.

Danion and Golon share a look.

"That will be tricky. We will need to make sure that this is not kept anywhere except in the *bellum* chambers and that only we nine have access to these chambers. We still have not tracked down the traitor who poisoned you. We know who he is but not where he is." Golon seems to be speaking partly to himself and partly to Danion.

"What? When did we discover who poisoned me?" I ask incredulously. Neither of them answers me, just share a look I can't decipher between them.

"Danion. Last you told me you suspected someone. Who is it?" I ask sharply, trying to fight my anger.

"We are almost certain that it is Shemir; he was responsible for the protection of all of these outposts. You have never met him personally," Danion tells me.

"Then why did he try to kill me?" I wrap my arms around myself, feeling vulnerable while the memories of my recent near-death experience come back to me.

"That we do not know." His words are grave. "It will be one of many painful questions he will answer once we apprehend him." His words are heavy with violent promise.

He wraps one arm around me and pulls me close.

"Do not worry, *aninare*, I will not let harm come to you again." I smile up at him in gratitude.

"OK, *animare*. I trust you." Heat builds inside his gaze and I avert my eyes from his. This is not the time or the place to become aroused and if I keep looking into his eyes, I am afraid I will soon be bursting into flames from the fire burning inside me. "So Golon, what were you saying? Something about how to put this grid correction in place?" I ask, trying to steer the conversation into safer, less sexy waters.

"Yes, we will need to move slowly, and only release the orders one at a time for the movement of the existing posts," Golon answers.

"Yes, I agree. We will have to reinstate the grid in increments. Also, the communication ships can't be moved from their posts until everything else is in place, or we will be even blinder than we already are," Danion responds.

"Yes. It will be difficult, but I would say that we can have this system up and running in about nine of your Earth days," Golon answers.

"That long?" I ask, dismayed. "Can we hold out that long?"

"We will have to," Danion says.

These words are met with grave nods around the table.

"My king, I will start with the preparations immediately." Kowan stands from the table and suddenly disappears from view. He had disconnected himself from the mirror table.

"Alright, it has been a long day. I will be taking Eleanor to eat and rest, and I recommend you all do the same." For a moment Danion's words surprise me. Then I remember that he said I have been working for twelve hours. I guess I have put in a full day's work, even if I can't recall most of it.

Danion stands and offers me his hand. I take it and he leads, me from the room.

Danion

As I lead Eleanor from the *bellum* chamber, I feel her try to pull her hand away from mine. I hold on to it tightly. Even though we are in a war and that we have several pressing concerns at the moment, I still crave some intimacy with my mate.

I know that she is not ready for a repeat of the physical pleasure that we can bring each other, but that is alright. Just being alone with her, learning her mind, and basking in her presence is enough for me. If the opportunity arises, I would not be opposed to stealing a kiss or two. What can I say? I am a male, afterall.

We continue to walk the corridors in companionable silence. It is strange, this sense of peace I feel when we are together. There is no tension or awkwardness that drives us to fill the silence with nonsense. Just serenity in being together.

I take us past the corridor that would take us to our chambers. I have a surprise in store for my mate. I hope she is pleased with it. I know that she struggles with her new role in life. With me even. If my plan goes well, she will begin to lower those walls she has up between us.

Walls that I myself caused. I know that I behaved badly. As my mate said, the bond madness is no excuse. I need to be better for her. I vow to stop making the same mistakes with my mate.

"Isn't our room that way?" Eleanor, ever the observant one, asks me while pointing behind us.

"It is indeed," I answer with a small smile toward her.

"Then where are we going?"

"Have you ever wondered how we have such fresh air on our spacecraft?" I ask her. I can tell by the look on her face that she thinks that I am changing the subject.

"I assumed that you had a machine that supplied it."

"Yes, but you might not know that ships that have purely machine-cycled air can be a bit unpleasant when you are on long journeys. The air grows stale. So, we have a rather clever way to aid our machines," I explain to her as we come to a stop in front of a large doorway.

Unlike the rest of the ship, which utilizes gold and other metals in their design, this door is made of a special *terra*-based material that is a rich brown in color and accented by a vibrant purple. This material lines the entire room we are about to enter.

"And what is this clever way you came up with?" my mate asks of me with an impish smile. Her beauty slams into me as I look into her mirth-filled eyes.

"See for yourself, *aninare*," I say as I open the doors with a smile.

Her gaze is fixed on the doorway, anxious to see what is about to be revealed. My eyes, however, are locked steadfastly on her face. I am awaiting the pleasure that is sure to come over her soon.

As the door opens she does not disappoint. She lets out a small gasp. Her eyes grow warm and widen in delight, darting from one side of the room to another. I try to picture the room from her perspective.

It is a lush paradise. Housed in the very interior of the ship is a garden so dense it can provide the entire ship with fresh air. The garden is overflowing with deep colors. Unlike on her home planet, these plants come in all colors. It makes for a surrounding rainbow of flora.

"It...it is beautiful," Eleanor whispers. Her body makes a slow circle so she can take everything in.

"Yes, it is. Breathtakingly beautiful," I tell her. However, my eyes are not on the vegetation; my eyes are only for her. She may not believe it yet, but she is the single shining star in my personal universe.

In my long life I have cared for few people on a personal level. Closed off from the billions I protect for my own sanity. In so short a time she has eclipsed every single thing I have ever cared for. No one and nothing holds a candle to the love I hold for her.

I know she is not ready to hear this from me yet. She still desires some distance between us. It goes against my nature to not take what I want, but I force myself to be patient. I rushed her before and I was met with disastrous consequences.

"Every ship has a garden like this?" she asks while her hand tentatively touches a large, bright blue leaf.

"Yes. Each of these plants are transplanted from planets that are exceedingly high in carbon dioxide levels. With their natural habitats being so concentrated in carbon dioxide these plants are highly efficient at breaking it down and releasing oxygen. It makes them exceedingly useful in our ships," I explain to her.

As I am talking, I grab her hand again and lead her along the garden path toward the surprise I had set up earlier. As a warrior I have cultivated very advanced senses and I use them to navigate the path without looking. Allowing me to keep my eyes on the gorgeous creature at my side.

Which is a good thing, as it allows me to see the shocked pleasure that comes over her face when we come upon the small stream that runs through the garden. Her free hand raises to cover her mouth before allowing a small giggle to escape.

"You have a river!" she exclaims.

"I would call it a stream, but yes, we do have one," I answer her with a small chuckle of my own.

"Does your homeship have one as well?" she asks me with a small accusatory glare. "The entire time I was on that ship I was longing for my river back home. Now you tell me that I had access to a beautiful garden and you never told me?"

"I might point out that you weren't speaking to me. You were actually actively avoiding me," I remind her. She has the grace to blush.

"Oh. Still, I mentioned to Amell how much I missed the riverbank I used to walk along. He never said a word!" Her pique of anger causes a smile to form on my face.

"Yes, and he would never point out that this was an option. It is not the job of a *praesidium* warrior to bring joy to a claimed female. That pleasure is left solely with her mate."

"That is a little selfish," she accuses. I try to fight it, but the pout on her face is too much. I let out a loud laugh at her expression.

"Oh, Eleanor, do you know that I can't remember the last time I laughed before I met you?" I ask her with a small shake of my head.

"That is very sad," she responds, her face dropping. A frown replacing the smile from before. I want it back.

"The life of a warrior is filled with many things, Eleanor. Laughter is not one of them." The laughter I felt has slipped away as if it was never there. "Even from a young age I displayed exceptional control of the lineages. After that...my fate was no longer in my hands."

I stare into the bubbling stream and remember the day I was told that I was a master of the elite level in all lineages.

"Why? Why did you have no choice?" she asks me while leaning her body more fully into mine.

"As small children every Gelder is tested. We have to know what kind of power they can call. This is as much for the child's health as it is for anyone else." I try to explain to her when I see she looks angry. "We need to know what kind of lineages are within ourselves so that we can learn how to channel power without having our *chakkas* exploding. To wait until we mature is a great risk."

"Yes, Golon has talked to me about *chakkas* a little bit."

"That is good," I say with a nod. I idly wonder when Golon talked to her about a subject as dense as *chakkas*. "As a result, children that have exceptional skill in any of the lineages are given the option to enter into the warrior path or not. Almost all go forward and become warriors, but there are other choices. *Scientia* for example, like Golon enjoys. Or they can study *hael* and become a healer like Jarlin."

"But you said you did not have a choice."

"Yes. Almost every child has a choice. Except those whose power proves them destined to be the next king or queen. Even as a small child my power had already surpassed that of the current king's. It was known then that I would be raised to rule. And to rule a warrior race you must be the strongest among them. In every way." I try to keep the melancholy from my voice in these last words.

"What do you mean? In what ways?" It was too much to hope that she would not have picked up on those words. Oddly, I find I am eager to share my past with her.

"I will tell you, but you must promise to stop me if it becomes too much for you," I warn her. She gives me a nod, signaling for me to continue. I wait until she speaks though; I want verbal agreement.

"Yes, I promise." I nod and begin my story.

"Normally the Royal *Chorus* is not completed until the celebration of our one hundredth *decapallie*. That would be close to one thousand of your years. Before me it was unheard of for a warrior to ascend to the throne any younger than this. I was...significantly younger."

"How old were you?"

"In your time? I would have been just under two hundred and fifty years of age," I answer her. "To you that may seem old, but to us? It is similar to putting a toddler on the throne."

"Why were you so young? Why did someone else not take the throne until you were older?"

"For Gelders there is no royal bloodline. We respect one thing and one thing only: strength. We believe that the Powers choose who is best fit to lead us and then gifts them with the most power."

"So you would have ruled anyway at that age? It was just your strength that caused you to rise up?"

"No." I have to take a moment before I can go on. It has been over two millennia and still the pain can cut me like it happened yesterday. "An attack on our people resulted in every high weaving member of our people to perish. I had to take the throne. There was no one else."

"No one?"

"None. At the time I was the only one being trained to rule. Not uncommon really. Strong lineages do not show up every day. Golon and Amell were the only other warriors that were master classes that had seen battle. They each were considerably younger than I."

"What did you do?"

"I did what any warrior would do. I led an attack so gruesome against our enemies that not one attack of retaliation was lodged at us for well over a millennia. The details I will spare you." I look out over the garden and recall those bloody days.

I lost myself to a rage. I was unable to control myself. I had lost everyone I looked up to and they threatened the last two souls I had to call friends. I fought for my people. I fought for our survival.

I never predicted what it would start though.

"It started the war. The war against the Erains. They were the enemies who attacked us," I admit to her. I have never said it aloud. This that I know to be true. I am at fault for the war that has spanned millennia and cost billions of souls.

"But you just said that they attacked first. How is it your fault?" she asks.

How easy it would be to agree with her. To continue hiding my shame.

"Because we were trespassing on their territory. The Erains had control of a very small, very specific portion of space. It was inconvenient for our space travels to avoid it. Going around it was made difficult by several high gravity voids—I believe you know them as black holes—so we had to go well out of our way to go around their small territory. One day the king who ruled before me decided he did not want to keep doing this. He decided to... renegotiate with the Erains. He took every master weaver we had in our population with him to do it." I let the words fall heavy.

King Jeekeir, my predecessor, might have claimed it was for negotiation, but he brought an army with him. He planned to take the space by force.

"Why would he do that? I thought you protect life?"

"We do, and by then we had our suspicions of what kind of creatures the Erains were. We all but knew the tortures they inflicted on the worlds in their region. The old king took in that knowledge and decided to attack. To overthrow them and take their planets and moons under Gelder protection. He never thought he would lose. We are the stronger of the two races."

"How did he lose then?"

"By the very thing he wanted to avoid. The Erains found a way to lure the ships close to the high gravity voids, and then somehow, they were able to transport the engines straight off the ships. With no way to fight the forces pulling them inside the voids, they were all ripped to shreds." I take a deep breath. "If I had stopped them from going, or if I had stopped to think before reacting, the Erains would never have been able to leave their quadrant of space. Never been able to take so many lives."

"How so? What do you mean?"

"There was a reason they only had a small section of space under their control. It was not that they did not want to conquer the galaxy. They did not have ships capable of faster than light travel. They approached it, but fell just shy of it. When they stole our engines, they gained the ability to travel the galaxy."

"It was not your fault." Eleanor's words are loud, firm. She believes what she says, but I know the truth.

"Yes, it was. If it wasn't for me, they would never have had the time to integrate the engines and never build up their numbers so large. I was so guilt ridden over my attack that I never stopped to wonder what they were doing for one thousand years. I let them become what they are today." I say these last words despondently.

As a warrior I always keep a calm façade up. But with Eleanor I can finally voice my regret. A regret that has been eating me for over two thousand years. It is freeing, even as I wait for her to reprimand me. To voice her disgust in me.

"No, you did not. No one is to blame except those monsters. You did not force them to kill all of your mentors. You did not tell them to go massacre entire planets of people. Their sins are on no one's shoulders but their own." Her words shock me. I never suspected that someone would defend my actions. Not once they knew the truth.

"You truly think so?"

"I know so." She wraps her arm around me and gives me a brief, but endearing, hug. "Now, are you going to show me the rest of this garden?" she asks, clearly trying to bring me out of my melancholy.

"Of course." I pull her back to the path and continue on to the surprise I have arranged.

Ellie

As Danion and I walk through this lush garden I reflect on everything I know about him. He is such a strong and fierce warrior. He is everything that a man should be, and he isn't actually a man. He is so much more.

He is honor bound and kind. Gentle when he can be and rough when he needs to be. He is able to rule an entire galaxy without falling prey to greed. I love him.

The thought comes uninvited, but once it is there, I cannot stop it.

I told you that weeks ago.

I know, I know. I wasn't ready to admit it. I still don't know if I can trust him.

You just were saying how he is everything a man should be.

I know but... it is hard to trust a man with your heart when you know that he does not love you.

How do you know he doesn't love you?

How could he?

You deserve love.

Then why have I never had it before?

I never get to hear the answer. My mind is distracted by the sight that greets me as we turn one final corner. In an open meadow in front of me is a blanket and a large basket.

"What is this?" I ask with a smile.

"I spoke with Joy and she said that this is called a picnic. It is a very romantic way to share a meal," he answers me with a smile. I can tell that beneath his smile he is nervous. He is worried I might not like it.

"I love it, Dane! I truly love that you did this." I reach up and beckon him to lean down closer to me. When he does I give him a chaste kiss on the corner of his mouth. He looks down at me with a small look of shock. "Thank you."

I walk over to the blanket and sit down. Danion follows and sits down across from me. I open the basket and start pulling out all the food that is packed inside.

"I thought it would be nice to share our meal here in nature, or as close to it as we can get in space. I would like us to learn more about each other," he tells me.

And so, we do. As we eat the delicious food, we share our thoughts on many topics, from things as trivial as our favorite plant in the garden to the more dense topics like what the war might mean for us. As we are wrapping up the food we did not finish, I remember something he promised me.

"Danion? Didn't you say you would explain how you measure time to me?" I ask him.

"I did in fact say that." At my pointed look he laughs again. "Do you mean now?"

"Yes, no time like the present." I smile back at him.

"That is true, I suppose." He finishes putting the food in the basket, then turns back to me.

"Before we took to the stars we had a similar method to yours. It was a solar-based time, based on our star and our orbit. But once we began traveling away from our planet we needed a new method. Seeing as how many Gelders are born on a ship and never travel back to the home planet it made sense to devise a new system. Also, since we are immortal we had need for a system that accounted for the longer periods of time we experience. To you a year is a long time, but to us? It passes in the blink of an eye," he explains.

"That makes sense."

"Yes, so we looked to the cosmos for an answer and we found it within a Pulsar Star. From that we ended up creating Pulse Time and our fleet, along with most of the glaxy now, recognizes this as the standard units of time. Though generally we will revert to using whatever form of time our mates are comfortable with. Since Joy has been with us for a century most of us are quite comfortable with Earth time." He says with a look, making it clear no one is expecting me to learn their time.

"Which is very considerate. But I want to know how to talk with everyone, not just those I have met so far." I answer him, I am determined to do this.

"Trust me, everyone can easily convert to your measurement of time."

"Danion. If it is easy for you to convert Pulse Time to my time why can't I easily do it in reverse? I am not saying I want a lecture on it. I just want enough to feel comfortable with it," I say with exasperation. You would think I am trying to have him teach me how to design a faster than light engine.

"You are right. I just don't want you to feel obligated to learn this." He reaches out to me and caresses my cheek. "You are perfect as you are. You have already done so much for our people. You need not learn a new method of time."

"I know I don't need to. I want to learn this." I say the words firmly.

"Very well." He adjusts himself so he is sitting exactly across from me. He opens his hand and then a small rotating orb is displayed. It seems to flash light at specific times, rotating in precise intervals. "This is a Pulsar Star. There are plenty of these in the galaxy, but we chose this one specifically because of its location. It is located near our home system. It rotates at the exact same time intervals, no exceptions. So, we based the simplest measure of time off of one rotation. Comparable to your second. Only this takes about five of your seconds. We call it a pulse."

"OK, so one pulse equals five seconds," I reiterate.

"Yes, very good. You have a mind to go along with your looks," he says with a seductive timbre in his voice. I feel something low heat up inside me. "So, for every one hundred pulses we have what we call a palse. Like how your minute has sixty seconds in it." I do some quick math.

"So, one palse is about...eight minutes?" I look to him for confirmation.

"Yes. Very good." He is staring at me with heat in his gaze. I know we are discussing time, but I find my minf drifting to something else entirely. "We then group the palses into a pille, which is one hundred palses." He breaks off with a choke as his eyes lower to my breasts and stay there. I realize I am not the only one whose mind is decidedly not focused on time.

"So one hundred palses...would be eight hundred minutes..." I trail off. I am incapable of performing that math. I am so focused on his lips.

"Yes, about fourteen hours." His words are abrupt and sharp. "We then group those into tens. So one pallie is ten palses, roughly fourteen days... Come here." Danion's words come faster and faster until he reaches for me explosively and his mouth is on mine.

My hands wrap around his head and pull him closer. I relax back into the blanket and rejoice in the feeling of his hard body on top of mine. His leg finds its way between mine and gently glides them open.

I offer no resistance. I am completely lost to the sensation of him over me. I am loving every moment of my warrior. Every moment of the exquisite feelings he brings out in me. His hands have found their way into my top and are causing the most delicious of sensations.

His large, callused hands are plucking at my sensitive nipples. Rolling them between his thumb and forefinger, then pulling them taut. I gasp for air as I feel wet heat settle low in my groin.

Danion pulls my top up and exposes my breasts to his gaze.

"Oh...*fiefling* Powers...you are exquisite. I want to *devour* you." His words are growled to me right before his mouth descends and pulls the tight, beaded tip into his mouth. His mouth and tongue are so skillful that my back arches up off the ground. I am a writhing mess on the blanket.

The only thing I am aware of is the pleasure he is bringing me. I spread my legs wider and move my body against his sensually. Desperate for relief from the overwhelming heat I am experiencing.

I run my hands up and down his back until I reach his buttocks. I am pulling him hard down onto me, desperately trying to bring him closer to the part of me that needs him most. As I begin to raise his shirt his hands are there to stop me.

"Eleanor. If I allow you to strip me of my shirt, I will take you here. Nothing would be able to stop me from ripping these garments from your perfect body and feasting on you.

From taking you over and over until I had my fill. But I know this is not what you want."
He raises his head, making eye contact with me. "Unless you want to take me deep inside
your body, I must stop you."

At that moment I decide that I would be OK with Danion being a little less honorable.
I want him to take the decision out of my hands, not leave it for me to make. With quite
a bit of reluctance I push at his shoulders, ending the delicious contact.

Chapter Twelve

Danion

As I watch my mate sleep, hours after our wonderful dinner in the garden, I pull my mind away from the pleasure of her body and focus it on her other perfect feature: her mind. The feat she pulled in the *bellum* chamber was beyond impressive.

I am also equally baffled by her innate ability to solve problems. She has no experience with battle strategy or war tactics, but twice now she was able to see more into the network than Golon or I. We were the ones who *designed* it, yet she is the true master.

Today was intense; nothing we did could stir her out of her single-minded determination over the grid. We were not even sure what she was doing until near hour nine. That was when Golon first suspected that she was designing a new system.

Until then I was gripped with terror, afraid something had befallen her when none of us could reach her. No matter what I tried she just continued on, relentlessly poring over the grid.

She seems so small and peaceful in sleep. Her eyes closed and delicate. Her eyelashes fanned ever so gently on her cheeks. It seems so strange that her eyes can see so much when they have lived for so little time.

A room full of the oldest and wisest warriors and she is the one who solves the question that has us stumped. And in just a few hours. Then she acts like solving the problem was as easy as a game of lunar toss. Nothing more taxing to her than the simple dice game that Golon and I played as children.

I have been watching her sleep for hours now. From her exterior appearance you would never suspect the power she houses within herself. I can barely recall what caused me to think her weak on our first encounter. Since then she has shown time and time again how strong she is.

The source of her power is a mystery. A mystery that needs to be solved. While my mate seems completely unconcerned with the threat of the ambassador, I do not take it so lightly.

The ambassador knew enough about her history to make up the story, if it is a lie. I am not so confident that it is. What finally convinced me to give in to her decision was the fact that she was right. I can't condemn an entire planet to that *infer*. Especially when there is obviously a cure, as Eleanor said, and Jarlin will most likely be able to heal her.

He was confident enough that he would be able to convince us to spare his life after the crimes he committed. If it was not for Eleanor, he would have learned he was gravely mistaken. I would have gladly separated his head from his spine for the abuse he caused my Eleanor.

The list of crimes he did to my mate is endless. Stealing the resources sent to her, allowing her to starve for the bulk of her life, raising her in a dirty, dangerous room. To call that building a house is a disgrace to the word.

My mind is awhirl with questions about Eleanor's origins. I rise from my perch on a chair in the corner. I give her a kiss on the forehead and quietly leave the room. I am going in search of the one warrior who may be able to provide answers.

I swiftly head to Golon's chambers and request entrance.

"Dane, come in. I have been expecting you to arrive sometime this evening." Golon's words come from inside the room. The door opens on its own. I enter and find Golon levitating above his sitting area.

Golon often levitates when he is in deep *medate*. A meditation so deep, Golon alone is capable of entering it. The concentration and discipline required are immense. He only enters into a *medate* when there is a matter of grave importance he needs an answer to.

"Golon, what troubles you that you are engaged in a *medate* when you should be resting for our struggles tomorrow?" I ask him. A *medate* puts considerable strain on his power.

"Dear *cognata*, while I am touched that you are so concerned with my wellbeing, I crafted the threads of the *medate* line of power with my own hands. I can wield it whenever I feel the desire," Golon responds with no small amount of indignation. "To answer your question, the reason I am engaged in a *medate* is that I am searching for the answer to the same question you have."

"Eleanor's origin? What have you uncovered?" I query.

"Many things. None of which can be confirmed without Eleanor's father's ship. We need to find that spacecraft." Golon is famous for never disclosing his suspicions early.

When someone possesses such a wealth of knowledge like Golon does he often has to be quite careful not to influence the decisions of others before he is sure of himself. In the past he has not been so careful, and it has resulted in disastrous consequences. Ones that still affect us to this day.

I do not even bother to question Golon further. I know he will not share anything more than precisely what he wishes you to know. I understand and respect his desires in these matters.

"How are Eleanor's family and friend settling in?" Golon asks me.

His question reminds me of the strange occurrence when we escorted Eleanor to her family.

"They are fine." I stare at him a moment, noticing how he averts his eyes. "Golon? Why did you give *etnai lef* to the human friend and her sisters? It is almost impossible to extract. It is one of the most sought-after resources any of us possess." Golon remains silent, so I continue. "You spent over three days inside that jungle searching for the plant. Not to mention the eleven days following that it took you to extract that amount. It is your entire supply. I have never seen you share your *etnai lef* with anyone," I question him.

"There is no more nutritional food in the galaxy. Marilee was starved, it was clear. I was concerned for her health. I know that your mate would be devastated if she did not survive so I took steps to ensure that she lived." His answers are stilted, defensive. His response could be the answer, but I sense that he is hiding something.

"And the sisters?" I ask him.

"Same reasoning," he answers with his back to me.

"Golon?" I wait until he turns around and answers me.

"What, Dane?"

"That is the biggest lie I have ever heard. While the human was starving, I am sure she was more than well enough to travel to the ship. Also, there are rations a plenty you could have given her instead of your own supply of *etnai lef*," I challenge back at him. I cannot think of an explanation why he acted as he did.

"We both know that *etnai lef* has medicinal properties as well. It can heal almost any ailment. I was acting logically, that is all," he still tries to insist.

"Golon, the human would have been fine—" I am interrupted by Golon's fierce words.

"Her. Name. Is. Marilee. Not 'the human' not 'Eleanor's friend.' Her name is Marilee." For possibly the first time in all the years I have known Golon I am witnessing his temper snap. Interesting.

"Of course, Marilee. Golon? Are you feeling alright?" I ask. Could it be he has taken an interest in the human female?

"I feel fine." He seems to be battling with himself, opening his mouth and then closing it again. Finally, he speaks. "About Marilee and the queen's sisters, how did the medical scans go? Was everything normal? Are they healthy? Strong?"

"The girls were all as good as could be expected. Nothing that rest, food, and relaxation cannot heal. The hu—" I catch myself at the look on Golon's face. "Marilee refused the scan. Said she... Where are you going?" I call after him. Golon does not answer as he strides down the hallway as quickly as he can.

Strange. I never even got to ask him what his plans to discover the ship were. I shake my head and begin my journey back to my sleeping mate.

Ellie

I awake to an empty room. I can still smell the unique aroma that is constantly around Danion, so I know he must not have left very long ago. I sit up in bed and look around slowly, letting my mind reflect on everything that has transpired over the last few days.

I remember the locket from my father. I have it stored in the vanity in the bathroom. I stand up and retrieve it from the drawer I tucked it into when we finished planning Sylva's mission. I realize that we should most likely be hearing from her sometime today.

I raise the locket to my face for closer inspection. Maybe my father did care for me a small amount. He did seem to take drastic measures to ensure this locket was received only by me. I do wish I could open it, but it is sealed tight.

I grip the locket tightly in my hand and walk over to the floor to ceiling mirror in the corner of the dressing room, connecting the bedchambers to the bathroom.

I study myself in the mirror. The markings on my torso are becoming larger and more defined. I can see the tips of the sweeping curls beginning to show over the top of my nightclothes. I wish that Danion or Golon could still read these markings so that I could know what they describe.

If Golon and Danion are correct this is essentially a family tree for me. I wonder if any of my ancestors would have approved of the woman I have turned into. I know my mother was not happy with this new me, but I cannot deny that I enjoy my new and confident self.

Perhaps my father would be proud of me. He was a warrior, we think, so he probably was a strong man. I like to think he would enjoy knowing that his daughter grew into a strong woman.

Why be concerned what other people think of you? Do you like you?

Well, yes. Yes, I do. Now.

Then what does it matter if your father would like you?

I don't know. I just think it would be nice if someone liked me for me and was proud of me for me. For what I can offer.

Well, you already have that.

I do?

Don't be obtuse. You know who I am talking about. Someone you know who values your input. Who compliments your strengths?

Danion?

Yes, of course Danion.

I suppose you are right. He does support me. And guards me fiercely and unconditionally.

Yes, yes he does. He also is a man above all other things. You need to let him know you forgive him for the argument you had. Let him know you love him. Let him love you. Like you almost did in the garden.

I never said I love him.

Yes, you did. The morning after you two shared bodies you admitted that you loved him. And in the garden only yesterday.

Oh. That.

Yes. That.

I suppose that is true. And now that I am not just a human, he might be able to love me back. I don't think I am ready to confess my feeling to him though. What if he rejects me?

You will have to confront your feelings, and the time will come long before you are ready for it.

I think I am done talking to you.

Need I remind you that I am you? So you are done talking to yourself.

Fine, then I am done talking to myself.

I pull myself out of the conversation with my inner self. I wonder, not for the first time, what Danion would think if he knew that his mate talks to herself on a regular occurrence. I smile to myself as I contemplate his possible reactions.

I am still holding the locket in my hand. I decide to listen to my inner self for once. It doesn't matter what people think of me. It matters what I think of me. I feel that my father would be proud of me, not ashamed. I am not going to keep the one memento of my father locked in a drawer.

I am going to wear it with pride. I decide to place the locket around my neck. I secure the clasp and bring the pendant around to the front, letting it fall between my breasts.

The second that the metal touches my skin the faint heat of the locket suddenly flares. It is burning the skin on my chest. I gasp and frantically try to remove the clasp from my neck, but it feels like it's been locked together. As the pain climbs higher, I cannot hold back an agonized scream.

Danion

I am just entering the level our chambers are on when I sense the pain coming through our partially formed bond. I am already running down the hallway when I hear Eleanor's scream of pain.

On a thread of *caeli* I send out a thought throughout the ship's communication system for Eleanor's *praesidium*, a call of alarm. As I enter the room, I throw open the door while crouched low to avoid any attack from her enemy.

I scan the room for an attacker but sense no one else. Eleanor is on the floor in the dressing room, tears in her eyes and clutching her chest. There is a white mist forming above my mate's heart.

I feel my own drop. Another attack so soon? Who on this ship would harm my mate? The warriors on board are made up of only my most trusted associates. I gather Eleanor into my arms and move her to the bed.

"Eleanor, what happened? What did this to you? Who did this to you?" I quickly ask her. I am relieved to see she is conscious. Her shoulders shake and her breathing is ragged. Her whole body is curled around her chest.

"My father did." Her answer baffles me.

"What?" I ask.

"I put on the locket that he left for me and the second it touched my skin it burned. I think he wanted to hurt me." Her words sound choked, like she is in the deepest pain. I can tell that her pain is not all physical.

"Eleanor, I doubt that is true." I try to comfort her. She is about to argue with me when the door opens and all of her present *praesidium* enter except for Golon. I had barely finished the thought when he comes bursting in.

All of the warriors have weapons drawn, ready to defend their pledge holder. I let them know they can stand at ease. No threat is present for us to do battle with.

"Etan? Please see to the queen's burn. Golon, can you decipher the mist that is floating around her?" Etan moves forward and raises his hand to her chest. As soon as he goes to remove the locket he is thrown violently across the room. He crashes through the wall with an explosion of power.

All of us stare at the wall that Etan was flung through with bewilderment.

"Golon? What happened?" Eleanor asks hesitantly. Golon silently looks from her to the hole in the wall before shaking his head.

"For once, I have to say I have no idea. I did not recognize the aura that threw him from you. But I was able to trace its point of origin. It was the locket," Golon says.

"Why would her locket attack Etan?" I ask Golon.

"I do not believe it did," Golon replies. "I believe it defended Eleanor from a foreign power."

"Why would my locket do that?" Eleanor asks.

"I am not sure. It would require me to examine the locket more closely," Golon says.

"Then do so. Try not to get thrown through a wall though," I say with a smirk to Golon.

Golon approaches Eleanor and moves to assist her into a sitting position. I step forward and block his hand. I grasp Eleanor near her elbow and shoulder and help her sit up.

"Could you please move the locket? I want to take a closer look at the burn." Golon says to Eleanor.

She tentatively holds the locket away from her body, displaying an odd-looking mark on her chest.

"Is that a burn mark?" I ask to the room at large, but not surprisingly Golon answers.

"No, not one that I have ever seen." His words are contemplative. "This mist is born from an aura so thick that even you can see it," Golon states. I know he is unaware of how his words sounded. The aura must be powerful indeed if someone who is not blessed with the gift of aura sight can see it.

"What lineage is it?" I ask of him.

"I do not know for certain," Golon says. "But given the nature of her injury, and the fact that I have never seen this weave aura before, I am confident enough to state the most likely weave source. *Lacieu.*" His words cause Malin to draw in a breath.

Arsenio is the only other one who knows of her suspected lineage, and Etan has not yet returned to the room. I suspect if he were here, he too would be showing his shock. Griffith seems remarkably not surprised by this knowledge.

"Why would my father go through all this trouble just to hurt me decades after he left?" Eleanor questions Golon and myself. Her eyes darting between us both.

"I am not sure he did, Ellie." Golon's words are soft and tender. "I believe that this is not only blessed, but also embedded with some of your own powers as well. It is meant to protect you. However, without the ability to channel powers within yourself the power brought you harm. Your father must have thought that you would be able to handle the power he placed within it." Golon gestures to her mark. "If you require further proof, that mark you carry is not a burn. It is frozen skin that ruptured. The locket became so cold it burned the skin it touched, but not with heat. With cold." As Golon's words come to an end the mist around Eleanor begins to flow rhythmically.

Orienting itself in a sphere shape, a rudimentary map seems to be forming. The symbols and weave threads are unmistakable. Before the question can be asked, I am speaking.

"That is an *orbis* weave," I say.

"An *orbis*? I have never seen one before. They are very difficult to construct, are they not?" the lecherous Arsenio states. I do not honor that question with an answer.

"What is an *orbis*, Danion?" my precious *aninare* asks. She is worthy of my responses.

"It is a type of map, but more like a detailed message meant for one person. It cannot be activated by anyone other than who it was meant for. Your father is leading you somewhere," I inform her.

My mind is quickly weighing each possible scenario. The most likely path is that her father is guiding her to either a safe haven or his ship. From everything that I have seen of the lengths that this mystery warrior has gone to for his daughter, he has something powerful set up to defend her.

For starters, a blessed item is ideal for containing a hidden message. He must have had the *orbis* buried under the protection weave. Once it activated it began to form the rest of the intended message, ensuring that only his daughter would ever be able to read it.

He must not have been worried about who could be with her when she received the message as well, since all of us are getting it loud and clear. There is no doubt in my mind that her father orchestrated something significant before he left. Whether or not it will be dangerous remains to be seen.

However, there is a chance that her father's good intentions have been misappropriated. Our powers are not foolproof. There's no proof that her father left behind the locket for her, someone could have planted it. My warrior mind begins to worry for my mate's safety. A trap could be waiting. One attempt on my mate's life is enough to make me cautious.

"Where would he be leading me?" she asks me.

"Wherever he wants you to go, it is of no consequence. It is too dangerous at this point. We will continue to research what might be there. If we can be confident enough in the safety of the location then we will follow your father's secretive map. Not a moment before. I will not risk you," I tell her in a voice that shows I am not to be argued with.

"It is *my* map from *my* father, I should have the right to decide if I go or not." My mate is stubborn to her core.

"You lack the experience and foresight to think clearly where your safety is involved," I explain to her. "That is why you have me. I can make sure you stop and think before reacting foolishly." It is a difficult impulse to control. It took centuries for me to firmly lock down the instinct to react before thinking. Luckily, we can use my discipline here to control her primitive impulses.

"Excuse me?" Her words are frosty. "You can stop me from reacting foolishly? Should I be grateful?"

"Yes, it is difficult for you to do so, understandably. But I do not mind," I explain to her. Everyone reacts foolishly in their youth. There is no shame in this. I have even told her about how I reacted without thought in the past and the repercussions we still face from that thoughtless action.

Eleanor does not respond to me this time. I give her a smile. I enjoy when she trusts my opinion. She is learning to trust her mate. "We will await Sylva's report before we make any further plans about leaving the safety of the ship."

"Sure. I wouldn't want to get in the way of your better instincts," Eleanor replies.

My smile grows. Our bond must be strengthening if her confidence in me is so complete. I feel very good about this interaction.

Ellie

I have been fuming all day over Danion's behavior in our chambers earlier. I had just been thinking that he respected me and was proud of me, but he proved me wrong. Again.

He thinks I am foolish. Oh, and that it is *understandable* that I can't control said foolish tendencies.

I have said it once and I will say it again.

Asshole.

This is what I get for trusting another person. I decide to avoid him all day. I decide to spend the day with my sisters and Marilee; they do not need me today in the *bellum* chambers and I have missed my family so much. I told myself it was so I could assure myself that they are fine after their ordeal on Earth Nueva, but I was really using it as an excuse to avoid Danion and his smug face.

Marilee and I are sitting together while all four girls are discovering the joys of a full bath tub. It is so large that they are all in the same tub, bubbles so high we can barely see their heads. Laughter is easily heard, along with splashing.

It has been so long since I have heard such sounds of joy from my young siblings that I realize I have not been listening to Marilee's story. I bring my focus back to what she is telling me.

"I was asleep, peacefully for the first time in what feels like years, and then there is a forceful pounding on the door! It was so loud I thought I was being attacked," Marilee is explaining.

"Who was at the door?" I ask her.

"That male that was with you when you first came for us. The one who gave us food. Golon. And he had a medical scanner with him. He forced me to undergo a full check just to ensure that I was recovering from my 'ordeal' correctly. As if my entire life was nothing more than an ordeal. Then he started demanding to know what I have been eating since I came aboard." Marilee says this last little bit with a huff.

"What did the scan say?" I ask her.

Just as she was telling me what happened after the scan, we are interrupted by none other than Golon himself. He approaches with a carefully blank face.

"Eleanor, you are to be under guard at all times. Even on board the ship." Golon says this to me, but his eyes never stray from Marilee.

"Alright, Golon," I say slowly. Golon moves back, positioning himself against a wall and making no move to leave. Normally my guards stay outside the room I am in. I am about to ask him why he is going to be in here with me when he speaks.

"You understand that under the circumstances we need to be extra careful. I will be right here if you need me." With those words Golon crosses his arms, and just stares at Marilee and me. Well, that is not strictly true. He doesn't spare me even a flicker of his gaze.

That is strange for many reasons, but paramount being that he is has never been my personal guard before. Normally one of the warriors in my *praesidium* is given that task.

Arsenio usually volunteers but I am slowly becoming familiar with all of them as each one has taken the duty at one point or another. Yet never Golon. Not before this. He is normally attending to other duties. It is a bit unnerving how he does not seem to take his eyes off Marilee. He is so fixated on her. I don't the he is even blinking.

"He seems to be very...domineering," Marilee whispers to me.

"He is actually quite sweet, and one of the people who has made me comfortable here," I whisper back at her. "This seems out of character for him."

"If you say so..."

"Ellie-Elle! Marilee! Come look! Savannah can make shapes with the bubbles!" I am distracted by Samantha's chortling laughter and both Marilee and I rise and cross over to where the girls are playing.

Too late we realize it was a trap and soon we are both covered in suds.

"Oh! You girls are so sneaky!" I yell at them while both Marilee and I reach for a handful of the bubbles, laughing the whole time.

I have never felt so happy or content. Danion may be an asshole, but he has brought such happiness, such safety, to my sisters. For that, I will always be in his debt.

After I spent the day with my family and we shared our evening meal together, Golon and I were summoned to the *bellum* chamber. We are standing outside now while Golon once again unravels the many weaves guarding this room.

I imagine Sylva has reported in and we need to make a decision on our next course of action. When the door is finally opened, we enter a room full of somber looks.

"What has happened?" I ask as I move around to my seat near Danion. I pretend I do not see the hand he offers me and sit on my own. Kowan is the one who answers my question. His face is locked into very tight lines. His jaw is clenched and his words are full of worry.

"It is Sylva and her team. They have not reported when we expected them to. We projected a thirty-six Earth hour window and it has now been forty." Kowan's words are strained.

"The mission could have just taken longer than we expected," I say with a hopeful look around the room.

"I am afraid there is more," Kowan says dejectedly. "We have been moving the outposts like you designed. One of them picked up a faint signal roughly seventeen hours after Sylva's team left. It took a while to decrypt it and then transmit it here. But it reached us moments ago. It was a distress call. Encrypted in Sylva's code. I believe she has been captured."

"No!" I gasp. I recall the prejudice against females that Kowan explained last time. The fear he had regarding what would happen to Sylva if she were to be captured. "What can we do?" I ask.

The warriors around the table all share a look, one that I really don't like. A look that drops my stomach to the floor.

"There is little we can do. Without more information, we know nothing of how she was captured. Any more warriors we send in will most likely be lost as well," Danion answers. "Lost to suffer the same fate as Sylva and her team."

"We cannot just abandon them there," I cry out. "We can't do that! I refuse to do that."

"And we won't." Danion attempts to take my hand but I move it away from him. "We will be sending teams to be stationed near the moon as close as we dare. If they see a way in, they will go and attempt a rescue mission." Danion's hand reaches out again, this time I am unable to avoid it. I sigh and let him clasp it around mine.

"For now, we can also function on the hope that she somehow evaded capture or that she managed to escape. Four hours is no great amount of time. She might return by morn and all will be well," Malin comments. I wish I could share his optimism. But I can't shake the feeling that something is very wrong with Sylva.

The next morning my worries are proven right when the dawn comes, and still, there is no word from Sylva. We are forced to accept that she was captured, or worse.

Chapter Thirteen

Sylva—*Forty Earth Hours Ago*

"We are on course for Paire, *ceps*. Should be arriving in about one and a quarter pille," Rale, my second in command, informs as he walks toward me. We have about seventeen Earth hours until arrival.

I am bone tired. I had only just returned from our central communication base, narrowly managing to escape the invasion that the Erains lodged at us. It was the closest call I have ever had.

When you are as successful as I am you can't help but be a little arrogant. Very little scares me in this universe, but that battle did. I watched souls I have known for over seven hundred years fall in battle. Souls, I called friends.

The battle raged on for weeks. They managed to take out the fusion power reactor on the first hit, but we fought for control of the base with our very lives. It was all for nothing. There were just too many of them to hold off. Eventually, we had to retreat.

What those blasted *veirman* could want with the Paire Moon is very concerning. I doubt they are planning on just sitting around, twiddling their thumbs until we all run out of *tatio*. My instincts are telling me they have something else planned. My instincts are rarely wrong.

I had only just made it out and was traveling to the nearest stronghold when I discovered Danion had a mission for me.

"Thank you, Rale. I am going to rest while we commute. I have a feeling we will need all our strength to face what awaits us. Wake me in one pille." I acknowledge his bow to me and head to my small cot, stationed in the one room that can be sealed in this small stealth ship we are in.

I need sleep desperately. I haven't had true sleep in weeks. Any sleep I can get has been plagued with dreams. I send a fervent whisper to the Powers that I can rest uninterrupted tonight. With one last sigh of hope, I lie back and close my eyes.

"So, we meet again." A lazy, sensual drawl rouses me.

I muffle a frustrated moan. Not again. Why have I conjured up some imaginary male to haunt my dreams?

"Strictly speaking we have not met. You are not real," I answer my imaginary mystery male without opening my eyes.

"You can believe that if you wish" is all the answer he gives me.

"It is not something I believe, it is the truth." I sit up and open my eyes. Looks like another night with no rest.

"Yes, so you say every night. But I am as real as you are," he says, just like he does every night.

Maybe I have conjured him up because I am lonely. Fighting battles is a poor substitute for companionship. Our race has few enough females and even fewer mated females. Most of them have heart bonded already since they have forfeited any hope to ever find an animare. *Perhaps I should not have scorned Kowan when he offered in our youth.*

"Kowan? Who is Kowan?" my mystery male questions.

"How do you know of Kowan?" I ask with a hint of suspicion.

"You just thought about him. Wishing you had heart bonded with him years ago." There is a distinct bite in his words.

"Why do you care about my past?" I ask him.

"Call it curiosity." His words cause me to stare at him in disbelief. "Fine, curiosity about the female who constantly invades my dreams. If you are promised to another why do you plague me night after night?"

"I don't plague you, you plague me," I remind him.

"Sorry, beb, *your mind is the one that pummels into mine until I let you in every night. It is more relaxing if I just let you in rather than fight it. I would really appreciate it if you gave me some peace." His words seem to ring true, but I ignore the thought like I do every night.*

"I have told you I don't like it when you call me beb. I have a name—Sylva. Also, I thought I told you I don't want to hash out my subconscious desires with you. I want what we have every night," I tell him with a meaningful look. *It might be unhealthy, and I might claim I dread to sleep now, but the truth is I am addicted to the satisfaction and pleasure I now get every night.*

"I will give you nothing until you tell me who Kowan is," my imaginary mate tells me.

"I have to give my subconscious credit, you have the arrogant, overbearing, and possessive male thing down pat," I say with a small chuckle. *I move to go to him and find my body suddenly locked. Not responding at all. I am frozen in place.*

"You don't move until you tell me. Who. Kowan. Is." He speaks each word with precision. *The words have a larger impact due to the lack of heat behind them. Before me is a male that does not need to throw his power around to intimidate.*

It is a huge aphrodisiac for me. In my world, the real world, I am often the strongest warrior. The only warrior I know who can intimidate me is our king himself. For me to feel an attraction to my imaginary man is impressive. Of course, my imagination did conjure him up, so I suppose it does make sense.

I study the male before me. I truly could not have created a more perfect male specimen. He is tall, with a sturdy and muscular form. His shoulders are broad and taper down to a lean and hard waist. His harsh features are softened by a full mouth that so rarely smiles. His eyes appear cold and hard until they land on me, their light blue color softening when they turn to me. His black hair has a light, almost white, streaks throughout, lightening the overall appearance.

"You know I hate when you do this," I say on principle when really I enjoy his control of me. *I am always the leader on missions. It is nice for the responsibility to be shifted. Of course, it is only nice to imagine, I would hate this in real life.*

"No, you don't, but I won't argue with you about it now. I will release you and give you what you want once you answer my question," he says again. *His appearance is so relaxed, as if holding me immobile is not a strain at all for him. Any fantasy male of mine is bound to be immensely powerful though, so it makes sense.*

"Fine," I say with a little aggravated sigh. *"Kowan is a friend, nothing more."*

"Try again. You know I am looking for more than that," he replies.

"There is nothing more than that. We trained together as warriors. Teamed up on our first missions. But we became estranged many years ago, due to a difference of opinion. Now we rarely speak, and see each other even less," I tell him.

"What difference of opinion?" he asks after a moment.

"Kowan wanted us to bind ourselves in the heart bond. A bonding of choice. While we did see each other briefly in our youth, and it was pleasant, I could not agree. He was not someone I felt I could bind myself to for all eternity, so I had to refuse his offer. It caused a significant strain on our relationship," I end lamely. A strain on our relationship is putting it lightly. Kowan and I are barely civil anymore.

"What does 'see each other' mean?"

"Huh?" It takes me a moment to pull myself out of the regret I am feeling about how far Kowan and I have drifted apart.

"You said you saw each other; I am not familiar with what that means," my mystery man says.

"Well, it means you spend time alone together. You know, like...alone." I am blushing. How a figment of my imagination can embarrass me is beyond me.

"Physical joining. That is what you speak of." His face has darkened into a black scowl.

"Yes, but it was over centuries ago," I remind him. I refuse to feel bad about my past, especially when I am not even talking to a real person.

"I do not like this, Sylva," he tells me.

"It is not up to you to like or dislike any of my actions," I remind him, irritation high on my cheeks.

"We shall see about that. So, this Kowan is no longer active in your life?" He won't drop this subject.

"No, he is not, I promise you." Why am I trying to spare the feelings of my fantasy male? He studies me for a while, then gives me a nod. Suddenly I have control of my body again.

I completely stand up and move toward him.

"Finally, you really shouldn't deny giving me what I want." I give him a saucy little smile as I sit down next to him. He moves over to make room for me.

"The same rule applies to you." He pulls me into his arms and the surface beneath us transforms itself into a luxurious bed. He curls himself around me and I wrap my arms around him just as tight.

"Nothing has ever felt more right than this." I sigh, resting my head on his chest. His arms tighten around me and he tucks my head under his chin.

"Hmm" is all the response I get. I could question the sanity of conjuring up a perfect male and then fantasize about doing no more than cuddling him for hours, but I choose not to.

I relax back into his arms and just bask in his glow. I focus on his even breathing and let him lull me into a peaceful doze.

"*Ceps*, we have only a quarter pille until we are at the moon." Kyel, the dual master of *caeli*, air power, and *anium*, water power, wakes me from my pleasant dream. I fight back a wave of regret that I never get to say goodbye to my dream male. Oh, well, I will see him next time I sleep.

"Thank you, Kyel. I will join you in the control room shortly," I respond to him. I slept fully clothed so I have little to do to get ready, besides force all thoughts of my dream male out of my mind.

Which is easier said than done. Even when I am awake my thoughts are dominated by his smoldering looks. His domineering attitude. His extensive power and control. It takes quite a few pulses to calm my body down.

Once done, I head out of the small room. When I arrive in the control room the rest of my team is already there. Rale, my second in command, master of *simul*, the combined power like me, is standing at the head of the room. He is studying the navigation system. Baer, dual master of *terra* and *vim*, earth and life power, is off to the left studying the scanners, alert for any enemy crafts that venture too near. Kyel is standing to the right of them both, beginning to sort the packs we will take with us to the surface.

"How are the scanners, Baer?" I ask him.

"Quiet so far," he answers with too much concern in his voice.

"Why do you sound worried about that?" I ask him.

"I am concerned with what we are *not* picking up. It is quite strange that the scanners are completely empty," he replies. I give him a moment to continue. When he realizes I am not answering he explains further. "We have had nothing reported on the scanners in the last half pille. No planets, stars, comets, asteroids, or anything. Normally our long-distance scanners should pick up evidence of some sort of celestial bodies. We were at the beginning of our journey, but now? Nothing. We are close enough that the moon should be showing up as well, but still nothing."

"What could cause the empty scanners?" I ask him.

"Damage could do it. Or something, or someone, could be blocking our scanners." His words cause mild concern.

"We are heading into enemy territory. There are bound to be some complications. Our ship is cloaked from all scanners as well. Even if we cannot see them, they can't see us either," I remind him. "We just need to be prepared for all obstacles."

Even as I say the words, concern slithers down my spine. Something feels off, but I can't place what.

Chapter Fourteen

Sylva

"We should have a visual of the moon base as we circle this planet, *ceps*," Rale tells me.

"Any signs of trouble?" I ask Kyel.

"Nothing so far," he responds. His tone speaks of his apprehension.

My senses are on high alert. Something feels wrong, and my instincts are never wrong.

"Sylva? What in the Darkness are you doing here?" an angry and somewhat alarmed voice rings in my head. A familiar voice. A voice I am not used to hearing outside of my dreams. I have trouble believing it.

"Sylva, answer me. What are you doing approaching the moon? Are you out of your blasted mind?" The voice rings again. I glance at my team and none of them seem disturbed at all. I am not sure how to respond, but I try thinking of a response.

"Who is this?" I think, picturing my dream male in my mind.

"Who do you think this is? The male you accost every night. I have no time for your contrariness. Now answer me. What are you doing here? You are in great danger," he tells me.

"Every mission I go on is dangerous. I am heading to the moon to do my job. How do you know I am heading to the moon?" I suppose I should be more shocked that my dream man is real, but deep down I always knew he was. I always knew he was more than just a figment of my imagination.

I never admitted he was real before because I knew that would mean I would have to give him up. I can't spend my dreams cuddling a real male. Pretending that he was just a figment of my imagination allowed me to cave in and enjoy him. Even warriors need comfort sometimes.

"You are being sent to the moon? By the Gelders? You are the one they call the Emper Elus, *the undefeated angel?"* He sounds alarmed now.

"Yes, that is me. Why?" I ask him.

"You need to go, Sylva. This is a trap. They are waiting for you; they've been tracking you for half your journey here. A scout ship is traveling behind you, blocked from your sensors." His words shock me.

I never even question him. Something about him is connected to something deep inside me. While I can't explain it, I trust him completely.

"We have an Erain scout ship trailing us. We need to lose them," I tell my team. No one questions how I know this. We have worked together for too long to second-guess one another. They quickly move into action.

"If they are locked onto the ship, we will have to disrupt their sensors," Baer says. "This planetary system circles a star of the extreme class. Their sensors will not be able to handle the intense heat and radiation near the star's surface. If we head close to it, we should be able to hide from their sensors."

"Can our ship survive traveling that close to the star?" I ask him.

"Yes, but we cannot be in the ship when it travels that close. It will sustain heavy damage and we need to send all energy to the shields. No life support or artificial gravity can be on," Baer answers.

"What is your plan for us then?" Rale asks.

"We jettison to the moon's surface by using the escape pods. The ship will be set to an automatic loop around the star, cutting back to us after it completes its orbit. We can then use the escape pods to return to the ship. It should provide us with enough time to do the mission and return."

"How much damage will the ship sustain?" Kyel asks. Together my team is a perfect machine. We work through the problems with no arguments.

"The engines will probably sustain the most damage. We won't be able to run the engines at full power. Or even half-power on the return trip home. We will be lucky if we can return to communications range within a week," Baer answers.

I think over the plan. As it stands it is a good one. The escape pods should be able to travel undetected. They are so small they are difficult to pick up on fully functioning scanners, let alone ones that are being blasted with star radiation. We can get to the surface without the Erains knowing we are no longer on board, perform the mission, and then rendezvous with the ship.

"Will we be able to escape efficiently without full use of the engines?" I ask Baer.

"Most likely. We should be able to skirt around the star long enough so that they have no idea where we are. The engines should survive a brief jump into hyperspace without too much danger. If we do a short jump in hyperspace, a few pulses at most, it should be enough to lose any scout they have on us, and then we will have to shut the engines down," Baer says.

"Alright," I say after a moment to weigh the advantages and risks. "We move. Baer, prep the systems. Rale and Kyel, let us head to the escape pods."

"*Ceps*? I am feeling very strange," Rale tells me. Both Kyel and Baer agree with him. We have been on the surface for only a few palses and I too am feeling the drain.

"Baer? Can you try to siphon some life energy from the fauna and rejuvenate us?" I ask of him. This would not be the first time that we have used *vim* to help give us the energy we need.

Baer nods and begins to weave his threads. Just as the power is called to his hands, thick, blistering boils begin to form all up his arms. Baer drops to the ground, his face that of a male in immense pain. Only his years of covert missions allow him to stop the screams he desperately wants to release.

"Baer! What happened? What causes these marks?" I ask, dropping to my knees beside him. My senses are on high alert, searching for an enemy to fight.

"When I summoned my powers, it felt like my body rejected it," he says through gritted teeth. I take *hael* ointment from my pack and spread it over the wounds.

"I will sense for poisonous threads near here," Rale says, and before I can stop him he is already calling the power forth. Blisters immediately flare up along his entire body. He collapses, Kyel lunging to catch him before he crashes to the ground. Instinctually he attempts to weave *caeli* to cushion Rale's landing, and whimpers in pain when matching blisters cover his hands.

"What is this?" Rale asks.

"Each of you attempted to use your lineages and immediately afterward you were covered in horrendous boils. Something is preventing you from weaving your powers," I reiterate to them.

"It. Must. Be. The. *Tatio*," Rale gasps out. His breath heavy. Pain racking his entire body.

I hear a noise in the distance. Approaching guards. Since Kyel is the least hurt I speak to him.

"I will help both Rale and Baer; you will have to walk on your volition. We must hurry or we will be captured." At his nod, I place one arm of each wounded warrior over my shoulders and we move silently through the brush, seeking cover.

I guide us through the overgrown vegetation in a zigzag pattern. I have to make sure the guards are simply on patrol and not tracking us before I allow us to stop to let my males rest.

Finally, I am satisfied with their relative safety and find a small notch inside the base of one of the giant, indigenous trees. As I lay my men down, and Kyel collapses to the ground beside them, I begin dissecting the events.

They let us approach the surface of the moon; they wanted us here. If they tracked us for as long as my mystery male told me they did they knew we were headed here. They could have attacked us long before we even reached this system. They wanted us to reach the surface of this moon.

It is obvious that our lineage powers are not available to us. They have found a way to make our *tatio* poisonous. But since I am not experiencing any terrible effects, it must be only after we channel our powers that it becomes unbearable. I feel ill and slightly dizzy but that is all. I look at the tense, pain-filled faces of my team.

"We need to abort the mission," I tell them. The fact that none of them question my command tells me I made the right call. If they were not in considerable pain, they would argue the decision. We have never failed a mission before. "You three stay here. I am going to do some reconnaissance and see if we can return to our escape pods and rendezvous with the ship early. It should be close enough to the moon for our pods to make it back to the ship by now," I tell them.

Just as I am about to exit the tree, Baer stops me.

"*Ceps*, we won't be able to make the distance back to the pods, but each pod is linked to the last user. You can set it so that they come to us. It is a feature that Golon and I just recently developed. It is only available on our pods. It connects our teleportation technology and our biometric technology. Let me show you how to activate it." He explains where to find the panel to input the command.

"I don't mean to sound ungrateful, because this little piece of technology is probably going to save our hides, but what is the use of a teleporting pod if you have to call it to you from inside the pod?" I ask.

"It is not finished. I am still working on designing the remote command. I didn't rush to finish the design before we left because I figured one more mission would not hurt. Sure is a pain when we are proved wrong, isn't it, *ceps*?" he says with a small smile. I pat his shoulder gently and offer him a smile in return.

"It is not your fault, Baer. At one point on a mission, everything is going to go wrong. We just have to keep solving the problems as they come until we get to go home." I look out over my team.

Their pain acts as the greatest motivator to finish this mission. "Alright, you three hang tight. I will get to the pods and send them back to you. Then we will head back to the ship. In any case, we have discovered what the Erains wanted with the moon. Mission accomplished." I make eye contact with each member of my team. "The most important thing is to get this information to King Danion. No matter what happens we need at least one person to return." After each warrior nods in agreement, I turn and disappear out the small opening.

I move as silently as I can through the vegetation. My mind is alert to both any sounds I might hear around me and the problem at hand. No lineage powers allowed. I have to rely on my other skills. Unfortunately for these Erain scum, I am stronger than just the powers I wield.

The Erains must have infected the *tatio* somehow. This mineral is the only reason we can channel the powers as we do. Now we are severely limited in power. We do have alternate weaponry that does not utilize our abilities, however, they are not our main source of strength.

This is a crippling blow to the Gelders. No powers means not only are we outnumbered, we are outgunned. I have to make sure that we make it back and report this to Danion. He has to know about this to prevent the entire fleet from becoming infected.

I don't know if my team will ever recover. I worry what will become of them if these wounds are permanent. I am just lucky that I did not weave any power. If I had, I would not have heard the approaching guards. We all would have been captured.

My ears pick up a sound in the forest to my right. I freeze and quickly dart behind a tree. I overhear two Erain guards talking. Luckily, I am one of the few Gelders who can speak the Erain language.

"Any sign of the filth yet?" one guard asks.

"No, nothing as of now. The imbecile pilots of the scout ship must have tipped them off that we were tracking them because they detoured into the star. We lost track but I am sure the ship will be circling back soon. It is only a matter of time," the other responds.

"I can't wait to get my hands on the *Emper Elus* and make her scream. A female like that needs to be taught her place," the first guard says cruelly.

A sexist group like the Erains would dislike the position of power I am in. I am one of the highest-ranked warriors. Few have better control of the lineages than me. In truth, my control is after only that of the king himself. And I suppose Golon as well. He may act the scientist but his control of *simul* is impressive.

I am sure that they have a particular hatred for our queen. If there is ever a soul evenly matched to Danion it would be her. Even through the connection of a mirror table, I could sense her power. Her strength. I have heard the tales of what she is capable of. Her strength and abilities are spreading through the Gelder ranks faster than wild *ignis*. I fear for my queen, what will become of her if the Erains learn of her strength.

I feel a small shiver coast down my spine as I contemplate what they would do if they capture me. Normally I would step out from behind this tree and challenge them here and now. But with no control over my lineages, I cannot guarantee success. It is a risk I can't take before I get the pods back to my team.

"I hope they come to the surface and prove that the formula worked. I can't wait to relish the sounds of their screams. To feast on the pain in their minds," one of the guards says.

"If it even worked. We have been given no proof yet that our new king's flunkies have been successful. That is why we wanted to lure them here," the other guard responds.

So they don't know if the poison they created is effective? Interesting. I might be able to use that to my advantage. The two guards' voices are beginning to sound closer and I try to move my body around the tree. I am stuck; there is nowhere to move without shaking the brush near me. All I can do is pray they do not look behind this tree.

My attention is pulled by a familiar voice. A familiar voice that should *not* be talking with Erain filth. No. My mind tries to deny what I am hearing. No. He can't be an Erain. Not him!

"What are you two *speins* doing standing still? You are supposed to be searching the forest and notify us when they arrive. Now move!" With his command I hear the two guards start to complain. The sound of their voices growing even nearer. It sounds like there are only a few meters left before they crest my hiding place.

"I do not listen to complaints or excuses. The next one who speaks will lose a tongue. Am I clear?" my mystery male asks. His words are barked, drawing the guards toward him. Fortunately stopping their travel to me.

"Yes, *Inus* Nix." I hear the sound of three sets of feet moving away right before his voice sounds in my head again.

"You need to get out of here. You were almost discovered," he says to me.

"Did you draw them away on purpose? Why would you do that Erain?" I can barely contain my fury.

He is Erain. A fanatical murderer who travels the cosmos looking for "inferior" life forms to enslave and murder. He represents everything I have pledged my life to fight. And for pallies I have been speaking with him, sharing secrets with him, cuddling with him in my dreams.

"Maybe I did. Maybe I didn't. Doesn't change the fact that you need to go. Now. Get to your pods and leave."

"Sure, *Inus Nix,"* I say with as much scorn as I can muster. He knew who I was but he hid his identity from me. His title, *inus,* speaks of how high in rank he is. It is comparable to my title of *ceps.* A title of command. He must be fairly high in whatever form of government they have.

I have no response from him. I wait a few more moments and begin to move toward our pods again. I manage to make it to where we landed without another incident. I move to the nearest pod, open it, and follow the instructions that Baer gave me.

Just as he described it would happen, the pod disappears in front of my eyes. I hope Baer is correct and this teleportation is working correctly. I make quick work of the other two, sending each of them over to my team. As I am sending the last one, I hear a noise.

I turn and my eyes scan the hill behind me, where fifteen Erain soldiers stand. *Dammit.* I break out into a sprint toward my pod.

Three of the soldiers are on me before I can make it to safety. I fight my instincts hard not to let my power flow through me. I can't risk the boils coming and weakening me even further. I got the pods over to my team. Hopefully, they are able to rendezvous with the ship and report to Danion in time. That is all that matters.

However, I don't plan to go down without a fight. I pull the steel strapped to my waist and strike out at the surrounding hands. My blade comes away red, stained with the blood of my attackers.

I manage to gain the upper hand briefly, but it is lost just as quickly. With every attacker I fight off, two more replace him. Soon I am completely restrained by seven soldiers. I see one take something out of his pocket, hold it to my nose, and then I know nothing but blackness.

Nix

I watch Sylva get carted away into the dungeons. I fight down the feelings this sight invokes. I did everything I dare risk to do to help her. I have worked too hard to climb this high, to gain their trust, to lose it all now. I am not going to risk all that I have worked for to save a Gelder woman.

I have my own goals that I will not disrupt because of some female who can't follow instructions. I told her to get away. I warned her to never come. I have no concern if the Erains are successful, truly I would rather they all burn. But some deals have to be made and some demons bargained with.

Her thoughts have been growing stronger every day. They first started when we attacked the main base that Shemir told us about. While I did not physically fight that day, I was present. I picked up her voice that day. Her melodic thoughts flittering inside my head, driving me mad with feelings of longing and lust.

I used to dread sleep. My mind was always bombarded with the horrors that I would overhear from my Erain half brothers. Never have I experienced such depravity than that which is inside my fellow soldiers' minds.

Now, with Sylva's mind reaching out to me, I was able to block their thoughts. I was able to cocoon myself with her for a few hours every night and just bask in the beauty of it all. The beauty of peace. Ever since my birth, I have never known peace. Never found solace from the unending darkness before I felt her mind seek mine.

I push it out of my mind and block the thoughts of what my people will do to her. I have heard their thoughts, and know of their plans. I know every twisted and sick thing they plan to torment her with. It is not my concern. She is nothing to me. I will not risk everything just to spare her life.

But maybe I can still help her. Maybe I can ensure her suffering is minimal.

Baer

"You couldn't have had these come a little closer to us?" Kyel groans. He is the least wounded of us all so I don't know why he is complaining.

"Just be grateful that they came at all," I tell him.

All three of us are trying to move toward the pods that appeared about ten meters away from us. It does not sound like too great a distance, but with the wounds we are suffering it feels like miles. The pods appeared several palses ago and we are still working toward them. I just hope that Sylva has made it back to the ship safely. I have a bad feeling in my stomach.

"You three are pitiful." A mocking, self-righteous voice causes all three of us to freeze.

"How did you get here?" I ask him. I have never been snuck up on in my entire life. My senses are second to none.

"You need to get into your pods and get out of here as fast as you can." The tall Erain soldier makes no apparent moves but suddenly all three of us are lifted off the ground and are being moved toward the pods. I stare at him incredulously.

"Why are you helping us?" I ask the Erain in front of me. I can tell by his attire and the marking on his right shoulder that he is a high-ranking officer.

"Your leader has been captured. If you are to have any hope of saving her you need to get in your pods and return to your king. Now go!" With those final words, he throws us into our pods and the doors slam shut.

The pods automatically activate and begin their journey back to our ship. My mind is still on the moon. Concern over Sylva is causing more pain than these wounds ever could. We all know what they do to females.

Nix

I am bombarded with pain the second I enter the complex. I have just returned from making sure Sylva's team made it off the moon and their ship is en route back to their own territory. Sylva must have ordered them to leave her if she was captured. Good.

I need to have her saved. If her team reports back to their king, a rescue mission will be organized. I can help in small ways to make sure that they are able to get her out. It took several hours to track the ship and make sure that it was actually leaving this system and not doubling back. In that timeframe, I had hoped that Sylva would not have been harmed too badly.

. From my senses I can tell my hope was for naught. Her soul bleeds, calling out to mine in immense pain. Begging me to help her. Save her. To stop the torment that is being rained down upon her.

Of course, no one is better with torture than the Erains. They are particularly good at causing pain. They crave to feel the suffering of others. Feed on it like it was the most divine of treats.

I try to block out Sylva from my mind. I do not want to see her pain. However, whatever link that's between us is too strong. I can't keep her out. My mind is bombarded with her agony. I am transported to the dungeon cell they are keeping her in.

"Your poison doesn't work. See? I am fine," Sylva taunts her tormentor. "You failed."

"How do you know about our poison if it doesn't work? And why have you not tried to free yourself?" Devve asks her. Devve is a sick ratshult *who is never happier than when his victims finally die from pain. There is not another soul in the galaxy I would avoid more than him.*

My stomach dives again as I realize what Devve has done to her already. I can see the room through her eyes. I can feel the pain that is racking her body. I try to assess her health and realize that Devve can be very efficient in just a few hours.

Sylva's raven hair is matted to her head, dripping red to the floor. I look for, and identify, the wounds that cause the blood to flow from her like a river. There are thousands of razor-fine cuts all along her face and body. Each one seeping blood.

My stomach heaves a little at the metallic taste creeping into her mouth. Every rib is broken, and breathing is almost impossible. I take stock of her major organs and I realize that Devve became so excited about torturing a Gelder female that she is already inches from death.

Gelders are notoriously hard to kill. One as strong as Sylva should have been that much more difficult. But with her power blocked and the poisonous tatio *working through her system, she is already depleted. Barely holding on to life. Her precious light is almost extinguished from this world.*

Fenke should be proud of his compound. It seems his poison also weakens Gelder cells as well as prevents them from using powers. I know that is the only reason her team did not travel to the pods together.

With Sylva this weak she is going to die long before a rescue can arrive. She may only have a few moments left.

"I overheard some flunkies talking about how they doubt your little poison will even work. I am here to show you it doesn't. I am fine." I wince at her words. *Taunting Devve is always risky but from a female? He will be beyond angry. It is almost always a death sentence to the victim who inspires this rage.*

"Do you know what we do to females?" Devve's voice is so deep it is like a growl. I can feel Sylva wanting to be strong but unable to say any words. She manages a small shake of her head.

"We throw worthless scum like you into the pit with the dregs, to do as they wish. They will use this revolting body of yours for hours. Non-stop, until you die. That is, once I decide you are no longer worth anything else to us. That is the fate that awaits you." He leans his face in close to hers. He takes his tongue and licks the blood from her cheek. Visibly aroused at the taste of her. *"Is that where we are right now? Are you worthless to me? Do you long to be thrown to the masses? Is your body to be abused until you beg for death? Maybe I will have to sample you before I let you be defiled by hundreds of my brethren."*

Sylva recoils, and I have to fight back the urge to race down there and physically push him away from her. The thought of Sylva being thrown into the pit is too much. Seeing her in this state is too much. As she shakes her head at Devve, I decide to throw my entire life away. Just to save a Gelder female.

"I am coming for you, beb. *Stay strong. I am coming for you,"* I send to her, she needs to know that she is not alone.

Sylva

"I am coming for you, beb. *Stay strong. I am coming for you."* I am so happy to hear the voice in my head that I don't even notice the endearment he used. I always tried to correct him in my dreams. He has not earned the right to call me *beb*, but I have no energy now.

It takes every ounce of control I have to stop my power from healing me. I am a warrior. This is not the first time I have been tortured and it is surely not going to be the last. I am determined to not let this be the last time. But this is by far the most horrendous. I know I am close to death. This has been a truly horrific session performed by a true sadist. What sets the Erains apart from other races is their pure enjoyment of causing pain.

There is not one other thing that brings them as much joy as torturing another soul. I don't know how they are so perfect at causing pain, knowing just how or where to hurt you to maximize the feeling, but they do.

"It is because they are telepathic. They listen and strike where they know it will hurt the most." Nix's voice floats into my head.

"Oh, that explains a lot." Any other time I am sure I would be excited about learning this secret. I have never even heard a whisper of a rumor like this. No one knows of their telepathic ability. Try as I might to avoid it, the pain overtakes me. I sink into an exhausted, pain-filled sleep.

"Sleep, my beb, *I will guard your mind for you. Sleep. When you next wake you will be safely away from this place."*

Chapter Fifteen

Sylva

I am floating in a painful bubble. I am aware of a burning sensation on my face, but when I try to raise my hand I notice I cannot move. It is restrained on the bed next to me. I open my eyes and look down at my body.

"No use fighting, you are more than secure." I look over and see the black and white hair of Nix. "You were thrashing so much I was afraid you would hurt yourself even further."

"So you are telling me you only restrained me for my safety?" I ask, my tone indicating that I don't buy that for a second.

"I could tell you that, but it wouldn't be the truth. While it was a reason it was not the only reason," he tells me. "To answer the question you are thinking, no I will not release you. I saved your life. Now it's mine. I didn't save it just to let you throw it away again. You obviously need a keeper."

"That is not your decision and I most certainly do NOT need a keeper! Let me go!" I rage while fighting uselessly against the binds. Pure agony rushes throughout my torso.

"I wouldn't fight if I were you. Your body is severely damaged." His words make me thrash harder. His saying not to makes me more determined to do so. All of a sudden my body is frozen. Just like in my dreams my body is completely immobile.

"What are you doing? How are you doing this? I thought it was only a dream?" I ask him.

"I am holding you still so you don't inflict even more damage to yourself. If you recall I told you Erains are telepathic. I am not an Erain strictly speaking and so my telepathy comes with a little added punch. Nothing dreamlike about my powers. Does that answer your questions?" he answers without even looking up.

"No, it doesn't. What am I doing here? Why did you save me?" I cannot even believe he saved me. Just then I realize something he said. "What do you mean you are not strictly Erain? I heard you called *Inus.* They would not appoint such a title to an outsider. They are fanatics that murder everyone who is not one of them."

"I saved you because I need your services for something else. That is all. No other reason," he says. Then he speaks again, low and almost to himself. "Absolutely no other reason."

"OK. I mean nothing to you, wonderful. We are on the same page. You are nothing to me, except an Erain traitor. Now that we have that cleared up, how about you answer my other question?" I challenge.

"Why would I do that?"

"Because you apparently need me so you will need my cooperation. Besides, it must take energy to hold me like this or you would have been doing it the whole time. So unless you want to enter into a battle of wills of who cracks first, let's make a deal. You tell me what I want to know and we try to compromise," I offer.

"I saved your life, you owe me. You will help me because I saved you. That is a life debt. I know how you Gelders love your honor," he tells me. His words are filled with pain and resentment.

"If you are an Erain I would never honor a life debt to you. My life is not worth the billions who have suffered because of you and your race. You want my help? You better answer my questions."

"You are stubborn to the core, aren't you?" he says, still never raising his head from his work on the table in front of him. "Fine. I was not bred like Erains are, I was born." He makes eye contact with me for the first time.

"What do you mean?" I ask him. "Bred? How are Erains bred?" There are so many rumors circulating around the biology of the Erains. Little of it factual since not much is known for certain.

Nix brings his chair forward and places it near the bed. I finally feel him release me from his hold and I relax down into the mattress to rest my sore body. I am lucky really, there is no way I could have held that for much longer.

"Erains are a completely male species. A form of cloning and genetic manipulation is how they reproduce. They never needed females for that purpose. In part that is why they are so hateful toward females of any race. They see them as something they do not have. They hate anything that is not within their power," Nix says.

"Then how were you born if there are no females?" I ask.

"My mother was a victim of war," he says with a meaningful look at me. I get what he means. She was captured and rape was used as a means of torture. He was a result of that torture.

"I am sorry." It is all I can offer.

"It was many years ago. Centuries even, and I never met her so your sympathy is misplaced." His words are cold, but his eyes tell another story.

"No, I meant I was sorry for your mother. The pain and suffering she must have endured is something no one should have to experience," I tell him.

"Hmm." I get a sound in response.

"So since you were born, you're not an Erain?" I ask.

"Not entirely, I am a half-breed. But while I share many similarities with them, their beliefs are not one of them. I have never killed an innocent soul and I do not torture victims for the sheer pleasure of it. I climbed to the rank I am because of my battle knowledge and my strength. If I was like the Erains I never would have saved you, would I?"

"You saved me so I could help you. You haven't told me what I am supposed to do yet," I remind him.

"That is on purpose, I do assure you. You will know in due time. You will know what I want you to know when I want you to know it," he says. I try a different route.

"When will we arrive at the Gelder base? Which one are we heading toward?" I ask him.

"It will be quite some time before we reach one," he tells me. I become irrationally irritated at his nonanswers.

"How much time?"

"Well, since we are not headed to one? Probably longer than you would like," he answers with a smirk.

"What? I need medical attention. I need to inform my people about the poison. I need to check on my team. I need to—" He cuts me off.

"I am sure you need to do many things, but you are not going to be doing any of it. Any medical attention you need I will perform. You are already well on the way to recovery. You are in much better shape than when I smuggled you out of there. Your team escaped and they will tell your people, I am sure. You, however, are coming with me."

"Nix! You can't just take me wherever you want to go. We have a responsibility to save the lives in this galaxy," I tell him.

"No, *you* do. Or more accurately, you did. You belong to me now. I have no responsibilities of any kind anymore. I gave those up when I saved you. You have nothing to worry about but me. Just as I have nothing but you."

"What?" I ask. "What do you mean?"

"Do the Erains strike you as a forgiving race? Look around you, Sylva. We are on a stolen ship. The entire moon was designed to infect your *tatio* supply and lure you—yes, you specifically—there and make an example of you. I rescued you before they were sure their poison was successful and before you were thrown into the pit. Succinctly ruining all of their plans. Add the stolen ship on top of all that and we are both on the top of their hit list. We don't want to meet up with them anytime soon, I assure you." He says these words with very little emotion.

"So where are we going then? They are sure to be looking for us. If we were to return to my ship we could have the protection of the Gelder army. We would have far better odds with their protection than on our own," I tell him.

"No. I told you, forget your Gelder roots. You are mine now." His words are forceful. "I don't have a destination in mind quite yet. All we need to focus on is keeping out of Erain hands. My plans have been moved up so I am not quite ready for what I need you for. We are just going to travel for a while. Skimming the outskirts of the galaxy. Biding our time," he tells me as he turns away disinterestedly.

"But we need to warn the king," I try to convince him.

"No, we do not. He will be warned by your useless team. It may take a while but they will make it back to them eventually. Until then I am keeping you. Your life is mine now." The sight of his retreating back is the last thing I see.

Ellie

"We still have not heard anything from Sylva and her team?" I ask Danion after another full day of waiting.

"No. We haven't had any news." Danion's voice is grim.

"We can't just stay here and do nothing. It is time for me to follow the map my father left me," I try to convince him. I can't just stand around and do nothing.

"No. I won't risk you. It is too dangerous," he says, his voice like stone.

"How is it too dangerous? What could possibly be down there that is so bad?" I ask exasperation high in my voice. "I lived there my whole life. I have been there a lot longer than I have been on your ships. That planet is as safe as any other. Your shields are still surrounding the planet. No one is getting in unless you want them to," I try to reason with him.

"You did not live there. You suffered there. Never again will I trust humans with the care of my mate." His lip curls around the word *humans*. At his blatant disgust with my species, my anger snaps.

"Yes, we have to be careful around all humans, don't we?! If we give them too much credit they might try to grab more of your attention than just your disgust." His look of confusion does nothing for my anger.

"What do you mean? Humans don't disgust me." He tries to defend himself.

"The fact that you don't even realize how prejudiced you are against them is worse!" I throw at him.

"I am honest with the failings of primitive races. There is a very big difference. I may not seek out their presence but I have dedicated my life to saving them from races of people who are truly disgusted by races like humans," he explains, his frustration beginning to seep into his tone.

His words ground me. He is correct. He may not respect humans or any mortal race for that matter, but he does not harm them. He actually risks his own people in the defense of them, something he does not need to do. They could retreat behind a shield and never leave their area of space.

"Fine, you are not disgusted by them. You do not hurt them. But you must admit you do not think highly of humans." I hold on to my belief. His words betray his thoughts. He is constantly speaking of the failings and inferiority of humans.

"It is not humans specifically, Eleanor. Mortals are always easily corruptible and selfish. It takes millennia to develop the self-awareness needed to accept your own frailty. Only then can a mortal race evolve," he justifies. "Once humans mature a few thousand years it will be different."

"You forget, Danion. I am mortal. I am human," I remind him, my voice bleak. This is the source of my frustration and doubt in our relationship.

"You are not human. You are Gelder. You are my mate." His words are sharp.

His vehement rejection of my species is enough to shatter my fragile hope for our future. It confirms everything I have always feared. He refuses to accept me as I am. He wants me to be more. More than a human, more than a mortal. Regardless of who contributed half of my DNA, I am and always will be human. No changing that.

"That is where you are wrong, Danion. You are Gelder. Golon and Amell are Gelder. Sylva is Gelder!" My voice is rising with every word until I am shouting. "I am HUMAN! My sisters, friends, and every single person who ever showed me kindness in my life before coming here is HUMAN! They are not all bad. You judge an entire people by the actions of a few. You call mortals narrow-minded but you see them with such a narrow focus you miss their beauty. The beauty of life. I pity you." I turn and leave the room.

This fight is worse than the one we had over Arsenio. It might have been brief but the wounds have cut me much deeper. I won't hide from him for a month like I did last time, but I am done with this conversation for now. I need to take a little time to come to terms with this, to figure out what it means for Danion and me.

"Eleanor," he calls after me. I ignore him. "Eleanor!" he says with more force. I ignore him again.

I hear his steps following me closely; I can sense he is about to grab me and force me to speak with him. I whirl around and scream at him.

"No! You are going to stay here and let me have some time. While you go rule your empire of superior beings, I am going to be visiting 'the human' and 'your mate's sisters,'" I say with scorn. "You know? The beings you refuse to call by their names? Let alone spend any time with."

His face looks so shocked, as if I hit him. He stands still as I turn and walk away, this time without interference.

Danion

I stare after my mate silently. I wonder if she has some truth in her accusations. Even if she does, I do not know why I should feel guilty. I am a king and I protect my subjects, even the ones who commit horrendous crimes. Like the ones I have seen every mortal race commit. I have seen firsthand the horrors that mortal races are capable of.

Stealing from their neighbors, committing hate crimes, forcing themselves upon their fellow people, and even killing one another in the most gruesome of ways.

These types of crimes are unheard of in the Gelder people now. It was not always this way. It took thousands of years for our people to finally evolve into a higher class of people. Like I tried to tell Eleanor, humans will grow away from such brutality, but it will take time.

I would never hurt innocent souls. I do not think myself better than other beings. I am nothing like Erains who think themselves superior to other races. I have sacrificed everything to keep people like her *humans* safe, to protect them from the tyrannical races like the Erains. They repaid me by harming my mate. They repaid me by lying to me and throwing her into the dirt. She is lucky all I did was exile that rat. He deserves the death penalty for his crimes.

I am not in the wrong here.

I turn around and stomp to the control room. I should check and see if there is any news from Kowan or Amell. A strange feeling is spreading throughout my chest. One I have felt much too frequently since I met my mate. I shut it down quickly. I refuse to feel guilty over my actions. I do not discriminate against other races.

As I approach the room I am met with Golon, who seems to be in a mood that matches mine. His eyes are hard, his mouth pinched at the corners, and his hands are fisted so tightly I see the whites of his knuckles. Golon has been very strange these past few days.

"Dane." He says my name with an underlying current. There is definitely something off with him.

"Golon," I reply. There is something off with me as well. I hate when Eleanor fights with me.

"No Eleanor today?" he asks without looking at me. His words bring the frustration flowing back to me. My mate should be with me. Most warriors claim their mate, join minds and bodies, and the soul bond follows soon after. I seem to be the only warrior cursed with an unfulfilled matebond.

The madness presses upon my sanity in ever-increasing waves. I know I am supposed to win her. My rushing her to join with me so quickly is the reason our bond is unfulfilled. I have no one to blame but myself.

If I could go back I would not join with Eleanor when I did. I would have given her time. Courted her as humans do. Earned her affection. Now I am a lonely warrior who knows the temptation of a mate but no love. Eleanor is not happy with the life I give her.

I may hide my melancholy from everyone else behind anger but I know the truth. I cannot hide it from myself no matter how much I might wish to. I am frustrated with the distance that I cannot seem to close to my mate. I thought we had been improving these last few days. Ever since she awoke from her healing sleep I have felt that we are slowly becoming true mates. But today it felt like every issue we ever had has blown up once again.

"No Eleanor." As hard as I try I cannot keep the forlorn note from my voice, I cannot exile it completely. It is noticeable enough that Golon in his distracted state questions me.

"Is there something the matter with Marilee?" he asks me with a note of urgency in his voice. I shake my head and let him know that is not the issue.

Even my cousin is concerned for the human...that is what Eleanor meant. Perhaps I am prejudiced against the mortal worlds. It is not that I truly think less of them, but I know what they will evolve into and I would rather wait until they get there. Compared to me they are infants. I have always thought of it as I am waiting for them to grow up before I engage with them seriously.

Perhaps Eleanor is correct. Perhaps I am judging an entire people by the actions of a few. A loud few who draw attention to themselves. Their actions do not represent the feelings of all of them. I am pleased with my mate after all, and she was raised as a human.

"Golon? May I ask you something of a personal nature?" I ask my cousin. Golon gives me a nod. "Do you think I think less of mortal races? That I act as if I am superior to them?"

Golon does not answer right away. He is taking the question seriously. Not rushing to reassure me but truly giving serious weight to my question.

"No, I do not think you do," he says thoughtfully. "I believe your emotions are indifferent to them on the individual level."

"What does that mean?" I ask him to clarify.

"I mean that you are very concerned about the species as a whole. You are focused on preventing the extinction of mortal people. You do not look upon the people as individual souls like you do of the Gelder people. They are just 'mortal' to you. Possibly because Gelder life is so infrequently created while mortal life grows larger every year. This may cause you to think of them as a larger entity than you do with the Gelders." Golon delivers his decision factually and precise.

I think over his words. I gesture for him to follow me and lead us to a small meeting room down the hall from the control room. I want to continue this discussion. Could Golon be correct? Do I rank mortal life on a species scale? As I reflect I realize that it does have a ring of truth. While I understand the advantages that mortals have, I focus on the failings more than I give them credit for the good things.

"Why are you dwelling on this, Dane?" Golon asks me.

"Eleanor and I had an argument. Again," I admit to him.

"About the same thing as last time?" he asks me.

"Partly. But this felt more real. I think the underlying problem is the same. She does not trust me. Previously, Arsenio was the catalyst of the fight. But this time it was her going to search for her father's ship. She has already been poisoned. I cannot risk another attack on her life. There is nothing I won't do to avoid feeling like I did when I thought she was going to die." For a horrible moment I thought I would see the death of my mate and I knew that I would not survive it.

I would take the galaxy down with me as well. I fought tooth and nail to contain my power. If she had slipped from this life I would have gone into a blood rage. I would have hunted down the entire race of Erains and exacted vengeance on each and every one. And be gone with the bystanders. I would not have cared who died along the way.

"I don't think Arsenio or the ship is what Eleanor is angry about," Golon says. He walks across the room to a nutritional simulator and begins programming it. He removes two Starskies, my drink of choice, and walks over to me.

It is moments like this that I regret the distance time has put between us. We are over one century apart in age, but in terms of our lifespans we were practically raised together. I remember when he was born. I was so excited. We enjoyed countless hours in our youth together. We went through our educations together, trained together, and even fought in battle together. We made a pledge to always remain by each other's side. No matter where life took us.

But as we aged and I ascended the throne not long before my two-hundred-and-fiftieth birth year, we began to drift apart. Golon, while the second most skilled warrior we have, dedicated his life to science. I, a man of war, soon had less and less time for pursuits of the mind. We have become close again since the decline of our race, pairing our two strengths in an attempt to save our people. Times like these allow us to enjoy the other's company and relish the support we will always give the other.

Golon is more my brother than a cousin. We both have no living relatives other than ourselves. Our parents all passed in the Great War two millennia ago when the Erains first began their quest to conquer the globe. We had an aunt who survived, but she died seven hundred years ago. Her ship was captured by Erains and there were no survivors.

Golon hands me one of the drinks and I take it with a smile of thanks.

"What do you think the cause of her ire is then, *cognata*?" I ask him.

"I believe that Eleanor is struggling to find her place in our world. There are ways you have of speaking that could indicate that you look down upon the mortal races." I start to argue with him but he keeps going. "No, listen to me, someone who is unaccustomed to our ways could easily think that your words show a dislike of mortal people. You know this is true." I am forced to agree with him, since he is right.

"I concede your point." I take a deep draw on the liquid.

"Eleanor may be trying to find her footing. She is being told she is a queen. By you, by me, by everyone. But whenever decisions come up that influence her you take charge of the situation. No discussion, no thought. You just do what you think is best. This is what happened each time you have fought."

I nod to Golon and we sit in silence for a while, nursing our drinks and brooding about our own worries.

Chapter Sixteen

Ellie

"I just feel that I have no control over my own life. He never seeks my advice or my counsel. My voice is the last one he ever wants to hear," I complain to Marilee and my sister Jaime.

After the blowup with Danion, I desired to spend time with my family. Marilee may not be my sister by blood, but she is a sister all the same.

"So he never asks your opinion on anything? Then what do you do all day? You could always come and visit with us here in our chambers," Jaime says, and she has a smile when she talks of their chambers. I can see my sisters flourishing as they always were meant to. Space to sprawl out and a bed to call their own have done wonders for them.

"Well, no. He does ask my opinion on strategies and I am usually in the war room during the day," I answer her. I suppose he does seek my opinion more than I give him credit for. But when he treats me like a child who can't be trusted to look out for herself I tend to forget his good points.

"Then what is it that he does that is controlling?" Marilee asks.

"When the decision is about my life he just steamrolls over me. As if I cannot be trusted to handle my own life or make my own decisions," I try to explain to them.

It is hard to put into words, but I desperately need to be allowed to make my own decisions. I need to stand on my own and either succeed or fail under my own merit. For too long I have skated the sidelines. For too long I have stood idly by when action was needed. For too long I kept my silence, but no more.

"What about us? Was it his idea to bring us on board to live with you? Or did you request that?" Jaime asks again.

"I suppose I asked him and he agreed." They both share a look of confusion. "It is the other stuff I told you about that he doesn't respect my opinion on," I say in exasperation.

"It sounds like to me you have a very masculine male *warrior* as a husband and he is possessive. Which is not that surprising. He is also a king. I imagine that he would have a very dominant personality. Like all of these warriors," Marilee says with a blush.

"What do you know about these warriors? Why are you blushing?" I ask suspiciously.

"I know nothing personally, obviously. I just mean that you are married to a king. He is bound to be controlling of things he considers are his. Maybe it is just his way of saying he cares," Marilee says.

While I appreciate her and my sister's words of comfort, I want to think of other things. I shift the conversation to the more benign topics, such as what hobbies they have acquired since coming here.

The rest of the day is filled with stories about how much they are enjoying ship life, along with all the plans they have for when we finally return to the home ship and have access to the material generators.

I allow my mind to wander as they talk but I can't let go of a certain warrior king. Maybe I am not giving him the benefit of the doubt. Maybe Marilee is right and he does not know how to let go or even that he should let go. Whatever the case may be I decide to approach Danion this evening calmly, and without accusations. Hiding from our issues last time sure didn't help anything. I won't hide this time around.

I awake to an empty room. After spending virtually all day in my family's wing of the ship I returned to our shared chamber. I was hesitant to enter because I imagined Danion waiting for me. But when I arrived he was nowhere to be found.

After waiting for hours, I finally decided to go to bed and speak to him in the morning. But now it is morning and I still don't see him, nor is there any evidence that he came in at all. I feel deflated. If I needed further proof that I was correct about him and not Marilee, this is it.

I sit down on the vanity in the dressing room and stare at myself in the mirror. I feel a lone tear escape and slide down my cheek. Depression is heavy within me. I place my hands on the vanity and rest my head inside them. I give myself a moment to wallow in self-pity.

"Eleanor?" I jerk up at the sound of Danion's voice right above me. I was so consumed with my melancholy that I did not hear him enter the room.

"Oh, hello, Danion." I stumble over my words. I am lost for what to say to him when his next words render me speechless. I try to subtly wipe the tears off of my face without him noticing.

"I want to follow the map your father left and go find his ship, Eleanor." I just stare at him for several moments, trying to recover the ability to speak. Finally, I am able to form coherent thoughts.

"Really? What caused this change of heart?" I ask him.

"I realized that you are right. I have been treating you like you have no control over your own life. Please, *aninare*, understand that it is not because I do not value you. It's quite the opposite actually." He moves to kneel by me and takes my hands in his. "In truth, it is because I value you so much that I cannot bear the thought of losing you," he explains.

"If that is the truth why do you treat me like a child?" While his words do funny things to my heart my brain is hesitant to trust him. I have only known him a short while and he already has the potential to destroy me. Not my body, I trust him to never use his strength against me. No, it is my heart that is in danger.

"I do not mean to. It is not a conscious thought that I have. I am so worried about your safety that I let my instincts take over," he says earnestly.

"I want to believe you, Danion," I say tentatively. I remember what I promised my sister and Marilee just yesterday. It makes the decision for me. "I am willing to work through this, but what does that mean for our relationship?"

"It means that I will try to control my primal instincts and restrain my impulses. It also means you must be patient with me when I stumble off the path as well. This is not an easy journey for me to take. It goes against the majority of my nature." He pauses and stares into my eyes. His hand comes up and cups my face. "For over three thousand years I have been the absolute power in this galaxy. No one challenges me, no one opposes me. You are asking me to change habits that I have had for three millennia. I am not saying that they are correct, you have shown me they are not. It will take work to change me. Golon asked me earlier if you are worth it to me. Do you want to know my answer?" he asks me.

"Yes." I am hesitant in my response. Do I want to know? I hope so.

"I told him that there is nothing in this universe I care about, save you. Some species have the ability to sense the emotions of others. I am glad that gift is not one that my people possess. Since meeting you I have ceased to care about anything more than you. It is not something I expected and not something that a king should ever admit to. But I cannot deny it. I can survive anything, except losing you."

I have a warm blossoming of emotion deep down inside. I feel a smile come over my face. I also feel very shy. I duck my head down, looking at my feet.

"That is very..." I search for a word. "Nice of you. I care about you a lot too. Thank you." I am stumbling over my words and I can't seem to stop the flow of them from spilling out of my mouth.

"You are most welcome," he says warmly. His other hand comes up to join his first and he cups both sides of my face, moving it back to look at him. "Now, we need to start fixing my bad habits. First order of business is to decipher where this ship is," he says with a smile.

I nod at him and rise from the vanity.

Danion, Golon, Arsenio, Malin, and I are all surrounding the table in the *bellum* chamber studying the image being projected from the locket. There is a three-dimensional display of Earth levitating above the locket now.

On the displayed planet there is a marked spot in the northwestern hemisphere in the middle of an ocean. It is just southeast of a peninsula on a large land mass. Something about this location reminds me of something I read once but I cannot place it. Malin is the first to speak.

"If there is no island or other land there I am under the impression we will need to go under several meters of water. It has not been discovered before so it makes sense for it to be hidden under the sea," Malin says.

"Agreed." Arsenio seconds his opinion with a brisk, sharp response. I can sense that there is some hidden tension between these two that I had not picked up on before. "The difficulty is knowing where the ship might be. This planet's oceans cover enormous caverns. Taking into account the several millennia that the ship has been stuck there, and possible volcanic activity, we have no idea where to look in this area. It may have been dragged away by ocean current even."

Well then. Someone is full of optimism. Of course, of the few things that Arsenio and Danion seem to agree on my not searching for my father's ship was one of them. Arsenio agrees that I need to be confined to the ship.

"Very possible," Golon agrees.

"No, *probable*," Arsenio counters. Golon shakes his head though.

"No, possible. This Jaeson went to extreme measures to lead Eleanor here. I don't need to remind you of the significance of blessing an item," Golon says with a pointed look at Arsenio. "I believe it is likely that he took similar precautions in ensuring that the ship would be there when she came looking." I decide my silence needs to come to an end.

"When do we leave?" I ask the room. Based on the blank stares I am given, I figure that if it was up to any of the warriors in this room next year would be too soon. "I am serious, warriors. I want to go soon. Now, even. I need to go. I need to see what my father left for me." I say this last bit on a broken whisper.

"I understand, but still we should send some scouts first. Maybe in a week's time...who knows? Maybe then, we will be able to send you down," Arsenio says. Malin and Golon nod, agreeing with Arsenio.

I feel my spirit deflate. I can't help feeling a strong pull to this area. Just as I am accepting that it will be a week yet, help from the most surprising of places comes to me.

"No, we will head out tomorrow morning. We will send a scouting party ahead today. I will give the order to leave immediately. But regardless of their results, we will travel tomorrow. We will take the queen's entire *praesidium* and see what we discover," Danion says with confidence.

Arsenio begins to open his mouth, no doubt to argue about the decision to leave so soon. Danion's words cut him off.

"Eleanor is your queen. It is your responsibility to protect her, not hinder or censure her. She wishes to seek out her father's ship. Her wishes are your command. All of your commands. No one among you has the ability to question her decisions. Not even me." He makes eye contact with each male in the room individually.

Slowly each warrior nods. As an act of defiance, Arsenio nods to me, not Danion. Stubborn to the end.

Danion

I glance over at Eleanor after the other warriors have filed out of the room. I do not want to alarm her like I did last time, but her mind has reached out to me again. It is a tentative and fragile connection. Fleeting even. I only get small, vague ideas of what she is thinking but it is still an improvement.

Even this small connection soothes the matebond madness within me. I keep a firm hold on myself so that I do not frighten her. If she knew her mind was reaching for me I know she would shut down her connection. It may be underhanded, but the longer she keeps her mind open to me the longer I have to attempt to decipher her hesitance to bind our minds. To accept the bonding of our souls together.

I offer Eleanor my hand and ask her if she would like me to escort her to her sisters and Marilee. From our connection I can tell that my use of her friend's name pleases her. She takes my hand and we walk from the room.

"How have your sisters been adjusting to life onboard?" I ask her. Again, I get a sense of happiness that I am taking an interest in her family. This bond of the minds is going to be instrumental in winning over my mate.

"They are flourishing. They barely know what to do with so much space." It is sad that living on a small ship provides them with more space than they had on Earth. "The older two girls, Jessica and Jaime, are learning how to sleep in their own rooms. They are used to always being with the other, same for the younger two. But Samantha and Savannah are not trying new rooms to sleep just yet. They both have been sticking to each other like glue. It is understandable though, given their age," she tells me.

"Yes, they are quite young. It has not been an easy life for any of you." I continue asking questions about her family. I discover that Jessica is the oldest of all four girls, being a few minutes older than Jaime. She is more stubborn and forceful than Jaime, who she describes as the heart and soul of the family.

She continues to tell me pleasant anecdotes about her life with her younger siblings. I even feel the muscles on my face move into a smile over some of the antics she observed Jessica and Jaime doing.

"And what of your youngest two sisters? Samantha and Savannah?" From our tentative bond, I can sense how comfortable she is discussing her sisters. Much more than when I try to steer the conversation toward her own childhood.

"Oh, they are the quiet ones. Savannah is the youngest of us all and quite shy. Samantha is quiet as well, but her silence comes more from observation than shyness. She likes to observe the world around her." I can well relate to this Samantha. She seems to be wise beyond her young years. I am interrupted from my thoughts by Eleanor's words.

"I am boring you, aren't I? You can't possibly want to talk about my younger sisters. They are even younger than I am." I speak quickly to cut her off.

"No, Eleanor, it was an oversight on my part to not become better acquainted with your family. They are my family as well now and I want to know them," I assure her.

"Really?" she asks me doubtfully.

"Really. I swear on the stars I never meant to seem as if I did not care for your loved ones." As I say this, I realize how wrong I have been. Eleanor has embraced my one family member, Golon. Gelders cherish family, and the fact that my mate has four sisters and a dear friend should have elated me as they are now my family as well. I resolve to construct tighter bonds with my new family mates.

"OK then. If you are sure." At this point, we are at the doors of Marilee's room. Eleanor gives a brief knock and pushes the door open without waiting for anyone to greet us. I motion for her to enter the room before me.

As she passes through the threshold I hear a cacophony of squeals and soon my mate is engulfed as four small females, and one larger one, hurl themselves at her. They are all laughing and smiling, sharing precious moments together.

I briefly wonder if this will one day be my greeting as I enter our chambers. Perhaps Eleanor and our children running to greet me as I enter. I am hit with a fierce, searing wave of longing for just such a thing.

As I step into the room after Eleanor the room goes strangely quiet. Five pairs of eyes stare at me with a mixture of caution and surprise. Eleanor breaks away and introduces me to the females. I realize that while they have seen me before and have in fact been living here for several days, I have not formally met them.

Not in the Gelder way. Not in a way to encourage a closer connection. Only briefly when we first met, and I barely spoke two words to them. Certainly not as their sister's mate, or husband as they will no doubt think of me.

"Greetings, ladies," I address them in a more mortal way. Hoping to set them at ease. "It is much too late for me to introduce myself properly to you, I have no excuse for my tardiness. I intend to make it up to you all." I then bow to the females before me and introduce myself to them. Not with my royal title, but with my personal title. No need to draft out all my battle etiquette.

As I am met by each sister I can now put faces to the names. I am ashamed to realize that while I met them on Earth, I never actually looked at them. It is remarkable how similar they all look to one another. After some rather awkward introductions, Marilee breaks the silence.

"How about we have a seat?" she asks, and we all move to the sitting area within her chamber. Once we are all seated, Jessica speaks to me. The first of the sisters to engage me in conversation. Interesting, but not surprising that it was Jessica.

"What can we do for you, Your Highness?" she asks me.

"Call me Danion, I do insist," I respond. "I am here for no other purpose but to spend time with all of you. You are now my family and I want to understand my mate's family better. My wife's family." I say the last bit with a smile, aimed in Eleanor's direction.

My words are met with a blush from Eleanor and girlish giggles from the other five. It seems that's what was needed to break the tension and conversation flows easily from that point on.

Eleanor and I share a pleasant day in the company of her family, enjoying good food, amusing stories, and pleasant company. Matehood is agreeable indeed. I feel the bond between us flourish. As I sense a wave of elation that rushes down the link to one another I relish our continued bond.

Chapter Seventeen

Ellie

Danion's hands massage my shoulders firmly, rubbing up and down my back with firm, confident strokes. I tilt my head to allow him more access to my body.

"I am so happy we have been able to put our differences aside," he whispers into my hair. "I have missed you, my Eleanor. Missed your body. Missed the feel of your soft skin under my hands." As he speaks his hands move around to the front of my body, continuing their sensual quest.

"Oh, Danion" is all the verbal response I can manage.

"Yes, Eleanor? What can I do for you?" he asks with a clear smile in his tone. His lips are grazing my neck and the soft skin behind my ear. "What can I do to show you how much I treasure you? How much I adore you?" His lips are traveling up and down my neck, his hands are caressing my stomach. Inching higher and higher, closer and closer to my chest where I really want his hands. Where I need them. Desperately.

"Answer me, Eleanor." He nips at my neck. A sharp sting to prompt my response, followed by a soft lick to soothe the burn.

"Your hands. Danion, I need your hands," I tell him with a flush on my face. I want him to just do what he knows I want.

"What about my hands?" he asks, determined to make me say it.

"You know what I want you to do," I beseech him. My body is tight with desire.

"Is this what you want?" My body screams in denial as his hands move lower and caress my waist.

"Danion!" I reprimand him. "Stop this. You know what I want," I plead with him.

"Then show me. Take from me. Take what you want," he says, his hands falling from my body.

I am so frustrated with him, my body so tightly strung I let out an audible sound of frustration. He knows my body so perfectly that he can weave desire on me as easily as any power he possesses.

"Danion," I try one last time to convince him.

"Eleanor," he mimics me with a warm whisper of air along my spine. It is the last straw.

I reach down and grasp his hands in mine and bring them up and over my body. I press his large, strong hands onto my breasts. Thankfully that is all the encouragement he needs.

His hands begin working my flesh masterfully. Kneading with just the right amount of strength. Just the right amount of pressure. I feel my eyes roll up inside my head.

I reach back with my hand and pull his head down to meet my lips, kissing him passionately while he continues his erotic torture of my body. I arch my back even further and widen my legs. I drag his hand down to the juncture of my thighs, pleading for him to put out the fire that is burning. Burning for him alone.

His hand needs no further prompting. His long, strong fingers slide down my front to rest in my most private place. He knows just how to work his hands. His fingers have found the nub of pleasure at the top and are stroking it with growing intensity. The desire rises so swiftly and so strongly within me that without conscious movement I find myself turned around and facing him.

I move my leg up to wrap around his waist, pressing the part of me that needs him so badly against him. My arms move around his neck and back and pull him tightly against me. I open my mouth to beg him to end my torment.

"Danion..."

I am jerked awake by the shaking of my body.

"Eleanor, are you alright? You have been calling out in your sleep and I could not wake you." Etan is standing in my room, hand on my shoulder, peering at me with concerned eyes. It is strange to see him so worried. He normally is so cheerful, masking his concern behind a smile. "I would not normally enter your chamber without your permission, but you did not respond when I knocked."

"Etan. No, it's fine. I am just a little confused. I apologize for worrying you, it was nothing more than a dream."

Yeah, it was. A hot, dirty sex dream. Proud of you.

Well, don't be. I don't know where that came from.

It came from sexual frustration. Caused by being married to a sexy, masculine warrior that you stubbornly refuse to sleep with.

You know why. We are not at a good point in our relationship. Everything has been moving so quickly.

Yada, yada. You know you are just being stubborn.

I cut off my internal battle before I worry Etan any further. I am happy that it is only Etan in the room. I don't know how I would be able to face Danion.

That thought is barely in my mind when the door bursts open. Not only does Danion rush in, but so does Golon, Arsenio, Malin, and Griffith. Everyone is here. Wonderful. I hope no one can see the pebbling of my nipples or the flush on my chest.

"Eleanor, what is the matter? Etan says he could not wake you," Danion asks me as he rushes to my side. I avoid his gaze the best I can.

"What symptoms did you have?" Golon asks me. His concern is mirrored by everyone in the room.

"I appreciate the concern, but it was nothing. Just a dream," I try to reassure them, hoping that everyone will let it drop. That is too much to hope for.

"What was the dream about? Dreams can often be more than they appear to be," Golon asks. I can feel my face flush with mortification.

"Nothing, I promise you it was just a normal dream." I drop my gaze to the bed, embarrassment high on my cheeks. I jump as a hand cups the back of my neck.

I look up and see Danion holding my neck while looking into my eyes. I watch his eyes dilate and he takes a deep breath. I don't know how, but I am confident he knows what I was dreaming about. He brings his mouth to my ear to whisper beneath his breath for me alone to hear.

"*Aninare*, anytime you want to make that dream a reality, all you need to do is ask." Then he raises his voice and speaks to the room. "The queen is fine. Continue readying for the journey to the planet."

If anyone argues with him I have no idea because I refuse to raise my head and look around the room. Once I hear the last footfall leave the chamber, I risk a glance up. The knowing, pleased smirk on Danion's face is enough to make me duck my head again.

"You should never feel shame over what we share between us, *aninare*. I would never think less of you and neither should you," he tells me, his hand on my chin, tilting my head up to meet his gaze.

I give him a small nod in response.

"Do not worry, *aninare*. I know that you still are hesitant to continue our physical relationship. We will progress as slowly as you feel comfortable," he reassures me. "But, I admit, I am very pleased that your subconscious knows what it wants," he says with a smirk.

"Thank you, Danion. It has never been that I don't...want...you. It is just that I am hesitant to jump into this physical relationship," I tell him.

"It is alright, *aninare*. I understand what you are telling me." He smiles at me. "Now, let us move along. If we stay here too long, with you looking so flushed, I might not be able to stop myself from ravaging you. We are journeying to search for your father's ship. The scout team that we sent down returned this morning with no memory that they were ever on the planet."

"What? How is that possible? Had they not left yet?" I ask him.

"No, they had, but they had no memory of anything that went on down there. They had to be brought back by another team. They were found traveling aimlessly out at sea. It seems that everything about the mission to Earth was wiped from their memory. A most strange occurrence. But otherwise, they were both perfectly fine." His response floors me. How he is not concerned with the danger this journey may cause to me is a mystery. A complete change of character from our previous discussions. Not that I will argue with him.

"Alright." I am hesitant to say more for fear that he will change his mind. "When do we leave?"

"As soon as you are ready," he answers while I smile. I jump out of bed and move to the dressing room.

I look all around me at the wide open sea. Nothing can be seen in any direction. We are on a small watership heading to the marked location from my locket.

"It is beautiful, is it not?" I turn at Malin's words.

"Oh, yes. There is a strange kind of peacefulness here in the open sea," I respond to him. Malin was my swimming buddy back on the main ship. "Could you imagine swimming here? With nothing to restrain you?" I ask him.

"Indeed I can." He smiles. "Have I told you of the emmortal world, Holos?" he asks me.

"No, you haven't." I smile up at him. Malin is always the warrior telling me stories and broadening my knowledge of the galaxy and its many people.

"*Holos* is a world that has no land above sea level. Of any kind. The entire planet is covered in water. The people live beneath the sea. I once lived there for an entire revolution. That would be equivalent to almost ten of your years. I immersed myself in the water to challenge my control of the lineage. I forced my body to become one with the water. That is why I am able to breathe underwater now. I can truly become one with it." He has a look of longing on his face.

"You must miss it." I place my hand on his shoulder in comfort.

"I do, but not so much the planet as the peace I felt there. They have such serenity in the depths of the sea. It is where I feel truly at home." There is a look of poignant loss on his face.

"Did you leave something there?" I cannot help but ask.

"No, I escaped the pain of losing someone by barricading myself there. There is a difference." He looks at me with a forced smile. "But enough talk of such sad topics."

"One day I would like it if you could take me to visit the *Holos* people. To share your peace with you," I tell him.

"One day, my queen, one day," he says.

With a sigh and a short bow Malin turns and heads to the opposite side of the ship. I notice that we talked for longer than I realized. We should have reached our destination already. As I circle the watership, taking in every nuance of the sea, I search for where my father's ship should be. Suddenly, behind our ship, I notice a strange floating city.

It is the strangest thing I have ever seen. It appears to be floating on the water. No land beneath it and it is very small. No bigger than a few hundred meters across. And our ship is traveling *away* from the city.

I rush over to Danion and Golon.

"Why are you leaving? That city must be where we are supposed to go," I ask them with a sense of urgency in my words.

"What city?" they both ask in unison. Both of them are searching the horizon in the direction I am pointing. Both of their eyes pass right over where it should be with no hesitation.

"What do you mean? It is right there." I point to where it is floating.

"No, we need to go the opposite way," Golon replies, almost abruptly. Danion is quick to agree with Golon, adamant that they must go another way. I start to get a feeling in my chest.

"Danion? Golon? Where are we going?" I ask them.

"We are...going home," Danion hesitantly says.

"We are not heading in the right direction to go home. We are just heading away from the city. Where we actually are going," I repeat to them.

At that moment I realize why this area on the map seems so familiar. I recall an old myth I came across in old ancient writings about a location at sea that sailors would travel through and never return. It was named after a triangle of some kind. And this city is in the very middle of that triangle.

No one knew what caused the disappearances. Some blamed methane vents, others claimed it was just a busy area so it was simply statistics, others thought aliens were to blame. Now I wonder if it is my father's ship that caused all those sailors to die at sea. I feel nausea rise within me.

"We need to head in the other direction. That is where we are actually going." I point out the city. Golon seems to be the first of the two to understand the significance.

"Yes. We are supposed to be searching for your father's ship," he says with a faint question in his tone.

"Yes. We are looking for my father's ship. And it is that way." Again, I point behind me.

Again, both eyes focus on the area I point to and confirm that they see nothing. I call Malin, Arsenio, Etan, and Griffith over to check if they can see anything.

Malin, Arsenio, and Etan are quick to say that they cannot see anything either. Griffith, however, has a slightly different reply.

"While I too see nothing, I do sense that there is something *to see*. It is simply hidden from me. But you say you see it, Eleanor?" he asks me.

"Yes, I am sure it is there," I reiterate.

"Then we must head in the direction of this city until we can all see it," Griffith announces.

"Agreed." This comes from Danion.

Without any wasted time Golon has turned the watership around and is traveling in the direction of the city. I have to correct his course frequently. Something about this city is hiding itself and trying to force us away from the center.

I stand right next to Golon in front of the wheel and correct him every time he begins to drift off course. Finally, we are at the base of the city when the boat seems to hit a wall. We are all thrown forward.

Arsenio walks to the front of the boat and holds out his hand.

"I can feel the energy emanating from the shield. It is a fine weave, that is for sure. I can sense the intricacies of the threads within it. It is meant to keep everyone out," Arsenio says.

Danion and Golon each move to the front of the boat and they too hold out their hands. They share a look before Golon turns and looks at me.

"Eleanor, come here please," he summons me. I walk up between them with a deep furrow on my face. I am not sure what they want me to do.

"Now, Eleanor," Golon says. "Place your hand up and try to push through the wall." He holds his hand up to me to demonstrate how I should do it.

As I raise my hand and reach out I encounter no resistance. No wall of any kind preventing my hand. I do feel a kind of warm sensation running over my body for a brief moment, but that is it.

There are six sharp, quick inhalations from behind me. I turn around and look at the warriors on the ship with me.

"Remarkable," Griffith says. "It is a truly powerful weave to have hidden all of this from us."

"So you can see it now?" I ask them, even though the looks on their faces are evidence enough that they can see the city.

I turn my attention to the ship; it seems that it's being pulled into the shield. We're slowly gliding across the water to the front steps of this glorious city. As our ship sails under the front archway, I stare up at the looming towers. What the city lacks in lateral length it more than makes up for in vertical height.

I once thought Danion pretentious with the amount of gold and precious gems he had on board his ship, but his ship has nothing on this city. The bricks that make up the stairs seem to be pure gold with several sparkling gems throughout them. The fountains in the courtyards appear to *actually* flow with liquid gold.

One thing you can say about Gelders is that they seem to love their gold.

"This cannot be." Danion is whispering.

"But it is." Golon's equally awed tone seconds his cousin and king's observation.

"What is it?" I ask them. I have to prompt them several more times before they answer. Danion steps out of the ship and onto the stairs, reaching down and lifting me out before he answers.

"This is the lost city," Danion says. Golon also speaks up.

"It must be. I have only read about its existence, but the similarities are too precise for it to be anything else." Golon's voice is reverent.

"The lost city? It has been missing for over eight thousand years. How would it be here? On Earth?" Etan asks. A good question, I feel.

"How can a city be lost to the Gelders yet turn up on Earth?" I add my own question to Danion.

"As you might know, when the Gelder people took to the stars or began traveling the galaxy by spacecraft, we transplanted many of our spiritual buildings onto our ships. For instance, the hall where we had our *cerum fuse* ceremony is one of those places. The lost city is one of the most well-known archives of our people's history." Danion pauses to look around. Golon continues with the explanation.

"You see, at this point in history, we had not fully transitioned into the true immortal forms we have now. Our people were going through the transition and there were some differences in opinion on if science should be used to speed up the transition process. We do not know much of what this disagreement resulted in, other than a splintering of our people. Many refused to listen to anyone who did not share the same side. However, after years of civil unrest, the side of science won out. We sped up the transition and evolved into our truly immortal selves," Golon concludes. Etan this time picks up the story while Golon admires the significance of where he is.

"Except there is some mystery about this time in our past. The archives are missing, especially about what was done to help us transition. It has long since been thought that this city was destroyed, and the archives along with it. Our history talks of it being destroyed in an eruption of our home planet's core. Yet here is the city. So many answers could be discovered here," he says with wonder in his voice.

I take a moment to look at the metropolis with a new perspective. This is like a new kind of world for them. Discovering a piece of their history they believed lost. We begin to slowly wander along the path that is laid out for us while admiring the surrounding beauty.

"Danion?" I ask him.

"Yes, my Eleanor?" he asks me.

"How did you transplant your spiritual places? How was this in space? How did this get here?" I ask him. This is a really big area to be moving around from planet to planet.

"Do you see the center structure there? The tall one jutting out from the middle of the city?" He points out the tall, dark pillar that towers over the rest of the city. I nod. "Well, that actually has the outer walls of the ship inside it. When it is ready to fly the walls will unfold from the tower and cover the entire city. In essence, this entire city is the ship." His words baffle me. I never would have thought that this could be a ship.

We come up to a door at the base of this tall tower. It appears locked; neither Golon nor Danion can open it. In unison, they both step back and motion for me to try to open the door. I have not even got my hand out yet but the doors open. With a quick glance around at the warriors surrounding me, we all enter the room.

Every panel that I pass by begins to light up as if this entire room has simply been waiting for me to arrive. I am so busy staring around the room that I do not notice the circular pattern on the floor. As I pass through it, it lights up with a holographic projection of a man.

I jump back with a small squeal of fright. The man is distinguished. It is the only word you could use to describe him. He has striking eyes, the same shade of blue I have. Thick billowing blond hair surrounds his head. He appears tall as well.

I am surrounded immediately by the warriors who came with me. All six of them have formed a complete wall around me.

"It is alright, everyone, I was just surprised." As I start to speak the display in the room begins to speak as well. But I do not understand the language. "Does anyone know what it is saying?"

"It is a *vim* weave. Very ancient lineages. It is attempting to learn your language so that it can pass the message on to you. It seems your father wanted there to be no chance you would not understand his message. You will need to continue talking until it learns the language," Griffith answers me.

"How will I know when I have talked enough? What am I supposed to say?" I ask him.

"Once you can understand the message you will know you have talked enough" is his response.

"I really don't know what I am supposed to say. Do I need to list a bunch of words?" I ask.

"No, *vim* lines are able to delve into the life energies. It can use the power of your mind to interpret your words. It only needs to assimilate the words of the mind with sounds. It rarely takes very long."

"I hope you are right—" I stop talking because the blond man that I suspect is an image of my father is now talking in my language.

"My dearest Eleanor. If you are here, where you were always meant to be, then that means that the war has come to a head. It also means that you must be claimed already. I am so sorry that I was not able to be present with you at your ceremony. Not there to help guide you through this new and unknown world. I know you have many questions and I will answer all of them in due time. But first, there is a matter of grave importance I must tell you before anything else." I inhale a breath at the gravity in which the projection portrays this.

"I love you, daughter of mine. You are a precious gem, the pinnacle of my entire existence. Everything in my entire life has meaning simply because it brought me to the point in my life where I was gifted with you. How I long to be able to hold you again. I must comfort myself with the memory of the one precious time I got to hold you in my arms." There is a pause in the message, almost like my father had to stop the recording to calm himself.

"But I know that there is much to convey to you, and not much time. Your life is in danger. Let me start at the beginning. I came to this world with exploration in mind. I was never meant to even travel to this system. But my ship was damaged, and my communications and navigation were destroyed. I had no choice but to try to land and repair the damage.

"Once I arrived here, I realized that I had drifted light-years away from where I should have been. I realized that this world was primitive. Extremely primitive. Fire had barely been discovered. I feared what my presence would do to the natives. So I hibernated on my ship. I tried to fix the ship so that I would be able to return to the stars. Unfortunately, years passed and I realized that I would never be able to repair it. I lacked the necessary materials.

"I came and I went from this ship every few centuries, spacing out my time in hibernation. I had a limited supply of a mineral we both require to survive. I needed to stretch it as long as I could. Your world here does not possess this mineral and it is something necessary to our survival. I have been rationing my supply, entering into hibernation to limit the need for the mineral in myself. But when I held you as a child, I could sense that you needed almost the entirety of my remaining supply. I never expected you share my dependence on my mineral and was terrified of what would happen to you without it.

"I have organized with the leading powers here to provide you with what you need. But your mate needs to be told that you are not human. Not Gelder. You are something better. Something stronger. He needs to make sure your powers are carefully nurtured. He needs to make sure there is enough of the mineral to wake me up. I am entering into hibernation now to await the time you come for me so that I can help guide you and nurture you. I want to help you understand what it means to be of an Atelean bloodline. Help you save the universe."

The room is quiet as the projection slowly fades out and is replaced by a pod rising from the floor. Inside is what looks like a sleeping man, but I know that he is in something much deeper.

"Did I hear him right? Did he say *Atelean* bloodline?" Arsenio asks shock and disbelief dripping from his words.

"Yes. Yes, he did." This is from Etan, who seems similarly surprised.

"I never thought this could be possible. That one was still alive," Malin says reverently.

"What do you mean? What does Atelean bloodline mean?" I ask. Danion is the one who answers.

"The Atelean bloodline is the original bloodline. The very first Gelders to master the lineages. The very first Gelders ever recorded. We thought that they all died out before the transition." Danion stares at me in awe. "You are the youngest member to the oldest legacy in the cosmos. You are the daughter of an ancient people."

To Be Continued...

Author Notes

Thank you for reading book two, I hope you are enjoying this series. If you are enjoying them, think about joining my email subscriber lists by visiting www.emjaye.org.

Other works by E.M. Jaye

The True Immortals:
The Claimed Queen
The Hidden Queen
The Lost Queen
The Mated Queen

Golon's Story

His Mate coming winter 23/24!

Gelder Warrior Stories

Etan's Hidden Pain

Other Works by E.M. Jaye

Lovers of Beverly Tennessee

Hate At First Sight- Coming Oct 27th 2023

Works Available as Early Access on Kindle Vella
Gelder Shorts:
Kowan's Anger
Etan's Hidden Pain

Gelder Warriors:
His Mate (Golon's story)

Lovers of Beverly, Tennessee:
Hate at First Sight
Longing at First Sight

Blackmailed Series (Dark Romance):
Blackmailed Marriage
Fantasy Romance
Dragon Reborn

Printed in Great Britain
by Amazon

30844120R00121